Judge of Saints and Sinners

Lords of the Underworld
Series Book 2

Maggie White

Judge of Saints and Sinners by Maggie White
Book 2 of the Lords of the Underworld Series
Story Copyright 2024 Maggie White
Editing by Jenny Raden
Map by B.C. FaJohn Books

Identifiers
Paperback: 979-8-9876093-3-0
Hardback: 979-8-9876093-4-7

The book you're about to read includes the death of a characters on page, references to heavy depression, moments of tension and danger, mature language and situations. For a full list of possible triggers, please visit www.maggiewhitebooks.com.

Contents

There are thousands of books published every day, I'm so honored you chose one of mine to share your time with. I have loved sharing my stories with every single one of you.

To my husband who doesn't have wings, or horns, but continues to remind me every day of how powerful love can be – I couldn't do this without you.

And to my parents, who never stopped believing in me. I love you…please don't read this.

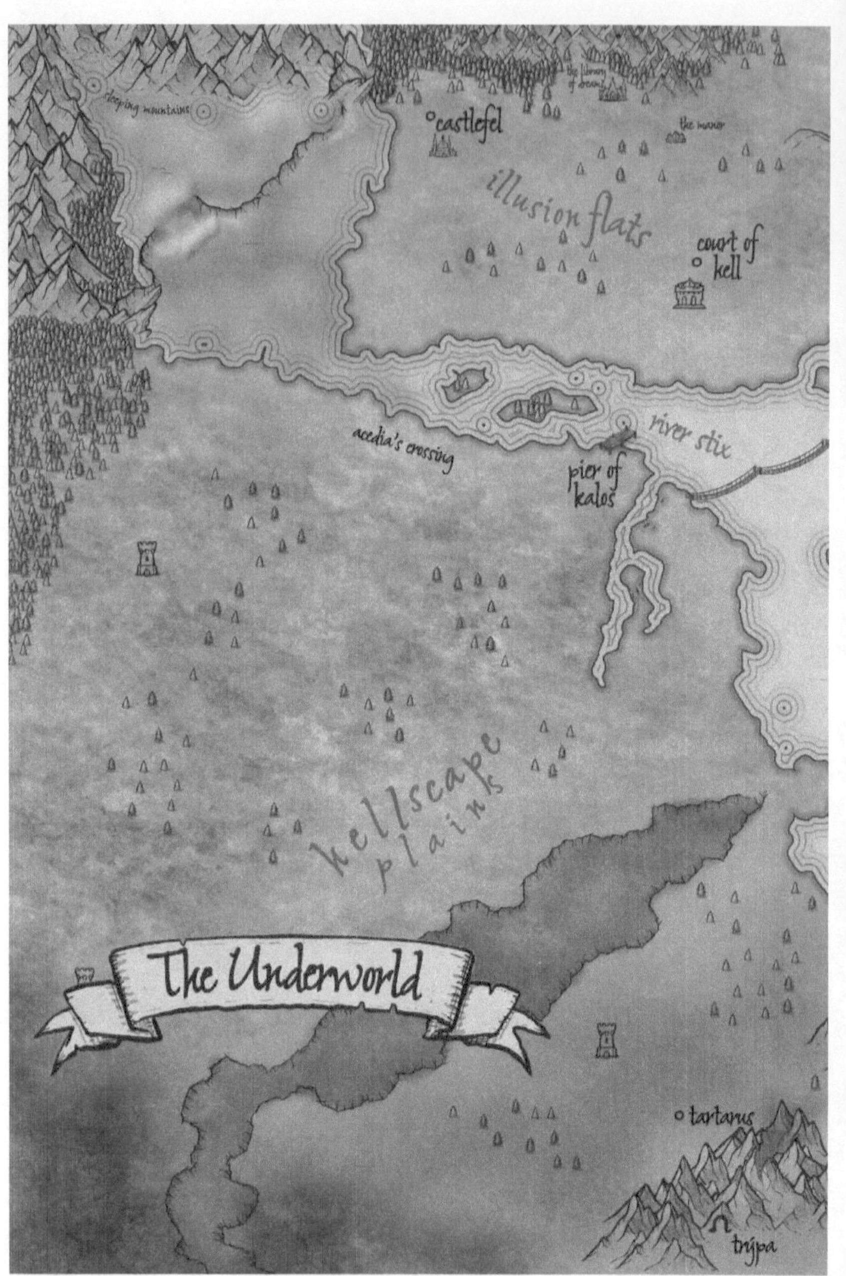

sleeping mountains
the library of souls
castlefel
the manor
illusion flats
court of
kell
river stix
acedia's crossing
pier of
kalos
hellscape
plains
The Underworld
tartarus
trypa

the
courthouse
elysium
elon's
isle
hell's
pointe
Wastelands

Prologue

Nephesh

The soul before me quivered, the faded outline of the human body that had once carried this soul—in this case, that of a middle-aged male—bald head and protruding belly still visible. He was kneeling on the dark-stained wood floors. He had dropped there, gaping mouth full of pleas and promises as I loomed over him.

And now, he shook. Funny, the belief that any of them had something good enough to sway me. If only they had treated their own lives with such fear and reservation. Then they would not be here before me. After all, it was only the mangled souls that were too tightly torn between good and evil that ended up here in my courthouse.

These souls, their scales so dangerously close to falling into darkness that my magic brings them here to the Underworld Courthouse. To my domain. It was up to me to decide if they would spend eternity in peace and glory, or whether they would suffer the consequences of a life of chosen darkness.

As for the rest of the souls, those that were so obviously dark or light, they were already taken care of. The River Styx, and the remnants of my magic, managed them—or at least, that's how I had intended it to be. As the gatekeeper of the Underworld, I was the final vote of a million considerations every moment.

In my youth, I had worried over each judgment. My magic had washed across the land as I obsessed about building the river's dam to filter the simpler souls, followed by my courthouse, and finally with housing a dozen souls here permanently. Each of them specifically chosen to help serve me in handing out judgment to those who were too close to darkness to be deemed worthy automatically.

That system was nothing but a distant memory now. Back when my magic had been wild and overeager, just like the demon who wielded it. Now I wondered if my father knew how little I cared about this process anymore. Or anything happening in the Underworld. I wondered every day if he wished for another heir. But that was too late now.

My fingers brushed across the face of the coin, the gold warming under my clawed grip.

"My Lord, Nephesh, you are scaring the soul."

I barely resisted rolling my eyes at my creature. Peter walked up beside me, the heavy robe that he always wore swirling around his legs. He was not a reaper like those

Kharon utilized. Or the mahrs that thrived in the dream realm. Peter was something else altogether. No longer just a soul, not quite a demon. I had chosen him early on, feeding the soul with enough demonic power that it had stabilized his form, his memories and his personality. My favor had allowed him and the others like him to stay and serve me here.

And unlike the pleading soul at my feet, Peter was more corporeal, his form more cemented, held in place by my magic.

I tossed the coin high, watching it roll over in the air before falling back into my palm. "When do I not scare them? Maybe if they had been more worried about consequences in their lives, then they wouldn't be here."

"Ever the optimist, sire."

"I'm a realist, Peter. Not a saint."

Peter paused, staring down at the crouching soul with pursed lips. "There is plenty of truth in your earlier statement, perhaps, but let's try to lessen the blow for…" He squinted down at the soul, a habit from when his eyesight must've lacked in the living world. "For, hm, Harrold, here."

I clucked my tongue, savoring the way the soul flinched away from me. He might not be worthy of a place in Elysium, but he was smart enough to know that I was dangerous. That put him head and shoulders above half of the souls who came through here. Many of them begged, pleading for another chance. Others simply screamed in fear.

But it didn't matter. My magic saw through all of that, to the core of them, where their scales reflected the actions of their living life. There was no hiding that. No ignoring the reality of their actions, and now they must face each and every one.

"Well, Harrold should've considered some of those aggressive tendencies of his long before he passed into my realm. Perhaps then we would all not be in this situation."

"We wouldn't, or specifically *you* wouldn't, be in this situation if you would just wake up the other jurors."

My temper begged to be released. To feel the heat and pressure of my true form as I let my body succumb to the demon that lurked just beneath my flesh. I slammed down on the control that kept the monster at bay, snarling halfheartedly at Peter.

He tensed but didn't back down. Even as I leaned in, pressing my fingers to Harrold's shoulders, which solidified under my touch. "Your judgment has been completed. Rise and face your future."

Harrold rose from the floor, his wispy face horrified as he stared up at me. I felt no doubt, no regret, as I released my magic, letting the soft red haze leak through my flesh until it coasted over him. At his center, the scales of life tilted precariously before a slow tilt left no question about who this soul had been at their very center.

Lacking.

Harrold here was bound for Tartarus, my brother Elon's realm, where he would spend time there until either he was able to recover and move to the glory of Elysium or offer up his soul for rebirth. "Ashes to ashes…" I murmured the common biblical line as my magic circled him, flames flickering up from the floor as it closed in on him.

Harrold, or the soul that was left, began to screech, throwing his hands out wide, tumbled words filling the courthouse as he begged and pleaded, his body pulled in on himself.

"Easy, soul. Your judgment has been cast," Peter echoed me, but as usual his words were more kind, more comforting than mine.

I removed my hand, letting the magic complete my judgment, dragging Harrold from the courthouse to the gates of Tartarus, where Elon's magic would find him a proper way to atone for his sins.

Peter and I stared into the now empty space, a small brush of ash still in place upon the white marble.

"Are there more?" I didn't look at him, just fiddled with my fingers, letting the flames scurry across my knuckles. I savored every burn from the brilliant red flames before calling it back to my core, where it danced along my maimed soul.

The one my mother and father had ripped in half.

"No more today." Peter's bearded face was guarded when he stepped away, moving across the vast inner chamber of the courthouse. More temple than courtroom, the vaulted ceilings displayed a variety of artwork from across the ages. Each painted by a soul coming to atone.

I glanced over my shoulder, through the paned window. The Underworld outside was dimming to a dusk-like color scheme.

The brilliant oranges blurred across the skyscape and blended higher and higher into a thick dark blue.

Almost like nighttime, like the rising and falling of the sun and moon. It was my father's little homage to the living world that he performed each day. He claimed that it comforted the souls we had in our care. But I wondered if perhaps it was a remnant from his days in Heaven with the seraphim that he kept to this traditional layout of time. Either way, it was doubtful that Lucifer would confess to me.

Whatever it meant to Father, it meant to me that I could rest. Recharge and await another day tomorrow full of exactly what today had been. "Goodnight, Peter," I said coolly, turning back to my head juror.

The willowy figure stared back at me, his endless eyes sharp. "At your leave, my lord." He raised his palms in a farewell. Along the immense back wall of the courthouse, an elaborate mural was painted. Upon it, there was a stationed jury, eleven members, their faces and emotions frozen in place. They were so life-like that even now, I could almost picture their faces moving, turning to look at me, begging me to free them.

The bright colors, the once dark and sharp lines of their forms, were beginning to blur and fade. Further proof of my weakness. My world was quickly becoming a relic. Something from another time, another world. I stared at it, willing the robes they wore to move, to sway, or display any of their former abilities to move or speak. But there was nothing. How long had it been? My head ached when I tried to remember.

The last fifty years had been—fuck, I couldn't think about that. My fists clenched, and I relished in the sting of my demonic claws digging into the soft humanlike flesh of my palms. My lips curled in distaste. I two parts of who I was were constantly at odds with each other.

No wonder I was a miserable bastard to be around.

Peter had reached the mural, turning to face me in a smooth motion. His ghostly fingers were steepled, and I could tell he wanted to impart some great wisdom onto me. When I was a younger male, I might have let him. But now, we were far past that. There was no room for growth in my life. There was only repetition and the dull gray of what passed for my normal now.

And yet. I owed him more than I had to give. Pulling my shoulders back, my lightweight shirt tightening across my shoulders, I nodded to him. Granting him the permission he requested. "What is it, Peter?"

With his back pressing lightly against the painted plaster, the juror's face turned stormy. "I can feel a change today, in the wards and"—he looked at me—"in you. Every day that I go to rest, I accept that I may not make it out."

"Peter, I—" I began, but he cut me off, speaking over me.

"I'm not worried for myself, my lord. I'm worried for you. You have not been the same, and I understand your pain, but sire…will you be alright on your own?"

I hated that his voice was worried, concerned.

My teeth ground, fangs catching on my lip as I snarled into the empty room. "That won't happen."

The juror's head tilted, his words low and rushed. "Someday it will, my lord, and I want you to be prepared—"

"Stop your prattling, old man. You do not have permission or leave to speak to me like this. I am still the lord here, not you."

Peter's chin rose, his dark gaze stilling on mine. "Of course you are." Slowly, haltingly, he bent at the waist. "Forgive me, my lord, Judge."

Shame, or the closest I'd felt to that in decades, filled my gut. But as I stepped forward, to demand Peter wait so that I could…what would I do? What could I do? My hesitation was all it took for Peter to bend his legs, holding at the knee as he released one last sigh into the Underworld air.

With a blink that ate up a century, Peter stepped back into the mural. The magic wall opened up, spreading around him like quicksand, the essence of his form, his appearance, even the worried lines at his eyes stretching itself over. Then color bloomed, filling Peter in until a lifeline image of him was painted in form, frozen in the moment, a monument to the power of my judgment and the courthouse.

I walked forward until I was level with the mural. I longed to reach out and touch the painted version of my jurors. There were twelve there, with Peter being the most powerful, the first soul I had brought here and granted an audience.

He helped me build this place, to create the process that all souls now experienced. The others I had added for various reasons. The barbaric warrior from a long-dead dynasty who possessed a depth of awareness and curiosity that had shocked and impressed me. Even the woman on the end, in her pearls and collar, who brought a sharp eye to every soul's judgment. They each served a purpose ,and when my power was there, they had been capable of handling nearly all the souls' judgment on their own. Between the courthouse and the dam, I was nearly out of a job for a few years.

And now…now it was a shadow of the system it had once been. My power was the mechanism behind all of it. And now, it just didn't move as it should. Perhaps the same as its master. My blood dripped from my palms to the floor, but I barely noticed, my eyes consumed with taking in every inch of the remaining mural aspects.

I wondered if they were watching me back, though I knew it was not likely. They'd always told me that they saw a distorted version of the world while they were in this form. I couldn't risk them knowing how much Peter's words filled me with fear, especially since it was the same worry that I'd been harboring for the past year.

My power, triggered by the torment of emotion, rumbled through my body. A mockery of what I once could do, but still, a testament to the heavy infusion of demon blood that coursed through my veins.

I longed to press my hand to the painting, to see if maybe that contact might awaken something once more. Back to how things were, when my power could easily free the twelve chosen who served on my jury. As my power had waned, I'd been slowly unable to call each of them from their rest in the cursed painting.

No, I couldn't risk them seeing me like this. Peter's obvious call out to my failure and weakness was enough.

Now, the mural was a painful reminder of what this world used to be. What Peter said could be true. Someday my ability to pull even him, the leader of my chosen, would be gone. And it would be my waning magic standing between a wall of lost souls and the afterlife. My claws dug into my palms once more, and this time I could feel the heat of my own blood as it spilled from my fists to the floor, where it slowly disappeared.

The Underworld was a part of me and each of my brothers. When our blood spilled, our world simply absorbed it once more, just as it always had done with our magic. Perhaps someday, I would simply be absorbed too.

I looked back to the painting.

"Goodnight," I whispered. "My friends."

I forced myself to walk away, to turn from the mural and move into my living quarters, a combination of rooms adjacent to the courthouse. Before I'd gone a stride into my private chambers, I was suddenly accosted with an enormous soldier in white, his dark hair swinging across his shoulders in neat braids. I clutched at his arms in an attempt to keep both of us standing then stepped back and released him quickly. Usually the Brotherhood members who served the courthouse stayed far from me. As the token peacekeepers of the Underworld, they were typically more occupied down by the bridge and the river, keeping the anxiously waiting souls in line.

"Atlas," I grunted, squaring my shoulders against the warrior. He was their leader, and therefore had to interact with me, much to his obvious dismay. "What the fuck are you doing?"

The warrior dropped to a knee in an uncharacteristic show of submission. I raised my brows.

"My lord, we have a problem."

My heart leaped in my chest. I mentally reached for the well of power in my soul. There wasn't much remaining after the number of souls I'd judged today. Without the jurors, that task wore heavily on me.

"What is it?" Had the corruption finally reached my realm? Or was there another issue with Arafel's realm? My stomach bottomed out as I considered what might have happened to my younger brother and his little human mate, Lucia.

I did not form attachments, especially to humans, but the smart, peculiar female human nearly had me convinced that she was strong enough to survive in our world. *Nearly.*

It would serve Arafel right if she were hurt. Hell was no place for a human. I had learned that; it was his own stupid fault for not learning from my mistake. Leave the bonding to the humans in the living world or the creatures of the Underworld.

Demons were not fit for mates, let alone being paired up with a human. My mother had believed we were, but then again, maybe that was why she was gone, then. Even the King of the Dead couldn't keep his mate safe.

What hope did my brothers or I have?

"My lord?" Atlas slowly stood once again. "I came to tell you that Cerberus has been missing for several hours."

I blinked. "You lost an enormous three-headed dog?" Of course they had. Cerberus was older than the Brotherhood. He was older than nearly anything else here. The equivalent of a boy asking for a puppy, I had asked my father for a companion early on in our existence.

He had given me Cerberus. The dog typically lounged around the Underworld wherever he pleased, but he was particularly fond of my realm. Something that made me rather proud most days. I couldn't hold much over my brothers, but I did consider Cerberus mine.

Atlas didn't meet my eyes but nodded just once.

I strode across the entryway to the office just beyond, raising my voice so Atlas could hear me. "Cerberus is a trusted companion, and he knows the Underworld better than most of its occupants. He will be fine. You are dismissed."

I didn't need to look at him to know Atlas hadn't left. Sighing loudly to be sure he heard me and my corresponding frustration, I turned to him.

"Yes, Atlas?"

"That's why I came to you, my lord. We have reason to believe Cerberus is not in the Underworld any longer."

That got my attention. I stalked closer to the warrior. "Rise."

Atlas moved smoothly to his feet, unencumbered by the armor. This time, I made sure to get uncomfortably close to the warrior's face before I spoke again. Inside of his standard Brotherhood attire—a tunic and lightweight black-dyed leather armor—the male was sweating. My nostrils flared at the scent of his fear, the demon inside me uncoiling and roiling to just below the surface.

"You are telling me one of my creatures is wandering around the living world and I'm just now hearing about it?"

Atlas nodded again, eyes fixed on something across the room. I could see his neck tighten as I growled. There, right there, his pulse hammered. It would be simple, one slice of my claws, one snap of my jaws. Unlike my more sophisticated brothers, my tastes ran more carnal in nature. More like my father's demon soldiers than the Prince of Hell. My exterior may be that of cool disinterest, but inner desires were as base as any demon in the Underworld.

With a growl, I spun away from him, forcing my heartbeat to even.

"Where?" I shook my head to clear the haze of fury that always accompanied my emotions. Fucking demon genetics.

"We think he's somewhere near a place called Omaha, Nebraska."

My feet skidded to a halt. And Atlas nearly bumped into me once again. He steadied himself, decorum faltering as he caught a look at my face. "Do you know it, my lord?"

"I do." I yanked open the door to my chambers. "That's where my soul bound was killed.

1

Justine

The sharp edges of the cardboard box bit into my palm as I walked slowly to the front of the store. My steps were measured, careful, the worn-out soles of my sneakers nearly silent against the pharmacy's thickly waxed tile floor.

One, two, one, two, I chanted to myself, forcing one foot after the other until I reached the counter. A grim-faced man stood there, his colorful vest and name tag a matching horrid shade of eggplant. *Ted,* it read in bold letters.

Seeing my hesitation, or perhaps he was just always upset, Ted gave a soft grunt and knocked his knuckles against the speckled laminate. "Right here, young lady."

"Just this, please," I said, leaning on the manners my mother had worked so hard to instill in me. Under the ripped jeans and too faded T-shirt, all designed to make sure I did everything to blend in, I was still my mother's daughter.

Ted grunted again, and I decided that it must just be his native tongue. I placed the box of cough medicine on the counter, and Ted quickly swiped it across the reader with a cheerful mechanical chirp, his gaze back on me.

"Your total is $9.42."

I laid out the amount in cash and coins, down to the exact cent, and while Ted made a big show of picking up each of the coins, he neither said nor grunted anything else. Still, I felt exposed, others joining the line behind me in an effort to check out too. I could almost feel their eyes on me. My fingers twitched, so I pressed them hard against my sides, remembering what the counselor had told me to do when I was anxious.

Touch something. Describe it to myself. Under my hand, the denim was soft, worn, the seams raised as the fabric was gathered together at the pocket. I ran my fingernail along the cut in fabric, willing Ted to move faster. I needed to get out of here.

Finally, he held out the loud, snapping plastic bag to me with my receipt in his other hand. I took them both, whispering a quick, "Thank you."

Ted eyed me, dull eyes disinterested as I moved to the door.

"Ma'am! Wait just a second."

I stiffened, freezing a stride from the automatic doors. If I ran now, I could probably make it. I just had to get around the corner, to the hiding spot I'd already scouted out. I had gotten fast. I could make it.

"Yes?" I turned, forcing a smile to my mouth as I looked back at the new voice. Another purple-vested employee was hurrying towards me, but unlike the checkout employee, he wore a wide grin on his face.

"You dropped this," the boy said, his cheeks an unusual shade of red as he held out a piece of paper to me.

My heart skipped a beat when I realized what he held, but I kept my face carefully blank, reaching out to take the slip of paper.

"How silly of me. Thank you." My eyes dropped to his name tag, reading Danny quickly before meeting his smile once more.

"It's okay. I do that kind of stuff all the time." Danny scrubbed the back of his neck, his eyes wandering over me appreciatively for a moment. Unlike his colleague, he didn't seem to notice my rundown apparel. I should be glad, since it distracted him from the evidence that I now held in my fingers.

I stepped towards him, letting my eyelids lower as I bit into my bottom lip. "Well, apparently you're my hero."

"Oh, it was nothing," Danny said, following the motion of my teeth with wide, dark eyes.

I contained the roll of my eyes that nearly emerged at his comment. But it seemed like my distraction had worked. Score one for me. Well, nearly. I still had to get out of this place. Which reminded me…

I offered my best smile. "Well, I've got to go, my brother needs this." To emphasize, I held up my bagged purchase.

Behind me, Ted was checking out another customer, the plaintive beeping blending into the white noise around us.

"Yeah, yeah, of course. Come back any time." Smiling Danny gave me an enthusiastic wave that I returned with far less gusto. I needed to get out of here. And soon. My feet carried me quickly down the sidewalk until I was turning, crisscrossing downtown Omaha. It was no New York City, and while I wasn't sure it was home, it was home for now. Or it would be, as long as I didn't get caught doing something stupid. Or rather, more stupid than usual.

I glanced over my shoulder. I kept hurrying, my backpack digging into my shoulder, as the sun began to fade, turning the already gray downtown into something dark and ominous. I was shivering by the time I reached my apartment building, and not just because my clothing was fucking threadbare.

Ever since my parents died, there'd been something, just there, right behind me. It followed me from Georgia to Tennessee. Then from Tennessee to Ohio. And now, just when I finally felt like I'd settled into whatever I could consider a normal life here in Omaha, it was rearing its head again.

I hated it.

I yanked open the door to the shitty apartment building that I'd been staying in since early summer. My neck ached from how I kept it turned as I climbed staircase after staircase after staircase. Instantly I regretted the fact I'd only had a package of ramen noodles roughly seven hours ago. I got a little woozy by the fourth floor.

I rounded the final turn and took a quick look around. No one. Perfect. I was in no shape to talk to anyone about why I had half a pharmacy shoved down my bra or why I was carrying cough medicine around like it was some kind of buffer against the world. Glad for the peace, I slowed my pace, skipping over the most squeaking floorboards in the hall as I approached Rocky's apartment. Instead of knocking, I took a spare key out of my jeans' pocket, pressing my hand against my breasts as I turned the old-style skeleton key in the lock and stepped inside.

The scent of old furniture crept over me—not bad, not good, just familiar. I shut the door carefully, eyeing the young child lying across the faded green sofa on the side wall. My footsteps were measured as I smiled, watching the distinct rise and fall of his chest. I was tempted to press a hand to his temple, to check his temperature, but I was sure that his grandfather had already done that.

"His fever is down, Teeny, but not enough," a gruff voice spoke from the side, and while I flinched, years of fear filling my bones at the proximity of the speaker. I hated being surprised. Even so, I managed to keep a smile on my face as I turned to Rocky.

"How's Jean?" I asked, my eyes skipping over Rocky's wild white hair to the door behind. His youngest grandchild, only three, slept in the bedroom just past him, a sliver of the living room lights illuminating a sprawled arm.

"Not so good." Rocky leaned back, his chin jutting out a little. I could almost see his pride faltering as he recognized his grandchildren's needs. "Did you, uh, have any luck?"

My lips curled in a halfhearted smile. Rocky was one of the good ones. Once a legendary boxer, he'd gotten mixed up with the wrong people, spent part of his life running into danger, the other half running from. But when his grandbabies had lost their parents, he'd come running, leaving behind whatever memories haunted him in Charleston, and took them in.

Money was tight. But these kids were loved, and their grandfather did everything to keep them safe. Rocky was obsessed with raising them as good or better than their parents would have. My eyes flickered down to the hands he'd made his living with, the thick knuckles, the permanent scars that seemed to cover every part of his pale skin, not blending in with the age spots that he often ran his fingers over.

The same hand that had reached for mine on my first day here then proceeded to open box after box, insisting he was raising good kids and that they would know how to take care of their neighbors.

His kindness was beautiful. It was also a debt. One that I would be paying off starting now. My throat ached for a moment. I was well aware of my situation, and having people like him nearby made me wish for more. But there was no one here to defend me, to make a home for me. Not anymore.

"I got a whole bunch of stuff." I reached up, shifting a little so I didn't show anything but a tiny slip of skin on my stomach as I hauled my haul out from under my shirt. "What do you think? I think I got everything…"

Rocky took each bottle, holding it up to the light and squinting at them a little. I mentally made a note to grab him reading glasses the next time I was doing a supply run. My stomach churned. They would be, just like these medicines, stolen. I didn't regret it—I didn't regret any of it—but I didn't want to tinge Rocky's life with my dirty hands.

Thief.

Runaway.

Emotional wreck.

Those were my three most prominent features, and while I had made my ability to multitask into a superpower, there were days, especially like today, that I wished I was doing something good with my life.

Jayden breathed in, the sound a rasp against the pounding worry of my thoughts, and I jerked back to the present, moving to lean over him. "How are you, big guy?"

Most days, the curly haired eight-year-old, a very proud second grader, would have given me the death glare for my almost babyish voice, but today he just winced a little, his clammy fingers winding through mine. Fear and anguish rushed over me. I looked at Rocky. "Which one first? You said he needed something today?"

It had been nearly impossible to steal the antibiotics. I'd had to wait around two different pharmacies, until someone inevitably came in to get their prescription before slipping it free and putting something else cheap and bagged into their clutches. I'd nearly given up a half dozen times, but there was no other way. Rocky was doing okay keeping the family fed and housed, but medical bills, especially for two little ones, would bleed him dry.

But now, my anxiety crept in back in. What if Jayden had a bad reaction to the medicine? My mother used to be allergic to one of those types. What if it caused Jayden to get worse? We were already walking the line between a random respiratory infection and pneumonia.

"One second, Jayden. We're going to get you all fixed up." Rocky grabbed the bottle then hurried over to the small kitchenette that lined one wall and got a small glass of water. I watched it all with nervous eyes, the delicate fingers in my grip weak and cool. "Here you go, baby. Let's get these pills into you. You're going to be feeling so much better soon."

I helped to prop up Jayden then watched closely as he swallowed, the pill making its way down his throat and hopefully making a beeline for the raging infection in his chest. I sent up a silent prayer to whomever was listening to me these days and then shifted away, letting Rocky keep the gentle weight of Jayden against him until he resettled the boy on the couch.

I began to back away, the feeling of overstaying my welcome creeping up on me like a dull chill until I hurriedly picked up my backpack and headed to the door.

"Teeny, wait, please." Rocky was there, his voice hushed, but his forehead wrinkles smoothing out a little as his grandson reclined in the background. "I need to tell you… I need to tell you."

I rubbed my hand over my lips as he looked down at me. Rocky had always been a towering monster of a man. But in his youth, I'm not sure I would've had the courage to approach him.

But I'd learned a long time ago that size was not related to strength. Not in the way it mattered. And so I reached up, patting his shoulder, feeling the lines of too-thin shoulders through the flannel top.

"It's okay, Rocky." I said, making sure my voice stayed flat, smooth, and unemotional. Because as much as I cared, I wasn't comfortable making this a big deal. "I'm glad I could help. He's such a good kid."

"Yes, but so are you, Teeny. I shouldn't have asked you to do this. I don't want you to be like me. I don't want you to—"

I cut him off, my chest aching. "I'm twenty-four, Rocky, and this was my choice. Hell, it was my idea to begin with. It's what I do best. It's good to keep these fingers fresh and spry." I waggled them his direction, trying to lighten the mood. It didn't work. He just stared at me with these sorrowful brown eyes.

"It's nothing, Rocky, really. If I'd had someone like you looking out for me when I was younger, maybe things would've been different. But I am who I am."

Rocky shook his head, eyes on the floor. "If you'd had someone like *you* looking out for you as a kid, things would've been different."

I tilted my head, a smile coming to my lips. "Did you just hear yourself? That doesn't even make sense."

Rocky chuckled, his stare rejoining mine. "Maybe, but all I'm saying is that you're a good girl, Justine, I can feel it, right at your core where it matters. You shouldn't joke about yourself like that. Not when everyone else around you can see just how good you are. I just wish you'd had a chance to do something with it."

Rocky patted my arm, and my whole body recoiled from the gentle touch. Not because I minded being touched, but something about the truth bomb that he'd dropped on me made my heart race with the need to run.

He knew too much.

He was too close.

Cursed.

The memory hissed at me from the recesses of my mind.

I could feel the world slinking across my brain, the visions from my life flashing behind my eyes as I watched Rocky open the door to the hall. This time I didn't bother looking to see if anyone was out there.

Nothing else mattered now, except getting away from here as quickly as possible. Rubbing my eyes, I walked down the hall to the next door on the right, the corner apartment, number forty-eight. A traitorous tear slipped out as I stepped in and closed the door behind myself.

The light switch was always wonky, and you had to flip it one or two times before the orange-toned fluorescent bulbs scattered across a dingy popcorn ceiling turned on. I was so distracted by the flickering light that at first I didn't notice the shine of two perfectly round orbs glowing back out from the corner of the room.

My heart raced, my palms grew damp, and my knees snapped together. Taking a short breath, my decision to run already in my head, I flipped the switch the final time, praying this time it would take.

It did.

My tiny, sparsely furnished studio apartment came into view. On the floor was the braided rug that Rocky had given me when he got another this past summer. A mattress was sitting in one corner, next to a clearance-sale bookshelf that held my most precious possessions. The kitchenette, complete with dripping faucet that looked like it was from the 1950s.

And right in the center of the space sat the absolute biggest dog I'd ever seen in my life. He stared at me with such relaxed countenance that at first I didn't move, didn't even breathe.

I didn't have a dog.

2

The wine splashed slightly when I poured it, staining the ornate stone countertops a pale red as I plunked the bottle down on the sideboard. My private chambers were on the top floor of the courthouse, along with a multitude of spare rooms that were so far untouched and unfilled. My needs were minimal, and the only reason I remained sleeping on this floor as opposed to below in my office space was the impressive view that I had designed outside the windows. I moved to one of them now, staring across the Underworld horizon. My realm was the center of the Underworld in many ways.

From here I could see the vast Styx, winding past the heart of this world, the Court of Hell, where my father ruled from. And as my brother Kharon patrolled the river, so did I patrol the dam, the magical filtering system that even now glowed in the dark night.

My magic hard at work. I snorted, choking down another sip of the liquid. My brother Elon was not home, as his home was dark tonight, perched atop the island that split the Styx.

No doubt he was chasing some rogue nasty who was attempting to escape from Tartarus. He had his hands more than full with the darkness that had crept into our homes, giving souls access to escape, to become corrupted.

We knew that the Drude was at the center of all of it.

But to what end? We couldn't decide. What we knew was that every time a soul was stolen from the Underworld, our powers dimmed. I palmed my chest for a minute, the pinching pain that was my constant companion was especially irritating tonight.

But then, losing your soul mate should hurt. Especially when it was my fault.

Lights flickered below, likely a change of shift in the battalion of Brotherhood warriors who served my realm. Their dancing torches distracted me from my pain as I looked down the trails that connected the courthouse to the immense dam. The dam, my most impressive creation to date, held fast against the constant onslaught of souls and water that beat upon it. This was where souls were sorted, the branching of the river slipping there, taking the good to Elysium and the bad to Tartarus.

For the good, there was a land flowing with milk and honey, or whatever the hell Elon was serving nowadays. And in Tartarus, those deemed too dangerous to be reborn and too difficult to be allowed in Elysium, those souls were kept in cages like the animals they were.

And all of that was decided by my magic.

The river itself was beautiful, the lifeblood and current of our world, carrying the souls of the living world right outside of my windows. I snorted, sipping the dark wine. The beauty of the river, or the ingenuity of my creation, wouldn't matter soon anyway. This world and our kind as its makers would cease to exist before too long. Unless my brothers managed to save us all.

Sighing, I turned back to my living area. I stared around with bleary eyes, trying to decide why this place irritated me so. The apartment itself was fine. Nothing like Arafel's castle or Kadmiel's tower. There were no twisting corridors or gaping darkness, thank Hades. I had had enough caverns and tight spaces to last me an eternity.

My magic had ignited a nearby sconce, the happily dancing flame glowing over me as I sat down, half-empty glass in hand. I eyed my stack of books. Mostly historical. A passing fancy to try to decipher what I had missed during the fifty years I'd been imprisoned beneath the Underworld.

In summary, I'd discovered that the living world was still a mess of their own making and I had very little patience or empathy for the way the human souls were spending their time. It was a disgrace. Even if I was powerful enough to go back to the living world, I would likely be disappointed by what I'd find. Once I'd been consumed with spending time there. Now I was more than content to stay here, watching my father's kingdom burn around us.

A rueful smile tugged at my lips. Of course, when I was in the living world more, I was usually attending to my father's business, and it didn't exactly leave a normal taste in any living soul's mouth. I was a monster at my father's command. Distantly, I wondered if he might someday confess who he had used while I was locked away. A devil without his weapons was a weakness.

And Lucifer hadn't done his own dirty work for centuries. Why would he, when he had five sons who were all more than capable of doing it for him? If I judged his preferences of weapons to be his affection, then I was his favorite.

But that wasn't true. When I had lost control, they had locked me below, far from the light and my family. They had chained and bound me for nearly fifty years. In all that time, Lucifer must've found another of my brothers to do his work for him.

Surely not my Dream King brother, though. Arafel wouldn't have the stomach for retrieving the Corrupted from the living world. These souls who had been stolen from the Underworld and given bodies to take over in the living world were an unholy combination of the knowledge that they couldn't be killed normally and the power of the one they would not serve.

I wasn't sure Arafel would be able to handle those tasks. After all, these Corrupted often looked like normal humans. It wasn't until you had them cornered that you would find out exactly how dangerous they could be.

But then, the same could be said about me. I was the firstborn son of Lucifer and the first witch, a product of their great, tragic love story. But I wasn't what they'd expected. And as my mother's belly grew again, my father assured me that he understood what needed to be done. Each of my brothers was less demon-like, more and more human. By the time they were done, they'd had the perfect little half-demon creations.

That plan resulted in Kadmiel, my youngest sibling. He was the most detached from the rest of us. Father kept him busy running errands from the Underworld to the Seraphim, our pompous sky-dwelling cousins.

Kadmiel spent more time among the living souls than the rest of us combined. Perhaps that's why he'd accrued the nickname "the guardian," a sort of dark avenger. He hunted those who were in danger from Underworld creatures and brought VIP souls straight to the Underworld. My father claimed he was the best at gathering souls.

That much was obvious. Kharon, my soul-wrangling, ferry-driving, gill-throated brother was not exactly palatable on his most human days. Arafel hated being in his human form, and Elon was the punisher. He hadn't been able to face the living world since the first great Underworld war, when he'd been injured beyond any of our magic's repair.

The Judge.

The Dream Lord.

The Ferryman.

The Punisher.

The Guardian.

All trapped here together in the world our father and mother made, surrounded by creatures and the forgotten souls of the living world. Heaven or Hell were fragments of speech. The Underworld was the destination for all souls.

And it was up to me to sort and categorize them based on their time in the living world. Once I'd been thrilled at the prospect of sorting the good souls into Elysium and the bad into Tartarus. But now, it all seemed futile. Once my brothers and I lost our powers, we would lose the ability to keep the souls where they belonged. We were seeing it even now.

The souls that were convinced by the Drude to push the boundaries. While we had a legacy of aggression and power on our side, it wouldn't last long once the souls realized how weak we had become.

Everything would be doomed. At least, that was what the Drude, a rising power that had begun to steal souls from the Underworld to do his bidding, hoped. Arafel believed that the Drude was a demonic creature like us. My father believed he was the first corrupted soul, meaning a soul that had gotten lost in the Underworld and had gained power by gathering more lost souls to themselves.

I didn't give two fucks what he or she was. They were ruining my plan at an honorable decline. By stealing more souls, they stole more power. When my mother had split each of my brother's and my souls, she'd unavoidably severed our magic in half. Only with our souls returned to us did we have a chance to fight the Drude and those they commanded.

Propping up a booted foot, I stared at my lantern light, letting the fire burn its way into my eyes before I slammed them shut. My fingers flew across the parchment that had been waiting for me. The bit of charcoal that constantly waited alongside this chair leapt into my fingers. They were still stained by the constant use, but I ignored that, focusing on the feel of the lines on the paper, the way my hands moved, without me even knowing it.

Up and down, smoothing across, filling in the blank part of the parchment as I shuttered my eyes. I didn't need to see the artwork to know where my hands were moving. This was the only part of me left, this useless talent that meant nothing for a judge of souls.

Even so, it was one of few things that still brought joy to my quiet, dull heart. My fingers flying across the parchment, I lost track of time, only realizing that it must've been hours when I finally looked up and saw that my candle had nearly burned out.

That and a demon leaned against the corner of the room, his features familiar. And irritating.

"Hiriam. What do you want?"

My father's second—or third, depending on the day and whether he or Alecto had killed each other lately—gazed at me with fiery red eyes. He was in the dark uniform of those who served the Hell household, complete with a cloak that pooled at his feet.

He clucked at me, the split length of his tongue softening the noise. "Always so suspicious, Lord Nephesh. So suspicious." One taloned foot stepped into the light, the shining black claws that adjourned his toes showing as he observed me with wide black eyes.

I groaned. Clearly, he was intent on staying. Setting my drawing to the side, I picked up my wine, sipping it as my gaze wandered down the now illuminated lines of the demon male. Once a great human king, he'd fallen into one of my father's deals and was now spending his afterlife running errands for my father's needy court and checking in on a bunch of demon children that the King of Hell hadn't wanted in the first place.

"Can you blame me? I have spent a lot of time alone lately, Hiriam." I nodded at the door. "And honestly, I'd like to keep it that way. Get out."

"You and I both know that I cannot do that. Your father sent me."

I stifled a yawn as I stretched languorously, knowing it pissed him off to have been so lackadaisical about his presence here, but I was tired, magically burned out. I didn't want to play his stupid games.

"And what does dear Papa need?" With a grunt, I heaved myself up and out of the chair. My legs were on autopilot, carrying me over towards the kitchen, where I refilled my goblet, downed the contents, and then refilled once again, emptying the bottle. One small perk of my powers receding, possibly the only perk, was that I could feel the beginnings of drunkenness. It had been exceedingly helpful on the nights that I attempted to lie down or rest.

Most days I didn't dare to close my eyes unless I was truly depleted or desperate. The nightmares would always come, no matter how hard Arafel worked to keep them out of my head. At least exhaustion left less of me to experience their horrors.

Hiriam was unfazed and followed me, a deep burgundy shadow, those claws clicking against the hardwood floors as he moved. "He heard about your little pet, that he's gotten lost in the world again."

I took a long, slow drink from my goblet. "And? What does he want me to do about it? He knows I can't travel into the living world right now. It would wipe me out completely. He should send a Brotherhood warrior or maybe even one of you."

"The Bane is busy elsewhere, and you know that the Brotherhood are all currently overextended as it is. Poor, poor little hellion, you're going to have to go on your own."

"Cerberus is a part of Hell and a part of me. He will come home. I don't know why my father is so concerned with this."

Hiram bared a mouthful of sharp teeth in my direction. "If you dragged your head out of your ass for half a decade, then you would realize that we need every creature, every soldier here to help. The Corrupted gain souls every day. The

Drude's power is growing, which means your father's is lessening."

My power flashed out of me in an instant, the flames wrapping themselves around Hiram and holding him aloft as the heatless fire wrapped keenly around his neck, an extension of my own flexed fingers. "In case you missed it, servant, until very recently, my father, and my own brothers, conspired to lock me up in a pit in the very bowels of this world. The only place I have my head is in the future because this world was destined to go down in fire and ashes. And if its time has come, then I will stand at the helm, in the position thrust upon me, wearing my family's shackles until the very end."

Hiriam snarled, the sound muted as I squeezed his thick throat. Then with a roll of one shoulder, I released him. "Now, run home to your master. I don't jump at anyone's command, not anymore."

Hiriam shot me one last murderous look then stalked back towards the window. He paused by my chair, his head tilting as he observed my drawings. Dread curled in my belly, and I barely resisted the urge to strike out with my powers.

But then, he would know what it might mean. What it meant to me, the last thing that really held value in my world. Thankfully, after another lurching twist of his body, his thick, leathery wings spread, taking up half the room and effectively shattering the window behind him. I didn't blink, unaffected by his destructive tendencies.

Once a spoiled human, always a spoiled human. He just had special tricks now. Just before he leapt into the darkened Underworld sky, a few final words slipped from his mouth. A warning, a dare. It wasn't until he was a speck in the distance, flapping obediently towards the Court of Hell, that I realized what he'd said.

"It serves you right to lose another one."

The words rolled over and over in my mind as I stalked back to my chair. Small bits of glass and wood from the shattered window lay across the page now. I brushed them aside, ignoring the pinprick of a sharp edge as I stared down at the flower I'd drawn. A lily, the petals bright in bloom, with one, delicate petal falling along the stem.

I tilted my head. Sighing, I tossed the paper down on the stack. I'd drawn this flower over and over since I'd been freed nearly a year ago.

She had carried lilies, her little boy's favorite flower, straight from the garden in her front lawn. I could remember that moment like it was yesterday, the pain greater than being gutted and twice as lasting. At least the dead couldn't feel anymore.

Because we, their caretakers, felt everything.

Fuck my life.

Relaxing my spine, my body fell back into the softness of the chair, a courtesy I rarely extended to it. But I wanted to think. I wanted to let those words soak in. So much had happened while I was imprisoned. And while I was concerned, I'd left part of my mind in that cave, I knew that the important things would come back to me. Making sure I was finally alone; I pulled my power from the lantern and threw myself into darkness.

My teeth gritted, my fangs a painful pinch as my eyes closed.

"Another what?" I asked out loud, as if I could command my damaged mind and its fickle tendencies to find me the answer.

My mind hummed, always anxious, always on edge these days, and even with my eyes closed, I was bombarded with the thousands of sights and scenes of the Underworld around me. There were souls arriving at the dam, the last step in their journey into the Underworld. I could hear Kharon's creatures, the reapers, herding them, guarding them from the corrupted souls that the Drude had turned against us.

The mysterious force had been around for almost a century now, a power that grew and grew until my father went from disregarding it as a deformed creature, to understanding that this thing could be the end of the Underworld as we knew it.

Souls powered the Underworld. The incoming souls paid a toll—one coin to the ferryman, one to the judge—but it was their passing through the dam that fed Lucifer and our powers. With the Drude siphoning off the power of those souls, we were weak. This meant more attacks, more souls being taken and changed. Suddenly, my father's last kingdom was too large, too cumbersome for the six of us to rule.

Not that it mattered now. Once upon a time, the life force of the Underworld had been the processing of souls, the guardians of souls as they healed or as they were punished. Then, when they were ready, they were ushered to the Pointe where they were sent back into the world. Some went on to become members of the Brotherhood. Some were chosen by the Seraphim. Others, the most obedient and deadly, were taken into my father's personal army, the Bane.

But all of it was cylindrical. A necessary part of life. We were meant to play our part. But I'd always known, always wondered, why the good souls, the rehabilitated souls that we were sending back onto Earth, were not getting any better. There was no bettering the world now.

It was a flawed system for a race designed to do only one thing. Live. Die. Try again.

I huffed out a breath, my body cooling as my power sank deep into my core, throbbing painfully as I tried to give my mind the quiet it needed to process.

Another what?

Fuck that male. I was almost in enough of a mood to chase him down and break a leg or two just to prove to Father how annoying his messenger was. But I didn't have time for vengeance. Not yet. There would be an end to the world. Then I could have my moment with that winged bastard.

Moving awkwardly, I moved to stroke a hand down my hair. It was long these days, a bright silvery blond. My fingers dug deep, and I swirled them at my scalp, thinking about how my mother had once treated me like this. She had been one of the few people who had never feared me. Even when I had been in my true form.

My eyes grew heavy as my mind dragged me through my memories. She had called me beautiful, her first and finest creation. The only female to ever use those words to me, until… My chest heaved as I threw myself into a standing position. Whipping my hand over my chest, I pressed hard at my center, waiting, hoping, unfeeling. There used to be a pounding there sometimes, a pull. But now, it was quiet, so quiet that I never would've guessed that I'd been experiencing nearly constant pain.

But now, nothing.

Perhaps it was that my soul, my power, was that weak at this point. I didn't doubt it. But even so, something raced through my blood, hot and urgent, as I stared into the darkness.

"Another one."

It couldn't be.

3

Nephesh

There was no proof about Arafel's theory that our souls, while still lost to us, could be reborn once again. But yet, this feeling… It was familiar. It felt…fuck, it felt good. Before I could think about the consequences, I was moving. Down the stairs, through the darkened courtroom, to the immense entryway, where I had once painted a small map of the Underworld. My palm burned with magic as I marched up, jabbing my finger above the depiction of a castle at the edge of a mountain. A breath later, I was braced against the smooth stone walls of Castle Fel's portcullis.

I barely glanced at the craggy, pine-covered mountains that spiked up from all sides. The Lord of Dreams preferred this vantage point, a guard tower against the River Styx, but also a clear advantage for when unfriendly creatures came calling.

"Arafel," I boomed, moving out onto one of the towers. My black-haired brother appeared instantly, his frame illuminating a floor below me as he looked up at me through a window. His pewter-gray skin nearly glowed in the dark as he yanked a shirt over his shoulders. Not fast enough, though. I could see the thick scrawling black lines, the deal he'd made with the woman who had carried his soul. His soul mate, Lucia.

She had saved his realm, given us hope when she not only gave him part of her soul, but also agreed to remain here, to rule the dream realm at his side, and therefore returned the whole of Arafel's soul to the Underworld where it belonged.

Because of her, we had a chance at this war.

And fuck, I wanted to hate her for it. But it wasn't her fault. She hadn't been here when my world came crumbling down. Perhaps if she had been, something would be different. Not likely, but I thought of it often.

"What are you doing here, Neph?"

My lips curled at the dreaded nickname. "I need a favor."

I could see Arafel stiffen from there, his black wings blooming from his back as he came closer. He knew that he owed me a favor. I had saved his mate in a time where he had been unable to do so. I briefly thought of the saucy dark-haired woman who had captured his heart. She was far less delicate now, the half of Arafel's soul that remained inside of her slowly spreading through her human self and making her into something altogether new.

She'd even learned to fly. Hades help my brother, who worried every moment about his sweet, smart little mate. And while I knew that every one of his instincts screamed at him to protect her and keep her far away from anything that might hurt her, Arafel was trying to be supportive. He'd mentioned the other day that Lucia had begun to dream walk on a regular basis.

I knew how significant having another dream walker would be, especially since the Drude appeared to be hiding out in the living world. We needed every pair of eyes and ears in the dream world as we could get. It was the safest, most efficient way to see what was happening in the living world without opening up the Underworld to potential invasion.

"Are you alright?" Arafel's voice was warm, gentle as he looked at me over, obviously expecting injury.

I smirked. My injuries had never been strictly physical. "Of course. I'm just here to cash in on my favor."

"As you mentioned. Do you want to come in?"

I looked past him, noticing for the first time that a slender shadow stood in the doorway to the tower he'd emerged from. A growl rumbled up in my chest at being watched, but I forced it down. If Arafel truly believed I was a danger to his mate, he would rip me to shreds in a moment. And he wouldn't even feel bad about it. I also wouldn't die, but it would take me a long fucking time to pull myself together.

Arafel stepped into my line of vision, blocking Lucia, his mate, from my gaze. While his posture remained relaxed, I could see the barely masked threat in his blue eyes. "I'll ask again, do you want to come in?"

"Such nice manners. I'm sure Mother would be thrilled." I folded my arms, putting my most aloof mask on my face. "No, I don't need to come in. What I need, it will take only a moment once you agree."

The tip of one wing twitched, a clear sign he was worried. He's always done that, even when we were young. "And what am I agreeing to?"

"I need to get into the living world."

"What? Why?" Arafel's hand slipped up to rub his jaw as he cast a wary look over me. "Why would you want to do that?"

I kept my face disinterested, even as the blood in my veins pulsed violently. I should tell him this part. Of all my brothers, he would understand. And even if he panicked and ran to Father…they would be too late to stop me. "Cerberus is there."

"Cerberus is in the living world?" Arafel's hands framed the dark curling horns on each side of his head. "With all three showing?"

I wished I was allowed to strangle him. But he was the only one who could help me tonight. I needed him conscious. "No, Arafel, I highly doubt he went into the living world as a three-headed, horse-sized dog."

"Then what's the problem? You said he always comes home."

"He does." I shifted on the stone, my leather-soled boots silent. "I believe he may have found something that belongs to me."

My brother tilted his head, bright-blue eyes flashing with carefully controlled power that nearly made me jealous, even if I'd never let him know that. "And what is that?"

I smiled, slow and full of fang. "My soul."

***

Justine

This was fine.

Everything was fine.

All I had to do was stay completely still until the dog just went away again. I pressed my back against the door, refusing to let my eyes budge from the enormous black and tan rottweiler that was still sitting in the middle of the room.

Why would someone put a dog in my room? Did that mean its owner was here too? I thought over the people who knew I was here, and the number was shockingly small. There was the team at the diner down the street that I worked at when they had open shifts. They had my address.

Had Dave, my landlord, suddenly decided to grow a heart and have normal human attachments? I snorted. Not likely. So that left—well, no one who would've left a dog in my apartment.

Swallowing the tremble in my voice, I held a hand out. "Hey there, handsome. Are you lost?"

The dog's tan brows moved a little, and then his jaws opened, tongue lolling out over dangerous-looking teeth. Encouraged that he hadn't immediately gone for my throat, I crept forward a step. Nothing happened. The dog continued to pant. I took another step towards him.

"Oh okay, maybe you're just lost. Did you come in off the fire escape maybe?" I guessed if the dog-sized rats in that alleyway could climb it, then maybe this dog could. I didn't think I'd left the window unlocked or open, but maybe. I could see almost every inch of my apartment from this vantage point, so it wasn't as if someone could hide from me while his dog lounged in my living area.

It was just the mystery dog and me.

Clearing my throat loudly, I gave into my intrusive thoughts one more time. "If anyone is living in my walls, or my closet or something, you can totally come out and get your dog. No harm, no foul. The front door is unlocked."

Nothing.

My shoulders relaxed a little and moved forward. "I guess it's just you and me then, huh buddy?"

I held my hand out, still a few steps from the dog, and waited. As if anticipating this moment, the dog bounded forward, causing me to shriek and dance around, unsure of what he was doing. I'd never had a pet before, and now that I suddenly did, I wasn't sure how to act.

The dog stopped immediately, haunches falling to the faded floors as happy, onyx eyes peered up at me. This time when I held my quivering hand out, the dog remained still, letting my fingertips brush lightly over the hard, boney line of his head. The hair was soft, of course, and I only had a moment to admire him before he turned his head and licked my palm with a slimy tongue.

I squealed, but this time in delight. As if he could tell the difference, the dog wagged his stumpy tail and moved closer, crowding against my legs.

"Well, since you're here," I said to him, both hands petting over his head now and down his thick neck. My heart lifted in my chest. "You might as well stay awhile." I reached back into my backpack.

"How do you feel about…" I read the label with a grimace. "Ravioli. Best you can get from a can."

The dog barked once, and I dropped to a knee on impulse, the can falling on the floor as I gripped both sides of his face. "Hey, hey, look at me. You can't be barking. I don't think animals are allowed here, and while I'm happy to keep your secret, the landlord lives right across from me, and I really don't need him coming in here. He's a dick." The dog woofed softly, as if to tell me he understood.

I swallowed, my fingers working that soft, thick scruff as I remained kneeling for another moment. As I stood, I swore that the big dog bobbed his head in agreement, but I chalked that up to having a very long, shitty day.

I retrieved the can from where it had rolled away and quickly divided my dinner between the two of us, adding some crackers from the cabinet to fill in any grumbling stomach gaps and watched some videos on my phone. As soon as I put my dish down, reclining back on my mattress as the day's woes sank into my skin, the dog wandered over and lay down at my side, his big head coming to rest on my calf as he stared at my door.

My gaze leaped to the door, visually double checking the menagerie of locks that covered every square of it. They were all sealed, locked, secured. We were safe. I pressed a hand to his back and whispered that to the dog, offering reassurances. And when I turned off the lights and peeled my outer layers off to crawl under the covers, my new companion immediately took the spot next to me. I huffed, but honestly his bulk was a layer of warmth that was unfamiliar but not unwelcome.

"Don't eat me or anything, okay?"

The dog just groaned, rolling over to his side as sleep finally claimed me.

The next morning, I shoveled some saltines and a granola bar down my throat as I held the end of the makeshift leash I'd made for the dog, who I had dubbed Clark. Grimacing at the dry throat that quickly followed, I pointed a finger down at the dog. We were standing in a small patch of grass, and I was attempting to get him to do his business.

"I'm no professional here, Clark, but I'm pretty sure dogs are supposed to pee out here." I pointed back at the apartment building behind us. "Not in there. Do you get it? Pee here, no pee there." Clark, named after the father figure from my favorite holiday-themed movie, looked at me with what almost appeared to be sorrowful eyes.

"Are you laughing at me?" The dog let out a soft woof, and my head flopped forward. "I know you are. I can tell. Okay, well, I have to go to work for a few hours, so if I come back to an enormous pile of—"

Clark cut me off, barking louder this time and making me grin. I jerked my chin at the building, and we were off, climbing each set of stairs with him by my side.

They were still long, but everything seemed a bit more manageable today, my body surprisingly well rested after last night. Turning onto my floor, I peeked my head out, holding Clark's giant head behind my hip until I deemed it empty and therefore safe. Side by side, Clark and I bounded down the hall to my apartment. The key slid in easily, and a moment later we were staring at each other once again.

"I'm going to go now," I announced, unclipping the belt and laundry line that I'd turned into a leash. Clark looked at me with disconcerting intelligence before wandering over to sit where he was when I first saw him yesterday.

"I'll be back," I said, my voice oddly thick. "Don't go anywhere, okay?" Those tan eyebrows rose and fell, but Clark remained where he was sitting. Taking a deep breath, I scurried down the hallway, past my landlord's door, holding my breath that the guy wouldn't open it. I couldn't afford to be late to work. I had the day shift at the diner just a short walk away from home. It was good work, real value, honest money. That was what I needed. Maybe someday, I could have a chance to prove to people that I was worth the second chance.

Maybe that'd be the day I would believe it myself.

The thing about having to survive on your own for such a long time meant that I had become a little immune to the whole principal of right and wrong. In my mind, there was only survival. Anything after that was just a bonus.

Once upon a time, I'd been like everyone else, living in a cute, quaint little house in the middle of nowhere Nebraska. Then it had been simple, the lines between good and bad clear as crystal. But now, I was here, scrimping and saving and stealing my way to survival.

After my shift ended for the day, I found myself staring down at the crumpled bills in my hand, dreading every thought that bombarded my panicked mind.

Because it wasn't enough.

My throat ached, but I pinched the bridge of my nose, a sad attempt to block the tears from leaving even as I desperately sorted through my mind for a new idea. One that didn't leave such a bitter taste on my tongue. All around me, people walked by, unaware of my crisis.

Brushing off my uniform, I swallowed my shame. Morally gray was the color of the day. Again. Forcing a calm expression to my face, I turned to the streets around me and looked for my next victim.

4

Nephesh

"Say it one more time."

I paused my pacing, aiming my most potent glare at my sibling. "In what language? I'm not sure how many times you want me to rephrase it for you, Arafel. The last time that Cerberus went to the living world and didn't immediately come back was when he found—" I swallowed, "—Anna. I think that while Hiriam is a living reminder of how shitty humans are, there's a fairly good chance he's correct and that Cerberus has found my soul again. And if Father has caught on, I don't want him going after them either."

Arafel regarded me carefully, perched in his big office chair, wings glamoured away again, as were mine. Otherwise, we took up too much fucking space, even in a castle. A flaw, but one worth it, especially for the ability to fly.

"Have you felt anything? Any pull?"

"No, not really, but after the cave"—Arafel's eyes flashed with something that looked a lot like regret before they returned to their iceberg blue— "my power has been drastically reduced. Especially on days like this when I'm personally processing souls by the thousand."

Arafel's head falls, staring at his black-tipped claws as he taps them against his desk. "I won't lie to you. It would make sense. Especially if that's how it happened before."

"It would. And honestly I don't need to explain anything to you. I rescued your mate, no questions asked. You owe me."

The tension grew between us, until finally he looked up at me. "What happens if you get to the living world, and you're stripped of your powers?"

"Well then, let's hope I find the soul bound or Cerberus finds me. Being around him gives me a small boost since he is one of my creatures. And if my soul is there, then I can only assume it will have the same effect that Lucia began to have on you as you spent more time around her."

"Let me get this straight. You're going to go up there, hope you can function, find your half-feral creature, find your soul, and what…? Drag them back down here and demand your soul?"

My eyes bored into him, fire licking at my fingertips as my temper flared. "I'm quite resilient, brother. I'm sure I'll figure something out."

"And if you find your soul, I know that Father has some concerns."

"Father always has concerns in regard to my soul, little brother. Which is exactly why it has to be returned to the Underworld."

"But not to you."

I snarled. "We will finesse the details once the soul is safely in my care. I do not trust Father's soldier or even my own for this task. And, as I was reminded last night, every other member of this Court is needed here. The dam will continue to do its work, as will my juror in my absence."

"Nephesh…"

"You won't even miss me. I will scamper into the living world, find my soul, capture it, bring it home, and then you and Father and the rest of the worriers can concern yourself with what to do with it after that."

Arafel sighed dramatically, and I knew I had won, "Alright, fine. How will you get home?"

"My most trusted Brotherhood warrior, Atlas, will be returning from delivering some Corrupted to Elon in a matter of days. He is still capable of shifting through the boundaries. I've already delivered his orders to retrieve me."

I didn't need to explain why I couldn't wait until he was back. The Corrupted had to be dealt with, and I couldn't let my father or any of my father's men find my soul before I did. While I was sure that he would retrieve it for me, I wasn't sure in what form it would be. Or what that would mean for me. I wasn't prepared to find out. I'd lost a part of myself already. Another would be too much.

If they thought there was nothing to me now, they hadn't seen anything.

"And if you're unsuccessful? What will you do?"

I smiled. "The same thing I'm doing now. My job, until it's all over."

"That's cheerful."

"Once upon a time, you asked for honesty. It has never served me well, but I refuse to go back on my word. Even now."

Arafel nodded, pushing to a standing position, the thick leather armor across his chest creaking slightly as he stretched his arms. Heavy wings, onyx black feathers to my pearl-white, slipped free from his glamor and stretched as well. A stab of jealousy drove through my chest at his ease. My brother was more comfortable in his natural form than I had ever been or could ever be.

My own wings were tucked away, a distant reminder of how once I had been a powerful force. Now I walked around, my appearance nearly human, sans the fangs and the black-tipped claws. Those remained, a reminder that I was neither man nor demon. Instead, I was some unholy combination.

"I'll send a note to Atlas as well. If he needs a boost to get into the living world, I can supply it."

I jerked my head in agreement as my brother came around the desk, his powerful arm extended.

I took it, my skin prickling at the unfamiliar touch of another's hands on my body. Nevertheless, I gripped his arm back.

"Nephesh, I—"

Bristling at the quickly approaching conversation, I broke in, "We don't have time for this. I need to hurry, Arafel. Please."

The plea slipped out before I could stop it, and I could see my brother register it, processing the way my fingers bit into his forearm. Slowly, he nodded, blue eyes closing for just a moment before opening, this time burning bright with the glow of his power.

"Be safe," he offered me, his power slipping over me with all the coolness of shade in the summer, tugging me into the shadows that covered my flesh.

"You, too, brother."

And then his magic surged up and over me, encompassing me completely as we fell through time and space and straight into the world of living souls.

The moment my feet hit the hard ground, I collapsed, pain filling my mind. Just before I lost consciousness, a powerful tug yanked at my heart.

They were here. And close.

"Cerberus, come to me." And then I gave into the darkness.

***

Justine

The first time I stole something, I was sixteen years old. I'd been freshly kicked out of the shelter for ending a fight another girl had conveniently started. I stood on the steps of that building, my lip split and bleeding, and decided that taking the high road couldn't always be my first choice. Not anymore.

And so, when an older teen, whom I had watched bully their friend for nearly an hour, left their backpack unattended, I picked it up. One stop at the pawn shop later, and I had enough money to get myself a sandwich, a jacket, and pocket money to keep me going for the rest of the week.

Physically it had been more than easy. But emotionally, I'd tortured myself the entire time. Every second I held that pack, I heard my mother's logical tone plead for me to do the right thing. I had wished with every part of my heart that she had been here in person to scold me. I would've gladly taken a thousand tongue-lashings than experience one more day without her. But that's not how life worked, and I needed a way to survive.

The habit of choosing my so-called victims remained the same. I would watch, wait until I could find someone I could justify they deserved it. Some days it was the asshole who didn't tip at breakfast. Others it was the one who scratched and dinged up other people's cars but forgot to lock their own.

While I shouldn't have been judging them, I did. And somehow it made it easier for me to shove down my morals and do what I needed to do.

Today it was a petite woman in gym clothes, her eager hands all over the man in the seat next to her. They had been clearly visible through the window of a popular coffee shop a few blocks from the apartment.

I had come in, ordered a small coffee, and seated myself at the next table over. I hadn't picked out a target yet…until I overheard their very loud conversation. I knew then one of them had to be the one for today.

She was his mistress. His family was at home, waiting for him to return. It wasn't hard to convince my already shaky morals to decide that she deserved my sticky fingers. When he got up to buy her a cake pop, I couldn't stop myself from sliding into the now-vacant chair.

For a minute, she stared at me, and then a clueless smile crawled across her vibrant pink lips. "Hi, sorry. Do I know you?"

"No." I fanned my face a little. "Sorry! I just had to come by and tell you how cute you and your husband are."

I could see the wheels working in her head, but thankfully it must've been a short circuit, because a second later she leaned across the little tabletop, Gushing, "I know! Isn't he dreamy?"

"So dreamy," I responded, eagerly eyeing the tiny little wallet she had hanging on the back of her chair. It was almost too easy sometimes. She opened her mouth, probably to gush further, when the man reappeared at her shoulder once again, a sprinkled pop in one large hand.

"Who is this? A friend?" He looked me over, a smarmy smile on his average-looking face. I could see him taking in my diner uniform. Something about his careful surveillance began to set off alarm bells in my mind.

Clueless leaned over, patting my arm. "A new friend. She just stopped by." She turned her attention completely back to me. "Can you believe he's a detective? Such a great guy."

Alarm bells weren't just ringing now. They were tolling in my head, dulling everything else as I glanced back up at him. But I couldn't back down now. Not when I was so close. If I didn't have rent, there was no telling what my landlord would do. I couldn't leave that up to fate.

"I always wanted to date a cop," she confessed, leaning into me. "You know, I've got a thing for men in uniform."

"Detective, honey, not a cop," he corrected her, setting the cake pop down in front of his date.

Adrenaline made my fingers tingle as my opportunity lurked. *Now,* my mind screamed to me. *Hurry.*

"I don't want to ruin your date. I just had to say something."

"Nice to meet you," Clueless said, waving at me.

I moved past her, one hand sliding her wallet into my armpit under the thin jacket I'd thrown on this morning, the other sliding over her shoulder in a friendly looking pat.

"Nice to meet you too."

Get out, get out, get out. My mind was screaming at me to get out of here. Hesitating, as if I were finishing the last of my coffee, I slid the credit card and her cash out of her wallet and straight into my pocket. Then I let the card fall to the ground. She would find it when she got up to leave, assuming she'd dropped it. I only needed cash, and thank God she'd had several neatly folded bills tucked in.

And it wasn't like she was going to be paying for anything with this guy around anyway.

With my head held high, coffee cup still in hand, I strolled casually out of the coffee shop. Taking in a breath of the rapidly cooling air, I cut down the one-way street just behind, adrenaline still coursing through my blood.

I was so close. Just a few more feet. Just a few more steps now until I could duck away. I squeaked in shock as a thick, heavy hand landed on my shoulder. I twisted away, shock making me stupid as I turned to stare up into the face of the detective from inside. My coffee cup fell to the pavement.

"You spilled my coffee," I said, my lips numb with fear.

His face was mottled with fury, big splotches of red appearing across his cheeks as he hauled me closer. His girlfriend was nowhere to be seen.

"You think I don't know that play?"

"What play?" I scooted away, trying to keep as much distance between us as possible. His grip was like iron, halting any thoughts of an escape.

"Try again, sweetheart."

I bristled at the nickname, my hand going to his and trying to detach him from me. "I have no idea what you're talking about. Let me go!"

His grip was moving, resetting until his fingers were digging into my bicep in a way that I knew would make him even harder to shake. "You whore. I know what you did. Not give it back."

Masking my nerves, I raised my eyebrows. "Let me go. Now."

"Not a chance." He began to walk. "My car is back here. We are taking you in. Your sticky fingers aren't getting the best of anyone another second."

My calm slipped, and panic throbbed in my throat. I leaned back. "You can't."

"I can."

"No. No, please."

His car was now in view, the black four-door waiting for him to throw me into the back of it. And that would be it. No more running. There was a strange relief to it. But then I remembered what could happen there. I would be a sitting duck. Those people, whoever they had been, had killed my parents, and I knew they were still looking for me. It might sound crazy, but I knew, more than anything else in the world, that it was true.

Closing my eyes, I threw my weight away from him again, my heels scraping against the loose gravel on the crumbling roadway. "You can't take me. Please. I will sell my soul to the devil before I go with you."

My heels slipped, and with a cry I went down. At least, that's what I thought would happen. Instead of the ground smacking into me, there was only a solid, hot form at my back. Slowly, I peeled my eyes open and stared up at the detective's face. His mouth was wide open, spittle leaving his lips as he shouted at me. But there was no audible shout. I followed the line of his throat down, realizing that neither his pulse moved nor his chest lifted. He was frozen, mid-act, fury shining back at me out of those dull eyes.

A deep voice spoke from behind me. "I hear you are in the market for a deal?"

I turned, as best I could with the detective's grip still heavy on my upper arm. At my back stood a man, his tall, broad frame blocking out any of the light from the gray day as he loomed over me. Everything about him was larger than life, from the broad, muscular chest, to the pair of arms that slowly crossed as I watched. But nothing prepared me for his face.

My stomach dipped. He was beautiful. Pale, silvery blond hair was long and loose around his shoulders. A straight nose, angular jaw, and straight brows captured a face that was both masculine and broad while still being immeasurably lovely.

His deep-amber eyes shone back at me with more than a little fire in them. As I took him in, he was doing the same to me, his eyes cascading down my body in sleek strokes that left me breathless. When his gaze settled on the detective's hand on my arm, something dark and dangerous twisted his stunning features. My belly gives a responding tug in the protective way his body bowed over me.

"A deal?" I tore my eyes away from him to look at the frozen detective. "What's happening right now? I'm so confused."

The beautiful man moved around until he was behind the detective. He had several inches on the man and at least fifty pounds. Carefully, he began to loosen a finger one at a time, freeing me from his hold. "Got yourself in a bit of a situation, haven't you, little thief?"

5

Nephesh

I didn't know what was wrong with me. When I'd crashed into the living world, I'd been hoping that Cerberus would lead me right to her. But that wouldn't be necessary after all. I'd barely gotten to my feet when I'd felt it.

A call? Not quite. More of a demand, and my chest and body had ached with the desire to find the source. I'd let my instincts guide me the short distance, parting the sprinkling of pedestrians as I followed the pull that burned deep in my chest.

I had only gone a short distance when fear had ricocheted through me, and I knew in a moment it wasn't mine. It was hers. And somehow, for the first time in fifty years, my cold heart bumped to life, adrenaline flooding my system as I grew closer and closer to the source of the pull.

And still, nothing could prepare me for when I turned the corner around the backside of an older brick building and found myself staring at her.

I knew her in an instant, every long-buried, choked-out instinct in my soul screaming for release as I watched a man put his hands on her. I swallowed the roar, her very presence filling me with not just strength, but with a sharp awareness of the soul that warmed her own chest.

Mine.

It took only a swipe of my fingers to freeze time. From the traffic noises to the male who dared to hold on to her. Everything except for her. I let my body buffer her fall as my hands automatically moved to cradle her slender form against me. My magic leaped in my chest as the soft pressure of her against me rooted its way into my mind, my soul, my fickle, traitorous heart.

For a moment, I wished I had frozen her along with her attacker, simply to have a moment to let my mind catch up with the very real carrier of my soul who stood against me now.

My soul bound. Likely my soul mate. Fuck all of this madness.

Against my body, I could almost feel her frantic heartbeat, and suddenly I was terrified. Of her. Of this entire situation. Before she could whirl away from me, I simply asked, "I hear you are in the market for a deal?"

She turned, satin strands of red hair brushing over my neck as she whipped around to face me. For a moment, I was worried I'd messed up the magic, because she seemed frozen as well. But her eyes were moving, taking me in, curiosity, interest, and confusion all wrapped up on that stunning face. And when she parted her lips, the soft pink reminding me distinctly of fresh rose petals, I had to cross my arms, tucking my hands in to make sure I didn't reach out to touch her.

Because I needed to touch her more than I needed my next breath. History and need battled in my core. She had called for a demon. It was sheer luck that meant I was the one who had answered the call. Then again, I was thinking a lot of things that had once looked like luck might just be some kind of divine intervention.

Whatever it was. I had to deal with it before this moved anywhere. I sent out a whisper of my magic, letting it settle over her as my natural abilities to sort the souls came front and center. Her scales were tipped to good, but there was plenty of darkness there. I took in the freckles on her nose, the way her chin quivered as she raised it high as I looked her over.

My throat clamped shut for a moment. What if my soul was responsible for that part of her? Responsible for her darkness?

Arafel's soul hadn't affected Lucia until she had given half of hers in return, but I knew without even talking to her that whomever this was, she was going to be a very different human than Lucia.

"A deal?" Her head tilted now, staring between me and the frozen man and back again. I could see the bright intelligence in her gaze as she attempted to take in all the new bits of information about the world around her. I saw the dip in her throat as she swallowed, and the insane urge to brush my lips over her there, against her pulse, nearly strangled me. Cursing silently, I tightened my hold over myself. I had to be very careful about all of this.

While this fiery little human may not know what monster she carried, I did.

"What's happening?"

Forcing myself to step away, I moved around the frozen man, taking in the shining badge at his waist, the ugly sneer on his lips, and the way she shifted nervously. Even now she was thinking about making a run for it. I almost laughed.

Of course my soul bond would be a pain in the ass. I was unable to keep the smirk out of my voice when I spoke again. "Got yourself in a bit of a situation, haven't you, little thief?"

She glared. "I was handling it just fine."

"Clearly."

She blinked rapidly then backed up a bit, raising one slender digit and moving as if she was going to jab me in the face with it. Humor sparked in my chest at the fierce look on her face. I smothered it with great effort.

"Excuse you, but you don't get to just show up and—" her throat bobbed as she looked around us once more at the frozen area "—do whatever the fuck this is."

I coughed to cover up my surprised laugh. Her hand suddenly slammed back to her face.

"Oh my God, am I dead?"

Now I did actually snort out a short laugh, dropping my chin to hide the smile that surprised me. When I'd collected myself, I met her eyes once again. "No, not dead. But like I said, you are definitely in a situation with this one." I jabbed a thumb at the male who had been shouting at her. "Care to explain?"

"To you?" She squared up at me again, sharp features tight.

"To the demon who has the capacity to get you out of it."

Her eyes darted around the alleyway then back to me. "Demon?"

I gestured down at myself. "Demon." Pretending my skin didn't prickle as her gaze coasted over me once again. I could see the soft pink tip of her tongue sweep out, brushing over that full bottom lip with a move that made long-dormant desire simmer to life in my gut.

"You don't look like a demon."

I huffed out a breath, a half snarl on my lips. "Because you've met so many."

She sputtered at me, which very nearly made another smile curl my lips. Cursing, I rubbed a hand over my face as she stomped a little in place before addressing me again. "Okay, fine, this is definitely weird. As long as I'm really not dead—"

"Not dead."

She nearly spat in fury, continuing straight through my comment, "Then you are here to…what? Offer me a deal I can't resist?"

I sighed loudly. "That was your idea. I just came for the deal. Any deal is fine. I'm not picky."

Dark-red brows crinkled as she stared at me. "So, what do I do now? Throw out some conditions and we shake on it?"

"Oh, it's far more complicated than that."

"Of course it is."

"First"—I mimicked her earlier pose, holding up one finger in front of her face—"you tell me what the fuck is happening here. Then I decide whether I'm going to help you. Then we put it in…writing. So, to say."

Her teeth were busy working her lower lip, which was more distracting than I'd like to admit. My chest felt warm and fuzzy as I watched her, which immediately pissed me off.

"Or you can try again with him? Since it was obviously going so well."

She considered me for a long time before her narrow shoulders dropped a little. "Fine. It's not like I have another choice."

I didn't answer but stood stoically watching her.

"I stole money from him. Well, from his girlfriend."

My brows rose, but I didn't move a muscle. There was more coming, I could feel it.

"He's cheating on his wife with that woman, and it was too easy." Her throat worked, but her chin remained stubbornly raised.

I still waited. Her blunt white teeth were gnawing at her bottom lip with an intensity that made me either want to scold her, first for doing it and second for not letting me. Fuck, I was messed up over this woman already. I'd only been around her a few minutes. No wonder Arafel was such an idiot for Lucia. I needed to make this deal and get the fuck back to the Underworld as soon as possible.

"I didn't make enough for rent. And it's due soon. I can't move again. I'm not ready. I just got here." She sniffled, tossing her head a little as a hand quickly brushed a drop of moisture away from her face as she did. "Is that enough? Any other part of my soul you want me to bare?"

"You have no idea."

"What?"

I hummed. "That's plenty. You stole his money because he's an idiot who cheated on his chosen mate and you needed it for your home."

Her nose wrinkled. "It sounds weird when you say it that way."

This time it was me who glared down at her. After a moment, her face relaxed and hot pink spots appeared on her cheeks. "Sorry, that was rude." Her delicate throat swallowed. "What happens now?"

What did happen now, I wondered to myself. I could remove his memories of the woman behind me easily enough. That wasn't the confusing part. But what I needed was both my dog back and my soul returned to me.

Fear tugged at my gut, and this time it was all mine. I could take her soul, just not absorb it until I was somewhere safe. That was what my father had wanted. And while I didn't trust him at all, I knew that there had to be some alternative. I could not be allowed to absorb the missing half of my soul. It was too dangerous. I could take it somewhere that I could trust my brothers to keep the monster inside of me at bay. That would be the safest way to go. Even if it meant me going back into the dark.

But then I looked over at her. She was the one my mother had chosen for me, after Anna. She was the one who was uniquely equipped to be mine. And suddenly I understood why Arafel was so obsessed with Lucia. Why he had moved worlds to be with her.

As I watched, her brows wrinkled again and she rubbed at the center of her chest, which immediately made my decision for me. Because as she did that, the bond at the center of my chest, the place where my soul was torn from, hummed to life. Aware of both the soul's close proximity and my mate's.

Fucking complications.

"Are you alright?" I forced out.

She gave me a small smile. "Yes, I just got a weird feeling. Probably just shock or something."

I breathed in, the scent of her washing over my senses and making every part of my body come to life. My power swirled to life in response, already growing from being near her for this small amount of time. It was intoxicating.

I needed a little more. Jealousy consumed me, reminded me of what my family had stolen from me.

"Here's the deal I will offer. I will offer my protection, and you will give me anything I want."

That look she gave me, I fucking loved it. "Is this some kind of awkward way to get me to have sex with you?"

I bared my teeth at her. "Do I look like I need help finding partners?"

"Not unless you talk to them first," she threw back at me, cheeks glowing pink even in the gloom of the day.

I sighed. "I will protect you, and in return I ask for you to give me something."

"Do I need that something to survive?"

Clever little thief.

"No, not at all. In fact, you don't even know it exists. But if you refrain from doing it, then our deal is void and I own your soul."

Her eyes went wide.

Slowly, I extended my hand. "Do we have a deal?"

"Nothing I need to survive, something I don't even know exists." She looked at me, then back to the screaming man, and then back to me. "Yes, demon, you do."

Delicately, she put her hand in mine, my skin burning at the first touch of our bare skin. With a soft growl, I yanked her forward against me. She gasped; her hands splayed over my chest as my magic whirled free, white flames flicking over her. If she hadn't believed me before, she did now, and I watched the stunned expression wash over her face, melting into something that was akin to awe.

I gave in, letting my fingers trail across her cheek for just a moment, passing it off as if I was brushing one of the flames off of her face. Under my touch, her skin heated, as if in welcome, and the bond in my chest screamed to be set free.

I gritted my teeth, forcing my hand to lower once again. "Your name, thief?"

"Justine Anders," she whispered, her chest rising and falling rapidly against my own.

Carefully, I changed the grip on her hand, moving it so that it rose between us, forcing her a step back.

"Justine Anders, do you accept my deal?"

6

"I do."

With my eyes on hers, I held the underside of her wrist close to my mouth. Her breathing was ragged as she stared at me. Deep in her chest, her heartbeat raced. Unable to resist, I let just a little of my demon loose, my fangs slipping free of the human glamor. Justine gasped, pulling back a little, but not before I pressed my lips to the thrumming pulse in her wrist.

Deals were simple magic, a binding contract, each unique and individual as a flake of snow. And while the signed deals that had sealed Arafel and Lucia together were a much higher power, this one was something any of the demons could do. It was how we gained power. The only sign of the magic would still be branded upon the human who initiated it. A living reminder until the deal was done.

When I pulled away, her pupils were large, dark, and held something that looked dangerously like heat. The answering pull in my own body made my cock ache and the bond in my chest hum happily.

Justine blinked rapidly, yanking her wrist back, and she looked down, brows furrowed. "A lily?"

Shock filtered through me, and it took every bit of willpower not to snatch her wrist back and look for myself. After a long moment, Justine tentatively held her wrist out, the intricate design only a few shades darker than her pale skin, the lines of the lily and petals so detailed that I nearly reached out to stroke her wrist once again.

It was identical to the ones I'd been drawing. My brows lowered to match her confused expression. Had I asked the magic to do that? I didn't think so. Justine brought my attention back to the present as she leaned over, prodding the shoulder of our still-frozen enforcer.

"Ah yes, our cheater." I moved towards him. "Let's take care of him, then."

With a wave of my hand, the magic released its hold on him, causing the man to stumble forward a step before he frantically looked around, first at Justine then at me.

"What the—"

My flames, invisible as they were, heated the air as I relaxed my hold on them. "You are having a great day. You've decided to donate to this young woman after behaving horribly to her and are now getting into your car, forgetting everything about the date inside and heading home to your wife, who you will inform of your improprieties and will bear whatever punishment she deems worthy of you."

I looked over my shoulder at where Justine watched with wide eyes, one hand over her mouth. "Enough?"

She nodded, a small giggle coming out as I turned back. I didn't stop the small smile that curled my lips as I faced the man once more. "You're dismissed." As my hands lowered, the magic retracted back into me, leaving behind the newly installed memories. The detective blinked then gave a strained smile to us both.

"Excuse me. I have somewhere to be," he said casually then turned on his heel, getting into his car and pulling out, all while Justine and I watched side by side.

"Oh my God," she whispered, "Oh my God, this is real. You really are a demon."

I shrugged. "I did tell you."

Then she was laughing, bent over, her hands on her knees as the bright twinkling tone of her joy washed over me.

I groaned, pretending to be irritated as the bond in my chest practically crawled out of my skin to get closer to her. "What now?"

"I can't believe that worked. I can't believe…" Her gaze caught on the tattoo of our deal on her wrist. "I can't believe any of this."

"But yet, you do."

Justine tilted her head. "I've always wanted to believe there was something else out there. I always said I was cursed, but maybe luck is finally on my side."

"Not luck, little thief… Just a demon in need of a deal." The lie felt like a hot poker behind my eyes.

Hands on hips, she grinned up at me. "Honestly, I think I'm okay with that." Her smile slipped a breath later, and I felt the loss of it like a stab to my heart.

"And now we just…what? Go back to normal? Until you ask for your thing?"

I nodded, the pull in my chest growing tight and angry as I began to step away from Justine. But when I contemplated leaving, my instincts threatened to overwhelm me. I couldn't leave. The deal wasn't done. And I wasn't talking about her part of it. I must've missed something, since my protection was still incomplete.

That meant I had to stay with her. With a grimace, I gestured to the street. "Lead the way."

Justine tilted her head again. "Excuse me, what?"

"You asked for protection, isn't that, right?"

Shock washed over her features. "From that guy!" Her slender fingers were pointing down the street down which our offender had rushed.

"You did not clarify that." I hadn't either, but no need to inform her of my mistake. I was quite sure a woman like her would need protection from something else soon enough. Then the deal would be done. Informing her of my mistake would only give her more ammunition against me.

"So, what, you're just going to follow me around?"

"If necessary. As soon as the deal is complete, then I will be able to leave."

"That is not necessary. Your end of the deal is fulfilled."

"I will decide that."

"Well, that's fucking great," she said, stalking off down the sidewalk.

I followed, my stride swinging and casual as I kept up with her furious stomping. After a block, her ire seemed to fade, and she slowed, letting me walk side by side with her.

"Where are we off to in such a hurry?"

"I need to feed my dog. Unless dog-care duties are a part of the package too."

"Not at this time."

"Well, too bad. You can at least help while you wait to save me from something." Justine eyed an incoming bus warily then looked back to me; mouth open. "What if…"

"It doesn't work like that. You can put yourself in as much danger as you'd like, and while I would be forced to help you because I'm a decent male, it won't make the deal any more complete than before."

Justine pouted.

"It has to be an authentic event."

"This is going to take forever, then," she grumbled. "I don't need rescuing very often."

I nearly snorted, blocking another passerby from bumping into her, my scowl making him scurry to the edge of the roadway. "I'm sure."

"Am I responsible for feeding you now?"

"I am not a stray animal, Justine, and am quite capable of feeding myself if the need arises."

She snorted. "Good, because I don't know if I can afford to feed you both, and I like the dog better."

Together, we wound our way up to an older building then up a rickety, loudly protesting set of stairs. Every once in a while, she would look at me, mouth open as if she might say something else but thought better of it. As for me, I was content to just stay at her side. But when her apartment door swung open to reveal one very smug and pleased-looking Cerberus, I couldn't stop the growl that slipped from my mouth.

Justine whirled to stand in front of him, her hands raised. "Now it's certain. I *definitely* like him better."

I glared at my pet, whose stubbed tail thumped the floorboards in welcome. "Most people do."

7

Justine

I should've run away, or maybe even slammed the door in his face. But instead, I stood there in between the dog and my newly acquired paranormal bodyguard and squared up against him. After what I'd just seen him do, I knew I should be freaking out, but maybe it was the survivalist in me or the fact that I'd always felt like there was something I was missing, but I held my ground.

After all, he was supposed to protect me.

He was bound to, right? That was part of the deal. "No fighting, you two." I spun to face the dog. "Clark, I know he's a dick, but he has to stay. At least for now."

The demon gave me an incredulous look. "You named him Clark?"

"Yeah, why not?"

Sighing deeply, he stepped into my apartment. I didn't have the time to be embarrassed until right now. Between the showdown with the detective and my panicked rush here, I now realized that I had a stranger in my home.

"I, uh, come on in."

Amber eyes crinkled, but his lips remained a flat line. "I'm already in."

"Good, good. At least you're not like a vampire or something, are you?" I hurried to close the door behind him then paused, "Oh shit. Vampires aren't real, are they?"

"No," he said dryly, moving into the room and dropping to a knee in front of Clark.

"Oh." I made a face at his back. "Just demons, then. How silly of me."

But he didn't answer. He was stroking the dog. I approached him carefully, still anxious about having another person in my apartment. It might not be much, but it was mine—for now— and having this larger-than-life person in here made it suddenly feel stifling, even with the temperamental heater in the corner out of order. I tugged at my uniform. "Are you going to attack me? Now that we're alone, I mean."

The man blinked slowly. "Why would I do that?"

"I don't know. I just don't know you. I don't really let people into my life very often."

Silence fell between us, and I started to feel awkward. My mouth opened, and then suddenly he was speaking again.

"I promised to protect you. Why would I attack you now?" He stood, coming to a stop before me once again. My neck ached as I attempted to look him in the face. I felt the white-hot rush of a blush crawling over my skin as the beautiful demon peered down at me, curiosity in every inch of his expression.

"You don't believe me." He didn't bother waiting for a response, his voice rumbling on. "I'm sorry. I should not have assumed you were ready for me to be here like this. How about this? If I attempt to hurt you, the dog will eat me."

"Bite you," I said quietly.

He regarded me closely, eyes narrowing as one edge of his lips lifted in the tiniest smile. I had the inexplicable urge to press my lips there, to capture that tiny bit of external joy.

"Sure, bite me."

I swallowed a laugh because this was not the moment to get a case of the giggles, but something about this whole night was setting all my emotions off kilter. "Okay, got it. But how do you know that?"

"Simple" he said, a hand rising to brush a wild strand of my hair out of my eyes. "He's, my dog."

Silence.

My mind scrambled. "You're lying."

"Not at all. Cerberus has been mine since my father created him."

"Cerberus?" My chest ached, my lungs desperately pulling air into my body as I attempted to process this last little bit of information. "But...but..."

"Don't worry. The stories are largely out of proportion. As you can see, he's completely capable of being a normal dog. Most days."

I started over at the dog, my mind growing fuzzy. There was a string of drool hanging from his lips as he watched me, black and tan head slowly tilting. This was the mythological guard dog of Hell? Because just yesterday, I'd fed him canned pasta, and the resulting gas had seemed real enough. That didn't seem possible. But if it was…

"Was this a setup? Did he find me for a reason?"

The demon shrugged. "He does what he wants. But I'm sure he's here for a reason."

"That's suspicious."

He didn't answer. He was circling the small apartment, long pale fingers skimming along the walls as he did.

"What's your name, anyway?"

He paused and then said after a moment, "You can call me Judge."

I rolled my eyes. "Fitting."

His sigh was deep and long, and I could tell he was completely exasperated with me. Probably the exact same way I felt about him. But even as he relaxed on the edge of the mattress, his back supported by the wall, his legs stretched out, deep inside I knew that he wasn't a danger to me. The danger that had followed me my whole life, the curse that I seemed to bring wherever I went…. I could feel that lurking behind me, around me, inside my shadow. But now, with him here, things felt different. There was a brightness in my chest that nearly made me dizzy at times.

And while I knew people had mentioned butterflies when they met certain people, this was something else altogether.

I stared at the beautiful demon, who was closing his eyes as if he had not a single worry in his entire being.

"Make yourself at home," I grumbled as I plopped my purse by the door and watched Cerberus move over to lie down by his master.

One amber eye flickered open in my direction before closing again. "If you think that I'm not going to watch you every second of the day until you fulfill my end of the bargain, then you have something else coming."

I crossed my arms, glaring at him. "You're serious about staying here, then."

He sighed again, the powerful muscles in his chest rising and falling. "Deadly so. To separate us would cause vast amounts of pain for both parties."

I gaped at him, at the dog, and then back at him until I realized my mouth was getting dry and Judge had done nothing but apparently doze off during my temper tantrum. I stomped over to the kitchen, banging my shitty pans around as I dug for something to fill my growling stomach. As I attempted to trigger the gas on my rickety little stove, my temper rose. "Should've stolen something precooked while I was at it."

I was still fuming when the demon moved through the apartment. Appearing at my side, his long-fingered hands swept across the oven, and instantly the fuse lit and my water jumped to a boil. I stared slack-jawed at him, a little shocked by another casual showing of magic.

"Oh, okay. Fine, you can stay."

Judge chuckled, the sound as rich as it was surprising, his body hot against the back of mine. I kept my eyes trained on the pasta noodles I was opening, dumping them into the now boiling water. But they strayed away, my chin twisting a little to see what he was looking at. He seemed fascinated by every move of my hands. And I couldn't deny the way that my skin flushed with every breath of his that hit the back of my neck.

"You don't know much about personal space, do you?"

Judge stepped back, but only slightly. I was surprised by the way my body clenched, missing the presence of him against me. "My apologies. I meant only to watch. I find your cooking to be fascinating."

"You've never made pasta before?"

"I've never made anything edible before." I heard him walking away, moving back to the window. I cut a quick look in his direction, watching as he leaned down, his palms flat on the windowsill as he stared out into the alleyway below. Shame filled my stomach for a moment.

"Sorry it's not much of a view."

Judge turned, sitting his butt on the edge instead of his hands, and regarding me carefully. "I find it rather beautiful." Was he smirking?

My cheeks felt too warm, and it had nothing to do with the stove in front of me. I forced my attention back to the pasta, stirring it aggressively.

"What's it like? Where do you come from?"

He didn't answer for a long time, and I didn't think he would for a minute. I drained the water, hissing at the steam as it warmed my face even further. As I was moving the noodles back to the saucepan, I heard his voice once more.

"Beautiful," he said, his voice emotionless. "Dying."

"Dying?"

His lips quivered as I poured some pasta sauce over the top of my noodles and added the chicken. "Just because our citizens are less…corporeal than your own doesn't mean we don't have many of the same issues."

"Sorry. I didn't mean to assume. I thought maybe it would be all…lava and grim reapers and such."

Judge lifted one shoulder, the muscle in his forearm jumping. "The reapers only serve my brother, and as for lava, it's not what you think."

I stared, attempting nonchalance, but my voice came out a high-pitched squeak. "Uh-huh. Sure."

"I've distracted you," Judge said, pointedly nodding towards my dinner.

"Shoot, shoot, shoot," I hissed, cursing at the stove, at the saucepan, and even at my own inability to stay on task. I dropped some of the pasta mixture into bowls and danced my way across the apartment to the floor, where I curled up at the edge, putting the bowl on the ground and sucking on the thumb that had gotten overly hot during my transfer from stove to bowl.

"Let me see," Judge said, coming to knee in front of me.

I almost flinched as he loomed over me. His hands immediately wrapped around mine, and my pulse leaped at the firm way that he gripped my wrist. When I instinctively jerked away, he tightened his hold, amber eyes hot on me.

"Please," Judge said. "Let me."

I froze, watching as his mouth got closer to my reddened thumb. Then, just before it was touching his lips, he retreated a little and then blew out a breath over my skin. Instead of the warmth that I had felt when he stood against me, it was icy cold, bloating over my meager burn and turning it dull and back to a soft throb.

"Uh, wow. Thank you."

"No apology needed, little thief." Then he rose, moving back to the window in a flash of white hair and dark clothes.

I ate my dinner quietly, casting the occasional glance his way as he wandered the small apartment, appearing to be content to explore the space on his own.

"So what are you going to do while you're here?" I asked him as I munched on my dinner. Each bite was still hot, and I spent half the time blowing on it, the other half attempting to not stare at the demon in my apartment.

"Keep you safe, clearly."

I halted mid-blow, frowning. "I don't need protection at night."

Judge raised a brow. "You also didn't need protection during dinner, and look what happened."

"You are equating a very small burn with life-and-death moments."

"And yet they all happened within hours of each other." Judge looked at me, curiosity making his forehead wrinkle. "Unless you are meaning to test me."

"No." I rubbed my eyes. "No, Judge, I'm not trying to test you. Unlike you, I'm not exactly sure how this whole deal thing works."

"I've already explained."

"Explain again, maybe? I had a boatload of adrenaline coursing through my body at the time."

Judge crossed his arms, leaning back against the wall with a soft thud. I flinched, afraid the wall behind him might give way under the weight of his body. But I didn't say anything. He was tense now, more so than before, and I hadn't gotten as far as I had without realizing when you should leave something alone.

Or someone.

"You agreed that you would give me something, and in return I would…how did you say it…bail you out of trouble?"

"That's it? Even I remember that part." I twirled my fork in the air for a moment then dived in for another bite, when a pair of black boots appeared in my vision. Again, he squatted in front of me, his jaw so tight I could see the muscles in his cheeks leap.

"It means," Judge said, his hand gripping my face with a hot-skinned palm and turning my face up to his, "that until we complete the protection portion of the deal, I will be right here, surely busy keeping you out of trouble."

I couldn't stop the cheeky response. "Seems like a bad deal for you."

"Maybe, maybe not. You never know when I might have a need for a short-tempered human thief."

"I am not…" I paused, glaring. "Short-tempered."

His brow rose sardonically, and I huffed out a short breath, pushing away my empty bowl. "Fine. I'm getting dressed for bed. I have no idea what demons do at night, but you are welcome to do whatever you want."

Judge's lips quivered, but he released my now cool finger. "Thank you for your permission, my lady."

"Ugh. You really are awful." Dropping my bowl by the sink, I marched the short distance across the floor and slammed the bathroom door. Once safely hidden, I dragged a brush through my hair as I raved about smug, irritating demons who didn't know when to stop. Pinning my mop of red locks on top of my head, I double checked the lock on the door, after which I admonished myself thoroughly because I'd just seen the demon stop time.

I didn't think a lock on a door was going to stop him from seeing me naked if he wanted to. But other than the touchy moments earlier, the demon had made zero effort to show me any kind of interest in me.

Which was good. It really was. I didn't have time for anyone else in my life. Let alone a cocky blond who clearly hated me. Or humans. Probably both.

After a long shower—or as long as I had hot water, which was only a few minutes-I did my usual nighttime routine. But today I took extra time brushing my hair, teeth, and giving myself a pep talk in the mirror. I left the bathroom in my overlarge tee and a pair of loose sleep shorts.

Judge had gotten comfortable, his long legs stretched across my mattress, one of my books in his hands. The size of his hands made it look like a child's toy instead of a full-length mystery.

Ignoring him, I flipped the lights off and threw my dirty clothes in the corner I had deemed my makeshift clothes hamper. I crawled into bed, my feet jerking to my chest as they encountered the demon still lying across the end of the mattress.

"I don't bite, I promise." His voice was a dark rumble that settled somewhere under my belly, making my breath hitch as I made a show of rolling over away from him.

Why was I a little disappointed? Covering my face with my sheets, I prayed for sleep.

8

Nephesh

She was a pest. A tiny, frail, pitifully dressed human pest. She woke me up every hour on the hour last night, and it seemed that she always waited until I was completely content and finally comfortable before she'd once again wake me up. I believed it was nightmares that made Justine cry out in her sleep, and for the first time in my life, I wished for Arafel's powers, to see what tortured her from the safety of her dreams. That way I could annihilate them.

Since I was nothing like my brother, all I could do was run a hand down her back, my power practically begging to be let free as I let it heat my skin up enough so that she could feel it through the thin nightclothes she wore.

I wanted to believe it had helped. Each time I had stroked her back, her breathing had slowed, her eyelids becoming less frantic. Simply touching her had left a gaping wound in my chest alongside the reality that this might very well be the only time I was allowed to touch her. But at least I could offer this comfort.

At least that was what I'd told myself as I had lain down beside her, my body turning to frame her as I did. It was easier that way, to keep my palms close to her, to feel the soft working of my magic as it had heated and warmed her sleeping body. She'd smelled like shampoo, and I hadn't stopped myself from breathing her in. I didn't sleep that night, but rather lay awake, thinking over not just the woman by my side, but our deal as a whole.

Clearly my magic believed I was supposed to be protecting her from something else. But other than myself, I couldn't think of anyone else who might be hunting her. But then I remembered that Lucia had once been stalked by the Corrupted. Justine's life appeared to be rather ordinary, but I couldn't deny that the bond keeping me here was rather strange.

I was a servant to the magic we had put into play. So until I had upheld my end of the bargain, there was no leaving. With or without my soul.

The early morning light was streaming in from the single dirty window, illuminating more of Justine's features. While I admitted that she wasn't exactly the most sturdy human model, her features were inexplicably beautiful. All that fiery red hair lay lush across smooth creamy cheeks and neck. Every bit of her seemed to be so soft, and from the moment I laid my lips against her wrist, I'd been fascinated by the feel of her.

I wanted to believe that it was the mate bond attempting to connect. Or maybe the protection deal that we'd struck. But I couldn't help thinking it was more than that. It had never been like this with Anna.

Not that we'd had time like this.

Justine's pulse had been racing when our deal was sealed. Even as she spat out orders and cursed my direction. A smile tugged at my lips. She was fire and ice with a tongue to match.

"Good morning," I said as she shifted, her eyes flickering open. I was vaguely humored by the way her eyes roved over me. My coat was folded in a corner on top of my shirt, my makeshift footrest at one point last night, leaving me dressed simply in a pair of denim pants and nothing else. Even my feet were bare. But that wasn't where her eyes rested as I smugly let the muscles in my chest flex and ripple as I stretched.

"Oh, I'm sorry. I didn't mean to stare. I just…" Her words trailed off. "I've not woken up with anyone for a long time."

"Consider me flattered."

She huffed out one of those little angry breaths, but it carried no venom. Justine pushed herself to her feet and began rearranging her clothes, but not before I saw the tease of one hip bone pressing against her sleep shorts.

I frowned. Her build was delicate. The bones I'd felt against me were long, fine, and utterly crushable. But she was too skinny. And something deep and primal inside of me stirred, a monster that demanded she be cared for. That I be the one to

care for her, starting with making sure she had a safer place
to rest.

I stomped down on the urges, focusing on the way that she
hurried away from me. First to the bathroom, returning
smelling of mint, when she took one look at my half-dressed
form again then went stomping from the apartment and, from
what I could hear from my position against the window,
down the hallway. When she returned a minute or two later,
her cheeks were noticeably pink. Even so, she looked over my
body again, making my muscles ripple and flex in response. I
couldn't find it in myself to hurry my shirt back onto my
body. Not when she clearly admired my form.

Justine held a pile of clothes in her arms, her body stiff as
she continued to stare me up and down.

"Is there something I can help you with?" I kept my voice
prim, even as humor threatened to fill my belly at her open
appraisal.

She pressed the clothes into my hands. "My neighbor, he
said you can borrow these. He's a big guy, but I'm not sure
they're exactly your size. I know for a fact they aren't your
style."

I took the clothes, noticing the way she carefully avoided
my touch when we exchanged them. She was wary of me.
Interesting. The pain in my chest throbbed a little at the
thought, but then, she was right to be wary.

I could easily be a monster. Or so much worse.

Clark whined at my feet, and we both looked down at him.

Justine spoke again. "I'll take Clark for a little walk if you want to take your time getting dressed. I don't mind."

I looked at the clothes. The worn cotton tee was navy but appeared clean and well taken care of. "That would be very kind. Thank you, Justine."

"Good, good." Justine hesitated, her balance shifting from one foot to the other and back again.

"Is there something else, little thief?" I stepped closer, rubbing a hand down my chest. Justine narrowed her eyes on me. "You can look all you want. Until our deal is done, I'm as much yours as you are mine."

"Of all the conceited…"

Her jaw went slack as she attempted to find more things to hurl at me. But I remained still, smiling at her until finally she gave a jaunty flip of her ponytail and marched out of the apartment. I watched her go, fascinated by the soft sway of her hips, and the way Clark, or rather not-Clark, trotted obediently by her side. The creature was obviously infatuated with the human he'd found.

The clothes in my hands were older, but she was right. They were almost my size. I was able to squeeze myself into the plain navy T-shirt and left my jeans on.

I was dressed and rummaging in her cabinets when she returned, this time with her nose a bright-red color. For a moment, anxiety filled me, and I stepped towards her. "Are you cold? Why are you so flushed?"

She fluttered her hands at me. "Just a cool breeze today. The sun feels great."

I nodded, patting my sides as the unusual feeling of being in such casual wear unnerved me. The flash of my own wrists caught my eye, just as they caught hers.

"Oh my gosh, Judge." She was immediately at my side, her tiny fingers against my pulsing wrist as together we looked down at my mangled skin. "What happened? Who did this to you?"

I stared at the skin. I could feel the bite of the metal against my skin, the burn and torture of unrelenting agony. But before any real imagery came to light, a sweet, blissful feeling slipped over me. The bond, our bond, bloomed between us warm and welcome and utterly terrifying. This wasn't going to plan at all. I ripped my hand from hers, massaging the wrist as I did. Justine didn't back down, though, and followed, holding her hand out.

"It's nothing."

"Judge, no, that's not nothing."

"It is now," I said stubbornly, even as I let Justine's hands find mine, slowly moving my hand in hers until she could see the vivid scars.

"I have scars all over."

"But these… These are so fresh."

"What do you know of scars?"

Justine looked up at me, my hand taking up both of hers as we stared at each other. "Not all scars are physical, Judge."

Her hands were so warm against mine, my chest hummed wildly at her touch. "But I'm so sorry that this happened to you."

"I'm fine," I said, but I knew my voice was softer now. "I made a mistake, and I was bound for it."

"I'm so sorry."

Breathing out, I said, "Don't be sorry. It is done."

"Okay." Her eyes snapped up to mine. "Did you get them back for doing this?"

"No."

"Well, if we ever meet them, I'll get them back for you. I'm a sucker for vengeance."

"I can tell."

Justine rolled her eyes, turning her attention back to the hand I'd left in her keep. Slowly she traced the scars there, from the chains that I'd been bound by. Her finger brushed against the pinched pink skin, reminding me exactly why I couldn't be trusted around any living soul. Let alone one like her, one that I could want.

One that I could love.

Creatures like me did not love. They destroyed. And once my soul was returned to me, the chances of failing her like I had failed Anna only grew.

Anna… The thoughts of her invaded my mind, making my chest ache in a whole new way. "Did you have plans today?"

Justine blinked. She released my hand, looking a little embarrassed. "No, not today."

"I'd like to visit someone, and since I cannot be too far from you…"

"I'm stuck going with you."

I grimaced at the word "stuck" but held my ground.

After a few moments of consideration, Justine's face brightened. "Sure, let's do it."

After something called a granola bar, which Justine insisted I eat, we were packing up our things when a heavy, pounding knock sounded against the door, causing it to rattle on its hinges.

Justin jumped, her body bumping mine as she did. With a quick look over her shoulder at me, she righted herself and checked that Clark was hidden away. I could feel the dread in her steps, the fear that thickened her scent on my tongue. My magic flared to life, running hot and ready to defend.

My feet braced against the floor as Justine stepped up to her front door and unlatched the bottom locks. With the door unlocked, it only took a moment for the person on the other side to push in.

Disgust and anger flooded my being.

"Hey there, lovely. Do you know what today is?"

A good day to die, I filled in mentally, watching as a thick-necked, heavily bearded man walked into the room like he owned it. It was early morning, and yet he smelled like a disgusting combination of vodka and sweat. I had the undeniable urge to throw him out the door he came in.

Deep in my chest, I was prepared to do what was necessary to protect Justine. The monster that lurked deep inside of me raised its head, no longer resting in wait.

Justine's body was stiff as a board, fear lacing her usually sweet scent as she forced her chin up to meet this newcomer's gaze. "Rent is due."

The new guy suddenly noticed me, a frown crossing his face. "Another one of your 'friends,' sweetheart? Send him out, and we can take care of this."

"I told you, Danny, that's now how I work."

"And I told you, that's how it could work." The thick man stepped closer to her.

"You think she will fuck you for her rent?" I said casually. "What a sad, pitiful excuse for a man you are."

The man's jaw dropped. "I'm her landlord, asshole. This is my place. I can do whatever I like."

"Correction," I stated. My hand dropped to Justine's shoulder and guided her back behind me. I saw the exact moment that he registered how far down the food chain he truly was here. "You could've. But not anymore. She is mine." The words fell from my lips, and my entire body vibrated with a combination of my temper and an uncorked pulsing energy that I could barely keep ahold of. "Do you understand me? You don't come here. You don't talk to her. You don't even look at her. If you do, I will shove your eyes so far down your throat, you will choke on them."

Urine. He'd peed a little.

I snarled as he cowered back to the hall. I followed, letting him see all of me. He needed to recognize what was changing here.

"Justine," I spoke softly, feeling her ragged breathing while she huddled against my arm, "We can drop your rent off today when we go out, can't we?"

She nodded.

I looked back to him, enjoying the way his pale forehead was mottled with red and streaked with sweat. "It sounds like we have a deal, don't we, Mr...."

"Danny Owens."

I hummed softly. "Say it, Mr. Owens." My magic simmered under my skin as the deal began.

"Deal. I'll—I'll leave Miss Anders alone."

My chest purred with delight, the deal warming my chest. "Good job, Mr. Owens. Now if you'll excuse us, we have somewhere to be."

Cerberus trotted out to take a space next to me, the growl in his chest ringing out. The landlord glanced down for just a moment, and then Justine's voice cut through the space. "The dog stays, asshole."

I grinned down at Cerberus then looked back at her. Other than being flushed and a little shaky, Justine's resolved pose never faltered. So I nodded. "Yes, the dog stays."

"Who the fuck are you? What are you getting into, Justine?"

I shook my finger in front of his face, loving the way his eyes jumped back and forth. "Danny, Danny, Danny. That's above your pay grade. I'm the Judge. That's all you need to know."

Reaching back, I gripped Justine's hand in my own and towed all of us out into the hallway, taking her key from her to lock the door after us. Without another word, we left Danny standing in the middle of the hall.

It wasn't until the fall-scented air of downtown hit my nostrils a few moments later that I realized Justine was crying. I turned to her, worry crawling through me at the sight of the thick tears on such beautiful, pure skin.

"What's wrong?" My anger replaced worry. "Did he hurt you?"

Deciding I didn't care, fury replaced all other emotions in my chest. I prepared to go charging back into the building. But before I could go anywhere, slender, band-like arms were thrown around my neck and I was being pulled into the most devastating hug of my entire life.

But instead of flinching away, I didn't stop myself when I leaned in.

9

Justine

He was so solid and strong against me. Immeasurably strong. I pressed my nose against his throat, my chest still tight and itchy with unexplainable emotions that had nearly burst out of me when he not only challenged my disgusting bully of a landlord, but when he'd delivered that final punch, building me up and letting me stand on my own.

Rather than feeling protected, I felt… God I felt cherished. When was the last time I'd felt that? Maybe never. It buzzed and jumped in my chest like a living animal, tugging me closer, and before I knew it, I was against him, on him, my arms sliding around his shoulders, my feet dangling midair. I knew he didn't mind, because he'd bent down just a little to help me capture a grip on him. Now as he leaned back, a warm hand pressed against my lower back, supporting me as my feet dangled in the thin air.

"Thank you," I mumbled against his skin, the rough texture of his jawline a pleasant scrape against my nose. "Thank you so much."

His chest rumbled under me, and while I wasn't sure I'd ever heard another man do that, I found that I liked it quite a lot. Under the fancy words and posh accent, this male felt…primal in a way that I had never experienced. I wasn't sure why that made me shiver like I did, but I liked it far more than I should.

"It's only right, little thief. It seems our deal remains intact."

I could feel the way his body began to tense. I'd hung on too long, and even though it physically hurt to release him, I parted my fingers, letting my weight carry me down until I was standing flatfooted once more on the front stairs of the building. Blinking, I stared around us. Why had it seemed like an entire world had just paused when we touched?

Judge searched my expression, and I offered a small smile in response. We needed to move, to leave this moment that left my blood rushing and my breathing shallow. I wasn't sure how much longer I could stay in it with him, without wanting…something more.

But first, I needed to clear something up.

"I need to tell you something." I gulped down some air, steeling myself for his disbelief, before pushing on. "I never slept with him, you know."

"You never slept with him," he echoed me.

"No." I shook my head. "He wanted me to, he wanted me to a lot, but I never did. I always had rent ready. Even when he messed with me about it."

Judge's dark eyes flashed and his teeth bared in a snarl, "Damn right. Males like him don't deserve females like you."

"I just didn't want you thinking I'd had sex with him."

To my surprise, Judge reached out, brushing a strand of hair that had escaped my ponytail back from my face. "The matter is resolved, Justine. You never need to worry about him again."

Well, until next month. But maybe, maybe now that Judge had said what he had said, maybe Danny really would keep his distance. Maybe I had a real shot.

I gulped. What if Judge was still around next month? Maybe then. I turned, taking in the mostly deserted Omaha city streets as I raised a finger to my mouth and gnawed on the broken edge of a nail. I was stupid to think that Judge would still be around next month.

The way my life moved, I wasn't even sure I would be here in a month. But deal or no deal, this male was changing my life. And while I knew I should be thrilled, I couldn't help thinking that there had to be another shoe ready to drop.

"We should go," Judge murmured, making me jump. He had crept close while I had been lost in my thoughts, and now, the warmth and weight of him was firm against my back. Seeing my reaction to him, Judge carefully placed a hand low on my back. "Are you alright? Should I simply end him now and forego any future concerns?"

"End him?"

"Honestly, I believe it would be a contribution to the human genetic pool."

A laugh burst out of me. "You're joking…"

Judge shrugged, appearing more human than he had so far. "Only partially."

"I'll think about it."

"Good. You do that." Judge cleared his throat, moving quickly out of the alleyway and into the bright daylight of the sun. Instead of flinching like I did, the man tilted his head back, his face turned up to the heat of the rays, and he sucked in mouthful after mouthful of the fresh air. I couldn't stop the smile that curled my lips.

"The sun feel good?"

"It does," Judge admitted. "I've missed it."

"No sun in the pits of Hell?"

One eye opened to glare down at me, but one side of his lips curled. "Not exactly."

I'd started to ask him to elaborate, when I noticed the Uber driver across the street was giving us an odd look. "Uh, yeah, Judge, we should probably get going."

Judge sighed loudly then offered me an elbow, as if we weren't wearing athleisure in the middle of a midwestern downtown center. It was something people did walking the red carpet or in medieval times.

Not here, and definitely not me.

Which somehow made it so much better. I grinned at him, which surprised him, and then poked my hand through to grip the smooth flex of his forearm. Judge looked forward again, his muscles tensing beneath my touch.

I didn't know why, but I ran my fingers over the forearm I gripped. "Hey, it's okay. I'm here."

"Do you truly mind coming along?"

"I truly don't."

"If it is my choice, then we are going to visit an old friend."

"Do you have friends?"

He grunted but followed as I stepped off into the sunlight once more. It was a beautiful day today, the crisp fall weather making it easy to convince myself that I was holding on to Judge because of the chill, not because he felt so damn good. But all too soon, we'd turned into a very old, slightly dilapidated-looking graveyard.

"You wanted to come to a graveyard?"

"This is—" Judge's throat worked "—where my friend's body is. Her family erected a stone in her honor. I've always wanted to see it."

"Oh." I blinked rapidly, trying to catch up with the wealth of knowledge he'd just dropped onto me. Judge had friends—human friends, by the look of it. And one of them had died. "Do you know where? What's her name?"

We had stopped at one row, and I could feel the tension radiating off Judge as we looked around. "Her name was Anna Stuart."

Something hung in the air between us, pressing down on my chest as I stared at the demon. He swallowed, a strange, wistful look appearing on his face. "And she was my soul mate."

Nephesh

It had been the wrong to say, seeing as I could actually feel the hurt that came racing through the bond between Justine and me. Her hand, which had been tucked in my elbow, dropped, swinging slightly by her side.

"Oh, of course. You said Stuart?" She turned stiffly and marched off down a row.

Groaning, I trekked after her, hoping to both find Anna's monument and to remedy the situation I'd just caused with Justine. "Wait, Justine."

But she was insistent, marching up and down the rows, her face turned down to the grave markers as she moved.

"Stuart, Stuart, Stuart," Justine was chanting. She stopped suddenly at the edge of the plot, her head cocking as she stared down at the last two markers. My heart thudded in my chest. I didn't need to ask her. Every inch of her body screamed that she'd found what we were looking for. Moving to her side, I let my knees fold. The earth under them was cold, damp, but I didn't mind. Because for the first time in fifty years, I was close to the living body of my best friend.

"Judge, I'm so sorry. Did you want me to go? I can wait over there."

"No," I gritted out, surprised at how difficult speaking was. "I want you to stay."

I reached out, fingers tracing the letters carved there.

Anna Stuart
Beloved Mother and Wife
1948-1974

"She never met a stranger. We met one night when Cerberus thought she was going to be hurt. I stepped in, and she thought I was an angel there to save her. But instead, I demanded the soul she carried, the one that bound us together."

I could hear the sharp intake of breath from Justine, but I pushed on. "Of course, she told me to go back to Hell. But if I wanted to clean up my act, then she'd buy me a cup of coffee. I didn't know what to say, so I agreed. And then we just talked for hours. She was happily married, with two little boys. Back then, demons could come and go through the living world whenever we wanted. I was invited to family dinners and even a birthday celebration one day. She was kind and saw the good in everything. I'm…well…me, and she was always convinced that I was so much better than I really was."

The grooves of the stones were rough there around the death date, the stone biting into my flesh as I pressed. "She was killed by a drunk driver on her way to meet me. I was late, too busy fighting with my father to realize I'd nearly forgotten her."

"Oh, Judge."

"She was so much better than me. And yet she considered me a friend, even at the end."

"Sounds like you were very lucky to have her."

"As it turns out, she was very unlucky to have me."

"Don't say it like that."

"I chased her soul, you know. In the underworld." My eyes closed, the memory so clear, so vivid I could almost feel the delicate weight of her soul in my arms again. Breathing deep, I let it take me away.

Back to the day I had failed her and my family in one fell swoop.

***

Fifty Years Before
Nephesh

In my centuries of life, everything had been gathering up to the point that I'd be granted a chance to reclaim my soul. And then I found her, my Anna, the first human I'd ever really known. The first human I'd really loved. My only friend.

Her husband had trusted me. Her sons had looked up to me.

And now, the only part of her left was the rapidly cooling blood that dripped down my fingers to the cement below. Lights flashed around us, the bright blues and reds that had brought the hoard of humans to my side.

Not that they'd been able to do anything. Nothing was done. Her soul was gone, her body cold on the ground. Nothing would ever be right again.

My head had slowly tilted back, staring up at the sky as I waited for one of the sparse clouds that were out to pass away from the crescent moon. My chest filled and expanded as I breathed in the fury and grief and let it course through my system. It wasn't power, this overwhelming emotion, but it was something else entirely.

I began to walk away. The humans behind me shouted, but I didn't care anymore. My legs carried me away, guiding me down to a deserted park a few blocks down from the park. There was nothing here, just singed grass and low-lying bushes. It was as ordinary and burned as everything else in the living world.

"Father," I said, kneeling in the stiff grass, "you would do the same thing. Forgive me."

And summoning every bit of grief, pain, desperation, I let my power loose. It moved and grew under my skin, distorting my form, distorting who I was. My heart ached with pain, the vicious muscle violently pumping blood through my form. A cruel reminder that it was my fault that hers no longer functioned.

And still, my power rose. There was no holding it back, no keeping myself under control. Grief was more than I'd ever known, even when my mother disappeared.

Even when I'd first been told what I was under my pretty exterior. This was beyond all of that. It threatened to override everything else I knew about myself. Releasing my grief in a flame of pure, raw power, I thrust my fist into the earth.

With a shrieking cry, I burst through the veil, falling into my father's kingdom. My wings spread, unfurling from my shoulders with another flare of long-dormant power.

Pumping the powerful joints, I banked and headed towards the mouth of the Styx. The pier of Kalos was my destination. And when my boots slammed into the soft soil alongside the pier, I knew I wouldn't have to wait long. Either Kharon was here, or he would be soon. My magic and grief swirled around me in a thick red mist, obscuring my vision and any remaining doubts I might have considered. Nothing else mattered except for undoing this horrible thing.

I was a son of Hell. The heir of the Underworld. What good did power and bloodlines do if not used to fix things? To undo wrongs

A new flare of power pulled my attention. I had company.

"Hello, Kharon."

I'd always been able to sense my brothers. Even as our power had waned, we were wired to find each other.

My younger brother, the middle son and resident peacekeeper, rose from the rushing water of the Styx. His torso was uncovered, showcasing the blue skin tone that had made him so unique among our brothers. Arafel and Elon had once teased him about it, and I had sent them howling into the fighting pits. If they knew what I looked like under my human skin, they wouldn't be able to look me in the face.

Kharon simply chose to ignore the human glamor our mother had given us. And since he rarely had reason to go to the living world, he had no reason to mask who he was. The souls that he met were already shocked enough. Seeing a six-and-a-half-foot male with gills rarely upset them. Even so, I envied him. Under my glamor, I was a monster. Under his, he was a uniquely designed master of his realm.

"Brother." His dark-blue eyes were suspicious, narrowed as his long bare feet carried him farther up the beach. No doubt word was already spreading, and I wondered if that powerful mind of his was reading mine yet. My shields had always been stronger than the others. But today, I didn't care what he saw.

He could see it all. It wouldn't stop me.

"I need your help," I said, approaching.

"No, brother," Kharon said immediately, his hands raised between us. "I can't do that."

My lips curled in a dangerous smile, and my magic pulsed under my skin. The monster inside of me crowed in desperate need to be freed. To fix what had been broken. For the first time in hundreds of years, I was tempted to free him entirely.

It would be so easy, even without the half of my soul that Anna had carried. "You can, and you will."

"You don't understand, Nephesh. She's gone." Kharon stepped towards me, his bare feet silent against the smattering of river stones that lined this part of the river. "She's at peace. I'm so sorry."

I snarled at his sympathy, holding my still blood-stained hands up for him to see. I felt my eyes shift, the edges of my vision blurring as the predator at my core grew stronger. "You are lying. She knew no peace."

Kharon's head tilted, the delicate point of his ears twitching as he observed me. I threw some of my remaining power into my mental walls, keeping his invasive power out of my thoughts. Her last moments may have been horrific, but they still belonged to me. "She worked her entire life to be kind. Her scales, Kharon, they were perfect. She was loving, she had her boys, she had a future." I ran out of voice. "You know what I'm asking. Do it, brother. For me."

Kharon's head lowered, his eyes never leaving mine. "I cannot."

"Didn't you hear me?" I roared at him. "She died because of me. Because I let him go."

"The fates are a bitch, Neph, but we cannot undo a life. We cannot undo everything that we stand for." Kharon stepped towards me. "Not even for her."

"You're a fucking waste of power," I snapped at him, leaping forward with a thrust of my wings and gripping his neck in my hand. "You think you're so much better than me, Ferryman. You are nothing but a speck in this world. Even Father will admit that assigning one of his sons to the river was a waste of his seed."

Kharon's face never changed, and the words kept coming, spilling out of me like lava, burning my flesh and my chest as they did.

"Did you hear me? Elon punishes, Arafel guides, Kadmiel guards, I judge…and you…" I leaned in until our noses were almost touching. "You fucking swim. Congratulations."

Kharon's lips parted, and for the first time in years, I saw the razor-sharp teeth that lined the gums of his mouth. "Say it again."

"You're a waste."

Kharon thrust me away, immediately following with his blade-like claws. They landed, slicing into the flesh of my side, and I snarled at him. He danced around me, his leaner form just out of reach of the long black claws that tipped my fingers.

"I may not judge souls or punish the evil in this world, but do you know why I'm not a waste?"

I growled at him, feeling the slick drops of my blood dripping down my sides, mixing with Anna's.

"Because at the end of the day, Judge, I know who I am. And I pity you."

Pain laced through me, but this time not done by claws. The truth in his words sliced further into my flesh and soul than anything else ever had.

My head fell back and my entire body tensed as something unfathomable pulled at my chest once more. Not pain, not grief… It was the ghost of a familiar urge.

The bond.

I reared back from my brother, shoving him from my person as he panted into the air. "She's here."

Kharon growled again, positioning himself between he bubbling edge of the Styx and me. "Don't do it, Nephesh. The river will reject you."

"No." I lunged for the shoreline. "She's coming. She's coming to me. This is my chance to undo everything. To give her another chance."

"Nephesh, don't." Something deep in Kharon's voice was pleading now. But I didn't turn. I didn't defer from my path. Instead, I continued on until the river's waves brushed up against my ankles. Again, Kharon spoke, his voice echoing inside my mind. "I can't let you do that, brother."

I didn't care. I was staring down the river. She was there, her soul a delicate swirl of muted colors, the features exact to the human I'd held minutes ago. But now, she was a ghost, a nearly transparent version of herself, the core of her being, traveling alongside the thousands of others on their way to the courthouse, to be judged by the jurors and me.

But she would never reach that.

I was going to pull her from the river. To free her from this place and send her back to the land of the living. It wouldn't be easy, but at the core of my power, I could feel it flickering back to life at her proximity.

Together, it would be easy enough to move through the world once more.

I waded out farther, the ice-cold water at my waist now. As if also drawn to me, her soul seemed to veer ever closer. I could see the shine of the buttons on her dress, the bright color of earrings in her lobes.

I could see her.

I would set this right.

I would free her.

"Anna!"

Her pearlescent eyes blinked and her head tilted, the current continuing to pull her towards me as I moved more quickly into the water. Souls moved around me, hands scraping as they angrily pushed at my lower half.

"Anna!"

Her soul came closer. This time her dear, familiar face was focused on me. And then it was easy to ignore the burning, the water's way of rejecting me and my presence there. In my head, I could hear Kharon talking, shouting at me through our mental link to get out of the river. That I was ruining everything.

Didn't he realize I'd already ruined everything? It didn't matter anymore.

Anna's soul slowed, her feet planting on the bed of the river as if they were still flesh and bone. Her shoulders rose from the waters, hands reaching out to press against my chest. I could see them there, but I couldn't feel them. Not anymore.

"Anna," I gasped, the tingling pain spreading as the river began to eat away at my magic. "I told you I'd save you."

"Nephesh." Anna smiled. "And I told you. You already did. I made my peace with this, Nephesh. I know where I belong."

"You belong with your boys, with your family."

Anna's face tilted, her smile growing sad. "My time is done, Nephesh."

"You are the only person who has ever—" my throat closed "—seen me. Or understood who I am."

Her hands raised to pat my cheek, the absence of sensation making the knife in my chest twist deeper. "I am merely the only person so far. There will be more, I know it. You have so much to give. Nephesh, you are the dearest friend I've ever had."

A choked sob broke free of my chest, and I let my head hang forward.

"But your journey is just beginning."

"Don't go."

Her gaze roamed to something behind me before returning to mine. "Don't forget, Nephesh, to see the good."

Her soul moved away from me, back into the current, where she slowly sank into the waves, rejoining the tide of souls all around us. "I'll miss you."

Her smile was brief but beautiful.

And then she was gone.

I didn't even flinch when Arafel's claws wrapped around my shoulders and yanked me from the river.

10

A warm hand wrapped around my shoulder now, the fingers nothing like Arafel's deadly claws. I looked up, pulled from my memory as Justine looked at me, her face pale and worried.

"Are you okay? You kind of zoned out for a while."

"I was remembering. Once you live a life like mine, there are huge amounts that become clouded or distorted." I swallowed. "And then there are parts that remain so painfully clear, like the day just happened."

Justine's knees hit the ground beside mine, and slowly she raised her hand to trace the lines of Anna's stone alongside mine. Her skin brushed mine a few times, her warmth a terrifying reminder that she was just as fragile as Anna had been.

I couldn't fail her. I had to complete this deal, ask for my soul, and get away from her. With no bond between us and the soul safely back in the Underworld, she could go back to her life. She would be safe.

"My parents were killed when I was sixteen."

I whipped my head around to stare at her.

"They hid me in our attic, but I was there when they were killed. The people… They were looking for me. They kept asking where I was. Kept saying that they would find me no matter what. But my parents didn't give me up. I can still hear the sound of the guns going off."

"Justine…"

"The people, they weren't right. There was something wrong about it, I could feel it. It made my head dizzy. And when I heard that they wanted me, that they wouldn't stop, I knew I couldn't just wait around for the police to help us."

"What did you do?"

"I ran." Justine's hand moved over to Anna's husband's name, Alec, continuing to trace the inlaid text. "And I've been running ever since. I can't get attached to anyone. I can't do anything right."

"What do you mean?"

"I tried to be good like my mother wanted. At first I snuck into schools or tried to get jobs where I could. But every time I did, something bad would happen. People would disappear." Justine shivered. "I had to start thinking about surviving. And nothing else."

Silence surrounded us, broken only be the soft sounds of cars on the road bordering the graveyard. "I don't even know if they buried them. I hope they were buried together."

"I'm sure they found each other in the Underworld."

Justine's eyes were bright on mine, "That happens?"

"Soul mates are always drawn to each other."

"Does that mean that you are able to find Anna?"

The bond in my chest hummed. "She's in Elysium, her soul healing and resting. Our bond wasn't that of romantic love, more of a platonic relationship. And nothing good would come of finding her now."

"Why not?"

"Because I didn't do anything she wanted."

Justine huffed, "Well, what did she want?"

"She wanted me to see the good in the world."

"That's not so hard!"

"Maybe for you. With what I see every day, it is…hard to remain positive at times." She had no idea what it was like day in and day out, making those choices. She couldn't. Even so, a half smile pulled at her mouth.

"Are you hiring? Because I can provide a lot of positivity. Especially if I'm being paid for it."

"I'm sure you could, little thief."

She tilted her head to rest against my shoulder, the intimacy of the movement making my chest fuzzy with pleasure. "Do you think that I would belong in Elysium someday?"

I growled. "Not for a very, very long time."

"But someday."

"No, Justine, I think you belong somewhere else altogether."

I moved, her head falling off my arm as I shifted to pull her to her feet. In my hands, her fingers were chilled and so small and precious. Her breathing spiked for a moment as I pulled her hand up to my lips, turning her wrist until I could press a kiss against the lily that was still inked there.

"Let's go home."

***

Justine

I woke up this morning to something I'd never once experienced. There was a man in my bed, and not just in my bed, but wrapped around me like I was his lifeline.

I gulped, my chest tightening as Judge shifted against me. I fell asleep early last night. My mind had been a scramble of emotions after spending the day with the demon. Not because anything significant had happened, but because it hadn't.

We had simply co-existed, talking quietly, walking Cerberus, and then at the end of the night, I'd attempted to show him how to cook scrambled eggs. To my surprise, he'd weathered my teasing like a champion as he burned the first egg into something charred and unrecognizable but then opted to trade me positions and instead doodle small pictures across the notes I'd left out.

They were beautiful, the attention to detail so stunning that I had nearly burned the eggs again when he showed me a few of what he called "scribbles."

One was a river, the waves looking like they were moments from splashing me off of the page. He said his home was there, by the River Styx. The second one, it had been a tiny portrait of a woman who he quietly admitted was Anna. Her features, so unfamiliar, made a spike of something run straight through my chest.

Not jealousy. It was something else. Something so much deeper and more important than any petty jealousy. This woman, she had carried Judge's soul. She was a part of him, and he'd lost her. And while their relationship had never been romantic, there was something so devastating about that loss every time I tried to bring up yesterday's grave visit that I gave up trying.

I knew his pain. I understood his pain. And God help me, it made me like him so much more. Because I liked Judge. I liked him so much that at times my chest ached and my stomach rolled. The need to be close to him raced through my veins with every heartbeat. I didn't know what it meant, exactly, but I knew that I wanted him here with me for as long as I could have him.

Which meant I couldn't be doing anything stupid and risk him saving me and thus breaking the magic holding him to me.

I shifted on the bed, and behind me, Judge's arm moved, reaching across my belly. His weight was warm and welcome, and I stilled, making sure I didn't wake him.

His breath puffed out the back of my neck, making goosebumps creep up and down my spine as I became more aware of just how many places we touched. His arm across my side, his legs cupping mine, one long, powerful thigh splitting my legs and pressing high against a part of me that throbbed with his proximity.

I wasn't very experienced. It wasn't as if I had time to date as I jumped and moved across the country hiding from my faceless stalker, but I knew enough to assume that Judge was far more experienced than me.

Not ti mention that he had to be so much older than me.

That shouldn't be as hot as it was.

"Hmmm," Judge said, his mouth moving close to the nape of my neck, where his face nuzzled into my hair. "What are you thinking about, little thief? I can practically feel the ideas rolling off you."

Ideas? Ideas of rolling you over, grinding down against your thighs. Maybe giving into the nearly painful need to press my mouth against yours and see how you taste.

I chomped down on my lower lip, making sure my hips didn't move an inch as I moved my chin so I could look back at him. His hair was braided back from his face, his expression relaxed, eyes still closed. "You're a blanket hog."

At that, his lips quivered and he snorted. "You think I chose this position? I had to get closer in order to have a chance at any blanket."

Blinking, I looked back and realized that I held most of the sheets and comforter in my fists, meaning I had truly stolen them from him. My cheeks felt hot as I pushed up, stammering an apology. "I didn't mean to, I don't usually—uh…"

His arm around my middle only gripped me tighter, and I was tugged back into the warm bed. "Calm down, Justine. I was just teasing."

I allowed him to rearrange me again, tugging me back into the frame of his form until we were paired up, close enough I could feel the way his chest moved when he breathed. My eyes clamped shut at the sudden need to memorize all of this, every moment. Who knew when I would experience such a divine pleasure such as this again.

I wanted to commit him to memory. The way his broad body cradled me. The way my hips felt tucked up against his. The way I could nearly hear his heartbeat.

Or was that mine?

"Did you have good dreams?"

Judge smiled. I could feel it. Something in the air changed around us, maybe in the way his body shifted ever so slightly against mine. "I did."

"What were they about?"

He grunted, "Another visit to the living world, another soul to steal at the end of a bargain."

I snorted, my eyes still closed as I focused on the gentle rumble of his voice along my spine. "That doesn't sound like a good dream to me."

"Humans… So judgmental."

"Sorry for my fully intact morals."

"Says the girl who was stealing from an enforcement officer."

There was humor in his voice. I was dying to turn and see if he was smiling like it felt. But if I did, I suspected it would ruin the moment. So I stayed put, soaking him in.

I didn't have anything to say to that for a long moment, and then I asked, "Do you think I'll go to Hell?"

His sharp intake of breath was undeniable. My heart skipped a beat as I waited for his words. "Judge?"

"No, little thief. I don't think you'll go to Hell. Or the correct terminology would be that I don't think you will go to Tartarus."

I felt his heart against my body. The steady beat.

Thump. Thump. Thump. Thump. "You sound so sure." *Thump. Thump.*

"I'm quite sure," Judge said, and something in his words told me this topic was getting too close to something he didn't want to talk about. He moved away so that his heartbeat was no longer recognizable. My body chilled, a spike of worry drilling its way through my chest.

Unable to resist, I rolled to face him. His heavy bicep moved to cushion my head in an instinctive gesture that made my heart nearly explode. Blinking up at him, I asked, "Are all demons like you?"

To my surprise, his mouth curled in a tiny, nearly indiscernible smile. "No one is quite like me. Human, demon, creature."

"Creature? There are more…types of things like you?"

Judge studied me closely as he nodded.

"Wow. I can't believe the whole rest of humanity is missing out on an entire world."

Judge breathed out in a short laugh, "Once we were more frequent visitors to the living world, your world, but we got too caught up fighting our own battles that we didn't have enough power or time to insert ourselves back into this world."

"What are some other creatures?"

"Hmm." Judge hesitated, and for a moment I worried I'd pushed too much. But then, he leaned in, as if telling me something in confidence. "There are entire tribes of succubus and incubus creatures."

"Oh my God. The sex dream things? That's *real?*"

He grinned, white teeth flashing, "And just as smug and sure of themselves as you'd imagine. And there are mahrs in my brother's court. They help to manage dreams. I already mentioned the reapers. Those are exactly as pictured in all your scary movies. And as for demons, the demons are not like me. They are…less human."

I couldn't stop myself from reaching out and running a finger down his cheek. "You look so human sometimes. Beautiful but human."

His hand left my side to capture my fingers, bringing them up by his mouth, where our eyes met in a brief, hot moment before he turned my wrist to plant a kiss against the lily ink on my wrist. "I am no human."

My words rushed out before I could stop them. "Do you really look like this?"

Judge smiled this time, actually smiled, and it felt like the wind was knocked from my lungs. "It took you long enough to ask, little thief. But yes. This is one of my forms."

"You have others, though."

"I do. This is my most human form." Judge released my hand to hold up his own. My eyes dropped to it obediently. "In the Underworld, I tend to look a little more demonic." As he spoke, black claws slowly moved forward, slipping from his pale flesh to tip every long finger.

I gasped but didn't move away. His hand moved back over my side, shifting himself closer until his face was only a few inches from mine. When he smiled at me again, there were long, sleek fangs instead of his formerly human incisors. They appeared like he was bearing them for me, and while I knew I should be panicking, I still couldn't find it in myself to move away.

Instead, my fingers moved again, bridging the breath of space between us and running my finger across his lower lip. He followed my lead, his jaw loosening further as the tip of my index finger ran over his lip. When I moved under his fang, I must've gotten too close, because with a pinch of pain, I realized the edge had caught my finger.

I yanked my hand back, my fingers nearly in my mouth when Judge's hot, slick mouth captured it and pulled me close again.

For a moment, very real fear slipped over my heart as my bleeding finger disappeared there. But then, nothing. His silky tongue lapped over the tip of my injured digit for just a second. Then his own clawed grip on my wrist slowly relaxed.

"I'm sorry," he said as I looked down at the tip of my finger. "I could smell the blood, and…my saliva, it has certain healing capabilities. Especially on…especially small wounds like this."

I stared at the finger in question. It was perfectly whole, no sign of the little cut that I'd seen with my own eyes. Swallowing my shock, I nodded. "Thank you. I think."

Silence grew between us, growing in intensity and tension as time passed. When I met his eyes again, my lips curled in a nervous grin. "You always seem to be fixing my fingers."

Judge relaxed at my casual tone, but something in his eyes was still there, dark and hungry. It made me shiver, the inside of my thighs clenching as we lay there together.

"Well, everyone knows that a good thief is nothing without their fingers."

"I don't want to steal things anymore."

"You can't steal what's already yours." And then his hand was on my hip, pulling me closer and rolling onto his back. He took me with him, my weight falling over his belly as I braced my hands on the heavy muscle of his chest. Under my palms, I could feel a rumbling, and then Judge reared up, his hands tangling in my hair, pulling it free from my braid as our faces got closer and closer.

There was a pause then, where my entire body was electrified by the prolonged contact of his, by the way that his entire body seemed to blend perfectly with mine. And when our eyes met, his amber faded into something more maroon, less human. I was even more drawn in, my tongue slipping out to wet my lips.

His eyes followed my tongue before finally, a ragged groan was torn from his throat. "Damn it all."

And then a seventy-five-pound missile tackled us both into the covers once again.

11

Nephesh

I didn't really need a guard dog. I had the Brotherhood in the Underworld. Not to mention my brothers. I could get by without the dog. Or at least that's what I told myself as I stared into the small mirror of Justine's apartment bathroom. Even in this dingy lighting, you could still see the rim of red around my irises, another hint at just how far my willpower had been stretched.

And as furious as I was with Cerberus for ruining what could've been the best kiss of my life, he had been right. I shouldn't be lusting after my soul bound. I was so close to getting my soul back, to taking it to the Underworld, where my father would be ready to receive it.

Justine would move on with her life.

I would move on with fighting my family's war.

I stared at my features, at the dropped fangs and the red eyes. I was too dangerous. Even now, I couldn't hurt her. Sure, things had been going well since the last time I had attempted to complete the deal. But my time with Anna had started out similarly, and look what happened.

My fists made the cheap laminate countertop creak as I hunched over the sink. The memory was painfully sharp, and I fell into it easily. Praying that I would remember the pain of it. That the pain was not worth it.

Cerberus had been with me then too. Whining at my knee, slobbering a little as I held loosely to the leash that I'd strapped onto him after several people had made comments about my dog being loose.

I leaned down, pressing my hand to his head and caressing the silky texture of his ears.

While he was in the living world, my faithful companion dutifully shrank himself to an acceptable dog size and glamoured the two spare heads that many living souls would be horrified to find springing from his fur-covered shoulders.

"Sorry, Rus. We'll be home soon," I whispered to him. My magic pulsing under my flesh, leapt to my core, curling there like a burst of heat. I was surprised at how easy my magic grew right now. In the Underworld, we were feeling the pressure nowadays, the ever-growing need for the other half of our souls dominating our every move.

And since today was the full moon, I'd be able to carry Cerberus and myself back home through the boundary in worlds and get back to the Courthouse. But I needed to get out of this rain, find a place where I wouldn't scar too many living souls as I walked through the shadows.

I turned a corner, staring down the street at a variety of small, striped overhangs on the buildings. They were visually appealing, and I tilted my head back to catch more of the rain on my face as I moved down the lane. We were only halfway there, a short distance from the entrance to the alleyway from which I had stepped through my world into this one, when Cerberus stopped fast.

I patted his head, tugging awkwardly on the leash. "This way."

But the dog didn't move. His dark, nearly black eyes focused on the alleyway ahead of us. The connection between us hummed a little. Dropping my human glamour, I let the leash fall to the ground.

"Show me," I told the dog, and he darted off down the street. I followed him at a slower clip, my boots splashing up water as the rain continued down. When Cerberus changed course and disappeared down the alley, I felt something deep in my chest, behind the muscles, where my magic usually dwelled.

But this was strange, more powerful than any lone emotion or magical impulse. I refrained from pressing a hand to it as I was compelled forward by more than just Cerberus now. I needed to get out of that alleyway. I needed to see.

My boots were loud on the sidewalk as I made my way into the darkness. A blink later, I could see it. I could see everything. There were three living souls in this alleyway. A female, at the back, her arms raised in a defensive position. The other souls were male, standing over her, their dark clothing and angry faces having no effect on me.

My magic slipped around them, and I took a breath in. These two were too easy, simple to weigh the scale of their worth. I could almost feel it, the malice of their desires, the disgusting needs that lurked below their fleshy exteriors… I judged them in an instant.

My fangs flashed as they turned to me. Their anger melted into fear as they got a good look at me. I'd done nothing to hide my red eyes, the snow-white wings that billowed out around me.

"Angel," one of them whispered, fear lacing through his scent.

I grinned at him, letting claws lengthen from my fingertips. I didn't even need to touch the first to vanquish him to the Underworld's court. To my court. The second was trickier. He was soft, fearful of his own actions. But still doomed to live out his life with my brother in Tartarus. When he dived for my legs, I simply brushed a finger across his shoulders.

"You've been judged and found lacking," I whispered into his face as he faded away into nothing. Into my world.

I turned to the woman, finding her kneeling on the ground. Cerberus stood over her, his hackles raised, but not at me. As soon as the living crashed to the earth, my dog's bristling jaw relaxed and straightened.

But for all that he relaxed, the woman behind him shrank away even farther. "Please, please, don't hurt me."

I tilted my head. "Hurt you? I would never."' And I wouldn't, because not only was the core of this woman glowing with the serenity and peace of a good-willed soul, but because I'd only come here to save her.

So why did my chest ache so severely?

Cerberus barked just once, rubbing his face against the woman's thigh. I reached out, my claws retracting as my hand fit around hers. Her face was lovely, kind. Her wide, dark eyes were calming now, and that too calmed me.

"You're safe now. I would never hurt you."

"What are you?" Her voice was shaking, but even so, something about it was so soothing that I nearly swayed on the spot.

"I'm…" I stalled, looking for an answer that would satisfy. Usually I would blurt out a passing reference to nobody. But with her, I strangely wanted to tell her. "I'm Nephesh."

"Are you an angel?"

Coppery blood covered my tongue as my fang bit down on my tongue. It was a common misconception yet never failed to irritate. But this was different. I wasn't upset. I just simply wanted her to understand.

"I'm not one of Seraphim. I'm—" I hesitated"—something else altogether."

"A demon?" she whispered. Recognition of something between us thrummed in my belly.

"Yes."

After a long breath, I moved to leave her. I had done my good deed. I had sent the lacking souls to the Courthouse. I could go home now and deal with them from there. But from behind me, her voice spoke up again.

"Please, wait. Oh please, wait."

A hand pressed against my elbow, just a touch, but it was enough to make me look sharply back at her. While she may have flinched, her feet didn't falter. "What is it, soul?"

"I'd like to thank you."

"Thank me?"

"Thank you." Her smile was tremulous and beautiful all at once. "You saved my life."

That pressure in my chest grew even more severe. I looked at her hard, wondering why I was so transfixed by her. I slowly crossed my arms. "I have. And now I demand payment."

"Payment?"

"Your soul."

"My soul? Oh my. I was thinking about a cup of coffee." The woman came closer, the darkness still swirling around us. But she was unafraid, a quiet smile on her face as she waited for my response.

"I don't drink coffee."

"That's a pity. Perhaps a piece of pie. Or a sandwich?"

Something about the earnest way that she looked up at me caused half of my soul, deep in my chest, to hum. It had to be her. I wouldn't have been brought here otherwise. I needed my soul from her, but…I wasn't ready yet. Father hadn't found a way to keep the monster at bay. And I wasn't strong enough to contain it either, not with my soul complete.

"I've never actually tried coffee."

The woman's cheeks rounded as she offered her elbow to me. "Allow me to introduce you."

I hesitated, and she spoke again. "Please, I can't afford to do much. And I'm not interested in giving you my soul, but I would love to buy you that coffee."

I nodded, the movement jerky. Stepping up, I took her hand and cupped it around my arm. Immediately she moved off, her staccato steps against the pavement setting the tone of our pace.

"What's your name?" I couldn't stop myself from asking as we stepped out back into the brighter-lit street.

"Anna," she said, grinning up at me. "I'm Anna Stuart."

Inside her chest, my soul glowed back at me, and I knew I would be staying in the living world longer than planned.

12

Everywhere we'd gone today, women's stares had been glued to him. As someone who hated being the center of attention, I found it highly problematic. Or at least that's what I told myself…instead of the rising threads of jealousy that had come to life as soon as women eyed him.

He was not mine, I knew that. But at the same time, this deal was keeping us tied together. That had to mean something, right?

Depositing Judge in the apartment and showing him the stack of books to entertain himself, I quickly threw on my uniform and hurried down to the diner. I had gotten lucky and picked up the night shift. A soothing chorus of hellos greeted me as I entered, making me duck my chin. Freaking Midwesterners and their *everyone loves everyone* attitude.

I pulled on my apron, picked up a notepad, and immediately dove into the late-night crowd, which was a delightful bunch of labor workers getting off work combined with high school and college kids who looked two seconds from a crisis. Later there'd be the post-bar crew, and I loved that even more. Those people consumed vast amounts of late-night breakfast food and left good tips.

The rush took over, and I let myself get swept up in it, enjoying the buzz and action of those around me. It was well past midnight when Lizzy, my no-nonsense manager, appeared at my side.

"That blond in the corner is staring a hole straight through you, sweetheart. Want me to scare him away? Or ask him to come closer?"

I jerked to look over my shoulder, a laugh bubbling up inside as I realized it was Judge sitting there, in the corner booth, elegant legs folded, with an air of disinterest, even as he stared at me hard enough to start an itch forming under my skin.

I grabbed a menu and flourished it toward the demon. "He's a friend. I can make him go."

"Oh no, no, don't do that. Keep him around. We don't need that booth and it makes the scenery all the more pretty." Lizzy leaned over the counter, unabashedly staring Judge down as she fanned herself with a stack of napkins.

I huffed a short laugh and picked up the fresh coffee pot before moving over to Judge's booth.

"Got a craving for greasy diner food? Or did you just miss me?"

His expression didn't change, and for a moment I thought he hadn't heard me. I shrugged, flipping the coffee mug over on the table and proceeding to fill it with the steamy brew.

"I was drawn here." Was he gritting his teeth?

I cocked my head, the fumes of the coffee winding up from the table, and furrowed my brows. "Drawn here?"

Judge nodded, the movement jerky. I finished pouring the coffee and sat down across from him. "I'm sorry I had to leave. I just... I need the money. If I don't, things get too tight at home." I curled my fist on the tabletop, frustration and anger building.

To my surprise, my new roommate placed his hand over mine, the warmth from his palm covering me and spreading up my arm as I looked up into those beautiful, unique amber irises. "I've said this before. You do not have to explain yourself to me. I am simply here, as it appears the deal requires it. So if you need me...you know how to find me."

My heart fluttered. I forced myself to push a smile to my lips, to stand up and check on my other customers a few booths away. I needed the space to think. I reminded myself that this demon was not mine.

He could never be mine.

I needed to stay away, to stay unattached. When I got attached, people got hurt. And I couldn't watch that happen. Not even to him. His magic was no match for what was after me.

My stomach clenched. While he appeared strong and savvy and capable, whatever this curse was that hung over my head, it was more dangerous than everything else. Well, more dangerous than most things.

My shift dragged after Judge got here, probably due to the bunch of wild latecomers who ordered half the kitchen and stared at me like I was dessert. When I finished dropping off their food, I moved behind the counter to make another pot of coffee, when I felt, rather than heard, someone behind me. Confused, I turned to find Judge standing at the bar, his bright hair gleaming, one fist planted on the counter.

Fury radiated from him in hot waves. Something deep in my chest twisted at his blatant show of emotion.

"Judge?"

He dropped his chin, white hair slipping forward over part of his face and hiding his expression. "They are talking about you."

I looked over at the group I'd just served then rolled my eyes. "Typical assholes."

Judge stiffened, face jerking up to meet mine. His eyes, which were usually that strange amber, were nearly black. Something in my belly tightened, and I could almost feel the shift of energy all around us. "Judge? What's going on?"

"I cannot stand it."

"No, it's okay. They're just dumb and half-drunk. They come in all the time. They'll leave soon."

Judge's eyes snapped to mine. "The things they say about you…" His lips quivered and drew back in a snarl that raised the hair on my arms. "They will be punished."

And before I could stop him, he was marching across the diner, stopping directly in front of the booth. I dropped the coffee pot onto the counter and raced around, watching as each of them registered this unusual-looking tall man standing in front of them, murder clear in his eyes.

"Hey man…nice hair—"

Judge cut them off. "I demand you apologize."

The one in the back of the booth, with a shiny bald head and blond beard, grinned at Judge. "For what?"

"For what you've been saying."

The others in the group smirked and looked at each other.

Lizzy and the cook, Gary, came up behind me. None of us speak.

"I don't owe her shit."

My jaw went slack as I moved to Judge's side, my fingers sliding into his hand and gripping him tight. "Come on, Judge. They aren't worth it."

"Yeah, pretty boy, you and your snotty bitch can move right along."

"What did you call me?" I turned slowly, Judge's bulk at my back so hot I felt like my skin was on fire. All ambitions of staying under the radar here in Omaha were forgotten as I stared at these men. I had been kind to them.

Too kind.

But suddenly the men froze, going a little pale, and at first I thought it was because of what I'd said. But I saw the very real fear in their gazes as they stared over me.

One or two of the guys made like they were going to leave. "Man, that's freaky."

Another started to stand, hands pushing at him to move out of the booth so they could leave too. "Cut that shit out."

Deep in my chest, something was bright and humming, that butterfly feeling but so much stronger. I couldn't stop the smile that appeared on my face. Even as I looked back to see Judge.

His head fell forward, and slowly, as if in a dreamlike state, he stared at me, blackness taking over his eyes until it was nearly impossible to see where his pupil began and ended. Realization of what I was seeing, that I should be afraid, sank into me. But I was not. My palm burned where I held him, and I could feel something deep in my bones twisting, pulling, and then suddenly, Judge whipped back to the table.

"What's wrong with his eyes?"

Judge smiled, so slowly that I felt like the movement drew me in closer. "You have all been judged and been found…lacking."

"Fuck you," the head idiot spat at Judge, shoving at his crew as they began to pile out of the booth.

The smallest one, who had been sitting on the end by me, stood and reached for me with a grunt. Judge didn't hesitate but sealed his hand over the man's collar and lifted him off his feet.

Dangling him midair, Judge seemed to breathe man in, and then with a grimace, he tossed the man aside. He slid on the dingy tile floor a few feet before coming to a stop. The sound of his body hitting the floor had an odd effect on the others still waiting.

They froze, staring at Judge for a long moment, ragged breathing breaking through the silence.

Judge inhaled, the sound making a soft whine as he rolled his head back, the movement purely predatory. "He was the very best you had to offer and therefore is a waste of my time. Leave, all of you."

They scrambled by, climbing over the backs of the other benches, stepping on each other's toes and hands as they frantically removed themselves from Judge's sight. One of the last to leave leaned down, helping his discarded friend to his feet before they limped out together.

A moment later, the bell chimed over the door and they were gone, sprinting down the street, the shapes of their bodies illuminated by the streetlights as they stumbled towards their cars. When I looked up at Judge, I found him staring down at me, a curious expression on his face.

"Judge, I—"

Cheering had broken out around us, scattered and a little arrhythmic, but it surrounded us nonetheless.

Judge looked surprised, his blond brows high. "They are…pleased, I see."

I shrugged, smiling. "I guess so. No one likes those guys."

Judge's eyes burned into mine. "I'm sorry if I acted incorrectly, but I couldn't stand by and let him disrespect you like that."

My hand was still neatly tucked into his. I squeezed it, which made a corner of his mouth twitch. Quietly, so no one else would hear, I asked, "Is the bond still there?"

Judge huffed. "It is."

"Well, I've never had someone defend me, and now, you've done it twice in one week. You better watch out… I'm not going to be able to let you go."

Judge's palm was warm as he curled his hand towards his lips, bringing me along with it so that I bumped gently against his body. I gasped in surprise, and then my breath caught at the smirking enjoyment on his face as he brushed his lips over my knuckles.

"Perhaps it is I who does not want to let *you* go."

We stared at each other, something between us changing, a strange sort of bond that seemed to grow within my chest until I was worried it might burst free and consume us both. But for the first time, it didn't scare me. For the first time in a long time, this made sense. It chased away the worries of what this meant, this relationship that had gone so far off the rails that I wasn't sure which way was up or down.

Only that I was beside him. And together we were stronger.

"Hey you two, quit mooning at each other," Lizzy crowed from the coffee maker. "I'll shut everything down tonight. You get home and enjoy your victory over the local scum of the earth."

I giggled a little, forcing myself to take a step away. Rolling my eyes, I moved to walk away, to release Judge as I did. But instead, he strode after me, the quiet strength in his hand making sure that we stayed connected, even as we walked over to the lockers, where I gathered my few things and then headed out the back door.

All the while, Judge's eyes burned into mine.

We tumbled into the cold evening air. Just before my ass threatened to hit the ground, Judge swept me up, pressing me against his body as once more he kept me out of trouble.

"You keep doing that…"

His face was so close to mine, I could see that his lashes were dark, thick. So at odds with the bright tone of his hair. "Doing what, exactly?"

"Saving me." I observed him closely, the golden flecks in that eerie amber gaze. "You know, I'm quite resourceful. I'm not used to having a full-time guardian angel."

He breathed out his nose harshly. "I'm no angel."

"You're so much better. I highly doubt any angel would give evil black eyes of doom to some diner asshole."

Judge raised an eyebrow, clearly amused. "Evil black eyes of doom?"

I nodded with a shrug. "Whatever you want to call it, it worked." After a moment, I added, "I think I'm starting to like this arrangement."

That made his steps falter.

Heart pounding, I pushed on a little. "I'm just saying, you could stay with me a little longer, you know. After the deal is done."

"Justine…"

"Only if you bring Cerberus, though." My words were rushed, falling like water from my nervous lips. "You don't have to. I'm not making it some kind of protection requirement."

Judge pulled me closer until our bodies rested against each other. My throat was tight and exposed as I kept eye contact with him. I was afraid to look away. If I did, this moment would be over. Both of us would be forced to fall back into our usual roles.

Me, the loner human. Him, the demon with other priorities.

Under my palms, I could feel the steady pounding of his heart. And something wistful filled me, so full that I could barely focus on anything else. I wanted to press my ear there to see if his heart raced like mine did every time we got close.

His nose brushed mine, our breath white puffs in the cool evening air as we breathed each other in.

"I'd like that, Justine."

"What? Really? You don't have to."

The corners of his eyes crinkled. "When will you learn, little thief, that I never do anything unless I expressly want to?"

Then his lips were on mine, the sweet bite of coffee and apple pie that I'd left at his table filling my mouth, coupled with the distinct and equally delicious taste of just him. Just Judge.

I moaned, and he took advantage, his tongue slipping its way into my mouth to stroke and play alongside mine. With a soft, strangled noise, Judge swept me up, higher, moving until he could press my spine against the back wall of the diner. My body bumped against it, but before he could stop to check on me, I whispered "More," and pulled him close again.

And there, hips driving between my thighs, he pressed me close. His mouth and tongue tangled with mine, coaxing my pleasure out, making me whimper and moan against the heavy weight of him. He was power and quiet dominance, cradling me as I gave in to the furious heat that arced through me.

And when he started to pull away, I couldn't let him. I wasn't ready to let go of this pleasure, this moment with him where it could only be the two of us, consumed in each other. His hand was at my lower back, protecting me from slamming into the harsh exterior wall when he rolled his hips against me.

"Yes, more," I whispered, only parting from him for a second as he responded to my words with a broken growl then granted me my wish. My hands were in his hair, the silken strands leverage against the roll of our bodies as we devoured each other.

I broke away from him with a soft cry as the hand tight on my hip pressed forward, the seam of my body grinding down against the hard length of him. My head fell back, and his mouth dropped to follow the line of my jaw straight to my throat, where he found a sweet spot that made my legs clench around him.

"Judge, oh God, right there," I groaned as he moved me against him again, his lips still torturing that spot against my pulse. Lips. Tongue. Teeth. I dropped my hands to his shoulders so I could get better leverage, arching back into his touch as his mouth moved lower still, to the junction between my throat and my chest, his tongue tracing the lines of my collarbone.

"Fuck," Judge groaned against my skin, the heat of his beath making me squirm even harder. "You taste so good."

The muscles in his arms leaped as he slowly lowered me again so that we were eye to eye, mouth to mouth, breathing in each other's air.

I panted, every part of me hoping he would kiss me again. "You are not what I expected."

His gaze was warm on my face. I saw the flash of something else there. "You are everything I expected."

My hands found the back of his head and pulled him in for another kiss. This one was sweet and slow and made my chest twist for a whole other reason.

13

Nephesh

This was a confusing place, that much was certain. But her, this little human who had so boldly captured me and placed me into her life… She was everything.

And now I had her, her delicate body wrapped around me as I kissed the lips that had been torturing me since the moment I first saw her. Sucking at her tongue, I swallowed the sweetness of her pleasure as she moved against me. Her taste was divine. The feel of her body against me, even through our clothes, was enough to send the sanest man to his wit's end. And I'd given up on my sanity a long time ago.

Whatever life I had before, it couldn't compare. That much was sure.

She whimpered under my mouth, her movements against my belly frantic and excited. I could hear her hummingbird for a heartbeat, so fast compared to mine, so excitable. I was addicted to the way her entire body wrapped around me, trapping me in her grasp, even as her whispered words begged for more.

I needed to return the favor, to make her understand this nearly suffocating need to be with her. It went beyond normalcy, and while I knew that obsession was something shared by many, I had never felt this way before.

"Judge," she whispered, breaking the kiss for a moment to press her face to my neck, where she nipped and played with my flesh there. I let my head fall back, something rolling in my veins, something harsher than arousal, more dangerous than anger. It built and built, making my head spin as I leaned forward against the diner's wall, keeping her flush to me as my vision blacked out then came back, blurred images and memories flashing across my mind's eye.

I could feel my soul through her flesh, through our touch. The bond that tied me to her was buzzing so loudly, I could barely hear anything else.

Take it, the monster in my torn soul demanded. *Take it now. Free us. Then we will claim our mate, our lady.*

No, I thought with panic, my skin chilling as I realized what would happen. What this could mean for Justine. Being tied to a monster was bad enough. But one that stood at the right hand of the literal devil was something else altogether.

She said she was strong. I knew she was. But she didn't need to be strong. Not for me.

I simply couldn't let her. With a strangled cry, I released the nearly punishing grip I'd had on her legs, shoving myself away from her. Our bodies broke apart at the same moment my chest ached with the break of my heart.

Because things had to change, starting now. There would be no going back if I let myself have her. Bending at the waist, I leaned over, dragging the cold evening air into my body as I attempted to ground myself in that simple fact.

I had lost my soul bound before.

I would not lose her Even if it cost me everything else.

"Judge?" A worried, soft voice was calling my name, gentle fingers smoothing my hair back from my face as I blinked quickly, trying to gain control back over my body and mind. Her body pressed into mine the moment I straightened. This time it wasn't passion, but concern in every line of her body.

Against my chest, I felt her heartbeat accelerate, her fingers shaking slightly as she pressed against my shoulders. "Hey, it's okay. You're okay."

I glanced down at her as she tugged her shirt back into place. Her movements were a little too careful, and I could sense the confusion blooming between us. But as soon as I reached for her once more, to pull her closer to me, to let her know that everything was going to be fine, something twisted in my gut.

I couldn't do that.

My fingers reached out, skin burning as a flare of sensation raced across my knuckles, dancing to my fingertip for just a moment, before I curled my hand into a fist and pulled it to my chest.

My power—fuck, it was growing back and with a vengeance. And while that strangeness still pressed on my heart, I couldn't help but feel the wave of satisfaction that my power had always brought me.

Now more than ever, I needed to keep my distance. Emotionally and physically. There was a part of me that no one else could ever know. A part of me that had disappeared with my powers but had come back just as quickly. I took a step back.

"What happened? I thought…" Her eyes followed me as I breathed in deeply, crossing my arms.

"You thought what?"

She blinked at the venom in my words, stepping back.

"I'm sorry if I confused you. I got caught up being around all these humans. It made me wonder. But none of that matters now. Demons do not get involved with their deals."

Hurt flashed across her pretty features, making my chest twist. Just a few minutes ago, I'd wanted to tear apart those who had hurt her. And here I was, the aggressor.

"You never said that. I thought maybe you liked me."

"I don't need to explain myself to you."

She blinked rapidly, and I could actually feel the stab of pain, an echo of her own, sounding in my chest. "Judge, what's going on? Did I miss something? Because…I'm sorry…"

"My name is not Judge."

"Okay." Her chin quivered, but she didn't break at the tone in my voice. "Great. Then tell me the truth. The whole truth. What is your name?"

I growled, my claws extending as I stared around us. There was no one. This wasn't the time, this wasn't the place. But suddenly nothing else mattered. She needed to know who I was so that she would understand why I could never be with her like that. That I could never be that person to her. I was not worthy of a mate. Even if my mother had attempted to make me one with her magic, I was too dangerous.

I would rather hurt her now than hurt her when my magic overwhelmed me. Because it would. It was only a matter of time. Especially now that I knew that her soul was accessible to me.

Our deal was done. All it would take was one brush of my magic, and my soul would be mine again.

Fuck.

"What is your name? Your real name. All of it." Her eyes shone with a kind of worry as I came to a stop in front of her.

"Nephesh."

Justine's brows flew high. "What?"

"Ne—" I held the syllable out "—fesh. Nephesh." There was a strained silence as she stared up at me, her mouth working the sounds out a few times.

"There's more, isn't there? You can freeze time and start fires. Your dog is a figment of mythology. You aren't just some casual demon who deals with damsels in distress, are you? God, I should've known."

My smart, smart little mate. "No, I'm not."

"So I'll ask you again, Nephesh. Who. Are. You?"

"I'm Nephesh. I am the Judge of the Underworld. A prince of Hell, the heir to my father's throne. I am his arm and his fire. I have spent my many lifetimes sending souls to their ends, all in the pursuit of power."

The soft sounds of traffic sounded behind us, but I saw only her. Watched the way her throat bobbed. There was fear in her scent, but she didn't show it. "Why are you here, then?"

"I'm here for you."

She took a step back, forgetting herself and bumping against the diner wall. I don't pursue because I couldn't stop looking at the way her face had gone white as snow. "I don't understand. Me?"

"You… You are not a normal human. You have something of mine, and I need it back."

"What? No I don't!" Something in the shadows shifted, and I tensed immediately, sending out a soft wave of magic to sense others around. There was nothing now, but that didn't mean there hadn't been a moment ago. The instinctive urgency to get us away from her rose up in me.

I didn't think twice before reaching forward to take her elbow. Justine jerked away.

"We can't talk here."

"Yes, we can. I'm done being lied to. We aren't going anywhere until you tell me the whole thing."

"I never lied."

"You also didn't tell me the truth."

"Semantics."

Her arms slapped at her sides in a frustrated gesture. "Semantics are everything, Ju—I mean Nephesh. Tell me. Tell me, and we will go somewhere else."

With a snarl, I paced a short line then turned around and marched back over it. "You don't understand the burden I carry, the one that I have carried every day of my life. I wouldn't wish that on anyone."

"What does that have to do with me?"

"It has everything to do with you. If I don't complete my mission, my family will suffer. If I do…"

"Fuck, Nephesh. I'm here, waiting. I want to help you. I want to know. What does this mean? Tell me now."

"I'm trying to protect you."

"You've been trying to do that for days." Justine held up her wrist, the deal mark still shining clear on her skin. "Something isn't working."

I stopped pacing, my head hanging as I tried to figure out our next move.

Justine only took a moment to read into the posture. "Oh my God, is the deal done?"

My lips curled in a smile, "You're not that lucky. Still binding, for as long as you live."

I paused as Justine wrapped her arms around her middle, rubbing her own skin a little. "You're cold." Self-hate crept into my awareness. How long had she been chilled like this? I stepped forward. "Let's get you home."

Justine stepped away from me as she suspiciously looked up at me. "How do I know any of this is real? The deal, I could maybe get around that. But this, this is something else altogether."

My mind was a painful blur, my power lapped against the will of my control, and I could feel my temper rising in my throat. Because even though I'd succeeded, I'd met my soul bound, I had kept her safe, why was I so deeply unhappy now that I knew who I was again?

I had known losing track of my memories had been a real possibility when I breached the boundary to find her. But I hadn't expected to be so pissed about it once I was myself again.

Fuck, I was confused.

"I'm not sure what to say. I just needed to tell you that…what just happened"—I gestured between the two of us—"cannot happen again. It's too dangerous."

The way her body stiffened when I placed a hand at the small of her back instantly cooled my temper and confused me even further. Distance. We needed distance. Too bad I was unable to leave her side for more than a few hours without the bond going crazy.

We were stuck in this loop, and I had no idea what to do. Until this deal released us, the bond was only going to grow. It would make my power grow even faster. The only thing short of having my soul back that would make me whole was to be with her.

Justine laughed, the sound hollow, "I can't believe that I kissed you before I even knew your real name. Oh my God, I slept with you before I even knew your name. You've been my roommate for all of three days, and I barely know anything about you."

"You know plenty." I knew my words were cold to her, but again, my power was leaping around in my chest.

I hummed under my breath, my eyes sweeping the perimeter of her building as we entered. Again, I couldn't tell if something had actually changed or if my senses were just firing at an abnormally high rate. But something felt different.

We started towards the front steps, when Justine stopped, turning to me and tucking a hair behind her ears. I was struck with the sudden overwhelming need to kiss her again. To taste her and mold our bodies together. Forget the consequences.

Oh Father Hades, that kiss. My lips tingled and heated at the thought of it. I wanted to do it again, to press into her, to find all the spots on her pretty little body that made her quiver and moan. I would savor and enjoy every single little noise I could wring from her.

I followed her up the stairs, trying to measure my steps. I didn't want to be too close in case my power bloomed again, but I couldn't seem to make myself stay back any farther either. Was this how Arafel had felt? This needs to be close. It was so different from my experience with my first soul bound that my mind could barely wrap itself around it.

Then again, it was different because *she* was different. Anna had been kindness personified. Justine was funny and awkward and generous, even when she was so far from comfortable herself.

She was good. Like Anna was.

I was meant to be with someone good, and the idea that my soul had managed to exist within two of the best souls I'd ever had the pleasure of knowing made me have hope for myself. Maybe someday, when I was whole again, I would have a chance at being the son I wanted to be, the brother they needed me to be. The ruler I was destined to be. Not the shell of a male who only understood judgment and anger.

We finally reached the apartment and went inside. I watched her make us some packaged noodles, my fingers cooling even in the early fall weather. Justine must've noticed me, because her face was apologetic as she handed me the soup.

"Sorry. The heating in here is a little nuts. I'll get out an extra blanket tonight."

My belly tightened. Right, for the night spent together on her sad little mattress. While it hadn't bothered me before to share this space, suddenly everything felt too close. Maybe it was because of how my cock twitched and ached in my sweatpants just imagining us curled together. I hadn't felt desire of any sort for so long, I almost mistook it for my power once again.

I turned to the window, pretending to stare out into the dark night, hiding my reaction to her words. "We'll make it work."

Fuck. My family. I knew that coming through the barrier would be hard for just about anyone. I'd already used Arafel's power in a way that would surely make my father set me on fire just for trying. But I also knew that my father would be looking for me soon. The Brotherhood reported on all things coming and going in the Underworld, and there was no way that Peter had been able to keep up with the soul sorting without me.

I cocked my head, deep in thought. Unless my power here also directly correlated to what was happening in the Underworld. Perhaps I could make the jump through the boundary. I looked at Justine. I wasn't ready yet though. She still had my soul, And I wasn't about to throw my memories away again trying to pass to the Underworld. Not when the new ones were so sweet and somehow more dear to me.

"What would you want to know?"

Justine looked confused, "About what?"

"About me."

An evil grinned pulled at her pretty lips. "Everything."

I rolled my eyes at her. "I'm hundreds of years old, we don't having time for that."

She studied me for a long minute, "Tell me about your family."

"My family?"

"Yeah," she shrugged, "How many times can you ask whatever you want about a family of demons in Hel?"

"Good point." I breathed out, trying to figure out where to start. "My brother's aren't so bad," Justine listened as she forked a noodle into her mouth, listening closely. "I'm the asshole of the family."

"I'm so shocked," she deadpanned, and I bared my teeth at her. She rolled her eyes, and the center of my chest hummed with the joy of having my soul so close. I'd felt the same way last night too, and I couldn't help but wonder if the soul was the only reason. What a confusing situation. I needed to get back to the Underworld so that I could ask Arafel what all of this meant.

"Justine…"

"Nephesh…"

I paused, taking a small bite of the still-steaming noodles. How she could eat them when they were so fucking hot was beyond me. But nevertheless, I needed to keep my body strong, especially now that my power was practically begging to be set free. If I wasn't careful, it would overwhelm me before I could find a way home.

"I liked it better when you called me Judge."

Her lips closed around another noodle, and she slurped it up quickly before coming at me. "Really? I liked it better when I didn't have a six-foot-tall demon stuck with me."

"Fair," I said, watching her eat another. "Am I really only six foot in this form?"

She narrowed her eyes on me. "Missing the point here."

I nodded, refocusing on the food in my hand. "And Rus, he's been with me his whole life. He's part of the family too. Best creature in all of Hel." At the sound of his name, the dog raised his chin from the floor, offering a wolfish grin to Justine before settling back down.

"And your family? Do they know you are stuck here? With me?'

"I'm sure they've figured it out by now."

"Will they come for you? I'm not sure Danny could handle more of you showing up here, attempting to protect me."

I snorted. "I doubt they would, but maybe. My family is a bit old-fashioned. They prefer the 'if you survive, you deserve to' motto about life."

"That sounds like a healthy family environment."

"Everyone has something."

"My parents were too, I think. Not living by that terrible family policy. I just think they were super old-fashioned. They didn't let me go out much. We were really close, but we didn't know anyone. When I lost them, I realized I didn't have anyone else to run to. "

I downed the rest of my soup then held out a hand to collect her empty cup. "You must miss them very much."

Justine squinted at me but handed me the trash just the same. "I guess so. Honestly, I don't remember much from the day it happened. We were always on the road, always moving, always in trouble."

My silence wasn't comforting, but I couldn't stop the hand that moved out to brush over her chin, up to her lips just once. "Has anyone ever told you how brave you are?"

"Because I dared to keep living?"

"Because you do live. Because you wake up every day like there is something to be made of it. Even when this world continues to shove you down. I don't understand it."

Her eyes sparkled up at me. "As long as you keep moving, there will be another chance for something better."

I pulled away, mock horror on my features. "Let's hope that the better thing tomorrow is soup, because this—" I held up a noodle "—is not edible. And why does it come in a cup? I feel like the time savings are not equitable to the utter lack of flavor."

Justine laughed. "Don't be such a snob, Nephesh." She grinned at me and the tension between us lessened. At least for now.

We took turns getting ready for bed in the bathroom, the other person babysitting Cerberus while he roamed the small back alley. When we finally fell into bed, it was the early hours of the morning, and I could feel the tension in her body as I stretched out beside her.

She eyed me. "What happened to 'I don't get involved with deals'?"

"I also cannot leave your side."

"You're giving me whiplash, Nephesh."

I sighed, my magic already seeping out of me in the darkened apartment to warm the thin mattress under her. "I'm giving *myself* whiplash."

She snorted, but her breathing was already slowing. The warmth from the bed and the long day was wearing on her.

I barely resisted rolling over to tuck in against her. "Goodnight, Justine."

"Goodnight, Nephesh."

I closed my eyes, tempted to take the rest while I could get it. Cerberus was on guard by the door. It would be as safe here as anywhere in the living world.

"Nephesh?"

"Yes, little thief," I answered softly.

"Is it because I'm a human?"

"No, it's because I'm a monster."

She snuggled deeper into my warmth, and my desperate heart thudded in my chest. "You're not a monster to me."

"You might be the only one who thinks that."

Justine yawned then elbowed my direction. "Then my opinion should be the only one that matters. Problem solved."

I waited until her breathing had slowed completely, her body slipping into the dream realm, before I leaned over her, brushing a kiss across the crown of her head. "Your opinion *is* the only one that matters, mate."

Swallowing the need to cradle her closer, even in her sleep, I carefully settled myself beside her on the bed…and let my body take me to the dream realm with her.

Arafel, if you are listening, I need to talk.

14

Justine

When I opened my eyes, I was sitting in a large bedroom, a fire burning in a heavy stone fireplace on one end. A wall of floor-to-ceiling windows lined the wall opposite. My heart pounded in my chest as I jerked to a sitting position.

"What is this? Where am I?"

"This is my home. Most specifically, my bedroom. Or at the least a very impressive duplicate of it."

I twisted to look at the demon who was perched at the foot of the immense four-poster bed. His long white hair was down and loose around his shoulders, blending into the loose cream-colored shirt he had pulled on.

"And why am I here?"

Nephesh looked at me, his face a little sad. "I asked a favor from my brother, but I didn't realize it would pull you in as well."

"What did you ask for?"

He considered it, finally saying, "Time."

"Time?"

"Time to explain things to you. Time to spend with you."

"You don't get mixed up in deals."

Nephesh dropped his head. "There is more that I haven't told you. Things that I know you need to know. And while our bond has continued to tie us together for the time being, I believe that maybe what I've been protecting you from is the truth. And that ends now."

I sat up, goosebumps erupting all down my skin. "But this feels so real."

"It is real, in a way. You are asleep, just like me, but we are sharing a dream."

"That's wild."

"It is, but I didn't know what else to do. Something keeps telling me that our time together in the living world is coming to a close. My brother's magic is specialized to dreams. He agreed to help us."

I nodded, shifting so that my legs were curled under my body. "So what is it? What do we need to talk about?"

Nephesh looked away towards the immense windows, where a warm light filtered in around us. "I'm not sure where to begin."

"Anywhere is good, Nephesh."

His wide shoulders nearly shuddered at my words, dropping low as he turned away from me. "I told you I'm the heir of Hell."

"Yeah, you sort of threw that out there."

"I meant literally."

"Literally we glossed over it?"

"No, that I am the heir to my father's kingdom."

"Your father is…?"

"Lucifer."

I swallowed. "What?"

"My father, the King of the Underworld, he is the ruler of all of this. He and my brothers, we rule this world together. Seeing as he is an immortal, it's not like he is planning on dying and leaving it to me, but there are certain aspects of my birth order that are less appealing than one of my younger brothers."

"You're saying Lucifer is a real person and you are his son."

"I am."

"Does he look like you?"

"No one is really sure. Only my mother has seen him without his glamor. But from what I've seen of myself, I'm guessing that his demon self is just as wild-looking as mine. If not more. Demons often have a more palatable form and then a more…aggressive battle form. My father and I are both blessed to have an additional form. A creature form. But unlike me, he has never been forced to use it."

"And who is your mother?"

"She was the first witch and an excellent cook. She loved us all very much."

"Past tense?"

"She was taken many years ago, before I lost Anna. My father has not been the same since."

"Who took her?"

"A powerful being called the Drude. They've been attempting to take power from the Underworld for over fifty years now. They are waging a war against my family, and we aren't even sure why. Other than the obvious need for power."

"I'm sorry, but at the same time, what does this have to do with me?"

"When the Drude began to gather power, my mother cast one last spell, to sever our souls in half, planting the other half of them in a human, who would be born when it was time for us to reclaim that half of our soul."

"That sounds intense."

A wry smile lifted his lips, but I couldn't see his eyes. "Mother was a powerful witch on her own, and I know that she and Father had the best intentions, but as you can imagine, removing our souls left my brothers and me struggling to manage the lands and tasks that had been given to us. So like any desperate fool, we began searching for our souls. Ironically, I was the first to be called to my soul. And it brought me to the living world."

"To Anna?"

"To Anna."

"She carried your soul? That's so beautiful." I blinked rapidly, crawling down to the bed to be closer to him. "But wouldn't that mean you would have your soul back already?"

"It would if we had figured out how to take it from her. But I lost her long before that."

"Wow, Nephesh, that is such a cruel twist of fate."

"Fate had nothing to do with it. I failed her and didn't deserve her friendship, or the power—my soul—would have returned to me."

"Arafel was next. His soul bound, she is everything to him, the perfectly designed match."

"So your soul bound… They are also like soul mates?"

"We weren't sure. Anna and I didn't share a romantic connection, but then, there's no reason that a friend cannot be your soul mate. But it didn't matter because we didn't complete the process. I didn't think I'd have another chance to meet my soul bound ever again. I thought perhaps we only had one chance."

My heart broke a little at how hard that must have been for him. I started to speak, but he continued.

"But then something happened that I never would have imagined."

Now my heart thumped as he looked at me. I couldn't stop myself from asking, "What happened?"

"I found my soul again. This time in a fiery little thief who made me question everything."

Everything around me seemed to slow to a crawl, almost as if time had stopped. For a moment, I worried because even my heart had sputtered. "N-Nephesh, what are you saying?"

"The deal I made, it might have been to protect you, but it was selfish as well. Because I had meant to ask for my soul back from you."

"W-Wouldn't that kill me?"

"No. Oddly enough, humans have proven time and time again that they don't need to have a soul to live." His jaw tightened. "Plus, your soul isn't damaged. Mine is simply co-existing alongside it."

"Wow…" I shook my head slowly. Curiosity, wonder, and trepidation were all warring within me. "I had no idea. But then, I guess that was the point. Something I didn't need or knew existed."

Nephesh nodded slowly. "I didn't think the deal would continue like this. I didn't want it to."

"Because I'm a morally gray human woman?"

Suddenly his eyes went dark as they swept over my face. "Exactly why. I was drawn to you so much more than I was prepared for. At times I couldn't tell whether it was the deal or my own desperate need to be close to you."

"Does this mean… Does this mean I'm your soul mate?"

Nephesh's eyes amber eyes flashed red now, but I wasn't afraid. "You are."

My chest was heaving as I stared at him. "But last night, after the kiss, you freaked out."

"I'm not well-acquainted with fear, Justine, and suddenly finding myself terrified of your every move and need is a lot for me. I had never felt any of these things before, I didn't… I don't know how to handle them."

"So, you invaded my dreams?"

"Arafel told me that your subconscious had to be open to letting me here in order for it to work."

I flushed, my skin hot. "Oh, gotcha. That's not embarrassing or anything."

"I'm quite flattered, little thief, but more so, I'm just relieved."

"Because now you know I dream about you?"

"Because we got to have this time."

"How long can this last?"

Nephesh turned to face me more completely, and my heart skipped a beat at the beauty and familiarity of his face. "Dream time is a sort of stasis. We can stay here for as long as we need, but it will begin to affect our physical form after what will feel like a day or so here."

"So let me get this all straight. If we wanted, we could live a day here and wake up just like it was one night."

He nodded just once. "Yes."

"And I'm your soul mate."

"Yes."

There was a heavy pause in the air between us, and I swallowed quickly after his confirmation of what was the only thing that made sense. Because even in the moments that I'd been confused by his presence or frustrated by his handsome smirking face, everything in me had always wanted to stay as close to him as possible.

"Hmm. That's a lot to unpack." Rising up on my knees, I let the blankets fall to the bed, slightly disappointed that my subconscious had kept me in the same ratty T-shirt and sleep shorts and didn't think to put me in something beautiful for this moment. But too late now. Nephesh's eyes were already devouring me, putting any concerns I might have to bed.

He cleared his throat as I stopped just shy of where he sat at the end of the bed. "Any other questions?" He appeared almost nervous, which only confirmed exactly what I'd been thinking.

"Do you want to kiss me again?"

"More than I can express," Nephesh said, one hand rising to cup my face. His claws were still visible, and I found myself briefly wondering what other characteristics he might show once he was more comfortable with me. I breathed in hard as he leaned into me. But then Nephesh hesitated, his mouth hovering over mine. "You really don't have any other questions?"

I wetted my lips, butterflies wild in my belly. "Oh no, I have a thousand, but they can wait."

"You aren't…how do you say, freaking out?" He stroked my cheek with his thumb, his gaze glued to my lips.

"I've told you before, I always felt like there was something more out there. That it couldn't just be this life for me. And now you're telling me not only is there an entire other world out there, but that I have someone out there who is designed just for me."

His brows lowered. "When you say it that way, it sounds simple."

"It *is* simple, Nephesh."

"Nothing with my family is simple. You'll see."

I settled back a little, and then ignoring the way he breathed out as I moved, I swung my leg over his lap and settled myself there across his thighs. "That's a little bit of a downer. Geez, Nephesh." Straightening, I found myself in the perfect position to slide my hands up over his shoulders. Nephesh' settled his hands on my hips, and I could feel every brush of his fingers as he gripped me there.

"Justine…" His voice was deep and rough. "I'm sorry. I just want you to know what you're getting into."

"I know enough." His hair was so soft against my fingers, I couldn't stop myself from toying with a few strands. Nephesh's eyes went half-lidded as he stared down at me.

"Enough to what?"

"Know that I want this."

He was already shaking his head by the time I finished my statement. "You can't mean that. This would never work. Outside in the real world."

"How do you know? You've never even tried."

"Because I know how dangerous I can be. I won't put you at risk. Ever. Not even for this."

"I lost my parents, have been moving around for years. Been alone for most of my life. From where I stand, it sounds like a worthwhile risk."

"I'm afraid you don't understand what you'll end up with."

I leaned in, hesitating to give him a moment to stop me, but he remained still. I pressed a light kiss against the side of his throat, where his heart rate surely matched the staccato pattern of my own. "A mate. A partner. A future."

He swallowed against my lips, so I settled back. "A monster in pretty clothes."

"Everyone is a monster on the inside. You have to be okay with that monster. I am okay with your insides, Nephesh."

"You haven't seen them."

"I don't need to." I purposefully closed my eyes, breathing him in, feeling the soft pressure of his fingers against my lower back. Here, we fit together. And while this conversation validated all those strange emotions that had come on so strongly, it scared me for a whole different reason than Nephesh's fear.

Because for the first time in ten years, I had someone to lose now too.

And I might already be losing him.

I was done not experiencing life. I was done hiding in corners and cowering at bullys. I was going to take what I wanted.

And I wanted him, any way and for whatever time I could have him. There was a pain in losing a loved one, but there was an even greater one in knowing that you never had them at all.

I refused to know that pain as well.

"Nephesh, tell me again."

"Which part?"

"That part about being yours."

I felt his smile against my throat as he hitched me up higher on his lap and pressed his mouth to my pulse. "You, little thief, are mine, just as I am yours. And no creature, human or otherwise, can come between us for as long as we live."

I kissed him then, yanking his face up clumsily until I could feel his lips against mine. They were hard now, desperate and hot. There was no more sweetness, not when there was so much to be done. So much life to be had. And such little time.

I dug my hands into his hair, letting my nails scrape against his scalp as I ground myself against his belly. My body was already on fire for him, my skin tingling everywhere we touched. But most desperate was the way my core throbbed as his hands slid lower, cupping my cheeks and spreading them wide against his body, bringing the most sensitive part of me flush against him. As he rocked up, I was acutely aware of his fingers, how they brushed low between my legs as they guided me up and down, up and down against him.

As he eased me lower, I had to break the kiss, my head falling back as a soft groan slipped out of my mouth. "Yes, yes," I encouraged him, the tiny muscles below my belly growing tight as Nephesh's mouth landed back on my neck once more.

"What happens, in the dream world if…"

Nephesh's deep laugh echoed across my throat. "All of the pleasure, but our physical forms remain sleeping."

15

Justine

I whimpered a little as he licked a trail up my neck to my ear, where his lips tugged at my earlobe. I could feel his razor-sharp teeth barely graze my skin—not enough to hurt, but enough to draw out my pleasure.

"I should wait, insist that we do this in the living world or even the Underworld, where you can be properly courted and wooed and fucking seduced. But I can't wait. When I was imprisoned, all I thought about was the fact I would be alone for the rest of my life. And then, here you are."

"Ruining everything."

"Absolutely everything. And I love it."

"You do?"

"I do. I'm going to keep pretending I hate it, but I love it. Never change, little thief."

"I couldn't if I tried."

And then, with a soft growl, Nephesh flipped me over until he loomed over me, his bulk blanketing me in a warm, solid wall of muscle. I shifted my hips, trying to get comfortable, when

Nephesh's hand suddenly gripped my hip where my shirt rose up, his claws biting in there. "Justine…I'm begging you."

"What?"

"You can't just…"

"What?" I did it again, feeling the thick length of him exactly where I wanted him. Damn these clothes.

"Fuck, Justine. I won't be completely unmanned the first time I feel you like this." His head dropped low, until his forehead rested against my collarbone.

"Seems like it's not your choice. It is my dream, after all. And I kind of like you like this."

"Pleading and desperate?"

"Maybe."

His tongue darted out and tasted my collarbone. "If I'm going to be desperate, then I'll have you the same way." And with that, he moved until his knees were bracketing my hips, and in a flash of fabric, my shirt was off, replaced by the silken heat of his lips as he traced his way down my body, between my breasts, across my hips, and low to my belly button.

"Nephesh," I whispered, my hands scrambling for his hair once again.

His tongue dipped into my belly button for a second before he traced his way back up over my ribcage to my breasts, where he paused. I could feel the burning heat of his breath on my skin as my nipples puckered.

"Beautiful," he whispered, and then his mouth covered my sensitive flesh, sucking hard as his hand moved reverently over the other, his fingers carefully stroking me while his dark claws played against my skin.

He switched sides, leaving a smattering of kisses between my breasts as one of his hands slid low, caressing across my ribs to my belly and then slipping just the tips of his fingers below my waistband. Nephesh teased me there, drawing tiny circles as his tongue lapped over the second nipple, making my hips rise and move in desperate little movements against him.

Why wouldn't he just move that hand lower? He knew I was dying for him to do it.

"Need something, little thief?"

I growled in frustration, to which the freaking demon actually had the audacity to chuckle. "Desperate yet?"

"You know I am."

"Oh, but I want to hear it. I want to hear from those pretty lips how badly you want me to do more."

I tossed my head back, my hands moving to his shoulders as if I could stop him from the torture session, but at the same time I really didn't *want* to stop him. I wanted him to keep going. I wanted it so badly.

"Nephesh," I said, and I could hear the begging in my voice. "Please."

"Please what?"

"Please, put your hands on me, make me come. Let me feel you."

Nephesh's mocking smile dissolved in a moment, his fangs flashing as his eyes glowed a brilliant red color. And then his hand dipped into my waistband, slipping over my pelvic bone to stroke me there, his fingers so gentle and careful against delicate skin that I nearly cried in relief when he finally pushed one finger then another into me.

"Do you like that, mate? Do you like feeling my fingers inside you?"

I nodded, my chin jerking as I was lost in the sensation of those thick, warm fingers pulsing in and out of me, barely moving, but at the same time sending waves of pleasure through me. I knew in a breath that even if this was just a dream, this was how he would be in the living world too. A little bossy, a lot cocky, and absolutely devoted to my pleasure. My eyes flickered open to find him there, staring down at my face. His eyes were still glowing red even as his expression was one of rapt attention.

After our eyes met, his smile turned smug once more, as he dragged his gaze down my body to where his hands were inside my pants, making my lower half jerk with every gentle pass. "Talk to me, Justine. Tell me what you feel."

"It feels better than good, better than I imagined."

"Good," he purred, his thrusting fingers pushing deeper. "So hot and slick here… I can't wait to feel you against my cock."

I groaned, my eyes falling shut again as my inner thighs quivered. So close, I felt the teasing edge of completion lingering just outside of my reach. And it was as if Nephesh knew it too. He slowed his movements, leaning over to kiss me once again.

I wrapped my arms around him, one leg coiling around his hip in a movement to keep him close, to help him rid me of this delicious and frustrating need.

"Do you need something, mate?"

"I need…"

"Say it."

"I need to come. Please, make me come."

Nephesh snarled, "Nothing would make me happier than to feel this sweet pussy gripping me like this every day for the rest of my existence." His words sent a shiver through my entire body, and a moment later, his fingers pushed deep, turning and teasing a place deep inside me that made my vision go white. Then every part of me exploded in a series of tense bursts of pleasure, each one better than the last, until I was breathing hard, my cheek resting against his chest as I struggled to catch my breath.

Nephesh drew my pleasure out with soft kisses and a slowly circling thumb over the center of my pleasure. But when it became impossible to stay still, I wanted only one thing.

Him.

All of him.

"Nephesh," I whispered. "Can I see you?"

He pulled back, a surprised look on his face. "You've already seen me."

"I mean, not all of you. I want to feel your skin against me."

Nephesh's eyes were hot on mine as he settled back, careful to not step on me as he shifted on the bed and rose above me.

His shirt came off first, and I couldn't stop myself from sitting up and running eager fingers over the muscles of his chest, then his belly, and then finally over the waistline of his pants as I saw the straining length of him right below my fingertips. "You're perfect."

Nephesh released a strangled groan, and then he was kissing me again, quick and hard, and his hands were busy, yanking his pants free of his body. Finally, there was nothing but skin on skin, and it had never felt better. I couldn't stop the sighs and moans that were coming out of my mouth, and I didn't know whether it was him or me, and it didn't matter.

Because we were one. Tears sprang to my eyes as I gathered him close. "Nephesh?"

His nose brushed mine as he held himself over me. "Justine."

I smiled up at him. "I'm yours."

"I-I don't want to steal you away from your life."

"You forgot already? What is already yours can't be stolen."

Nephesh lowered his head, his lips caressing mine with a sweetness that made a single tear slip free from my eyes and race down to my hairline.

"Mine," Nephesh whispered, breaking away as his knees sank between my thighs, and I felt the head of him between my legs.

"And mine," I said, breathing in sharply as he sank into me with one hard, deep thrust. For a long moment, I could do nothing but savor this feeling, the complete rightness that swept over me like a blanket, sealing in the heat of the moment and the comfort of him against me And then he was moving, his mouth by my ear, whispering things that make my soul and my heart swell in ecstasy.

"Sweet, sweet mate. Fuck, you feel so good. You're gripping me so hard, little thief. Relax so I can make this even better for you."

"Better for me?" I whispered finally, looking down at where he had driven himself into me. "It gets better?"

Nephesh's low chuckle made me moan as it settled over us. "It gets so much better."

***

Nephesh

This was a dream. But it felt like the real thing. It felt like we could make this work for real. Because there was nothing like being with her. Not just the kissing and then touching and the way her pussy gripped me like a vise as I moved inside her. There was something that went so far beyond all of that.

It was madness and reason. Pleasure and pain. It was her. And she was mine.

I shifted my hips back then thrust forward, my eyes glued to the perfect way her breasts moved as I drove into her. She was hot and slick and clenching around my cock, and I knew it would take only seconds for me to finish if I wasn't careful. And while I had no idea what the dream realm's rules on recovery were, I wasn't risking it. If we lost this dream and were forced back to the real world, real-world issues would follow.

But we had agreed to this. And I understood that she wouldn't know my fears until she was faced with them herself. I would be there to protect her then too. Even without our deal. Because I was hers. Through the good and the bad.

"Nephesh," she whimpered under me, and fuck if it didn't make my chest burn with pleasure. I was doing that, making my sweet, fiery little mate call out my name in pleasure.

Wrapping an arm around her waist, I rolled us until she was back on top of me. For a moment, she was caught off guard, and I saw the nervousness dance across her features. I slid my hands around her until I was cupping the perfect handful of her breasts. "Mine."

Her smile sent a bolt of warmth straight down my spine, followed by a rewarding clenching of pleasure as she rose up over me then bent her knees, driving me back inside her with a soft noise.

"Right there. Take what you need."

Justine's head fell back as her hands found my belly and pushed off the muscle there as she took herself up and down on me, repeating until we were both breathless and weak.

"I can't. I need…"

"Let me," I said, grinding my heels in the bedding and arching up into her.

Justine gasped, her body clenching tight around mine.

"Come apart for me. Let me see what I've dreamed of every night since I met you."

Her soft cry broke me, and I could feel the fluttering of her body as she came, shattering over me as I thrust blindly into her, so obsessed with getting as close as I could. I wanted to be deep inside her, to feel my body lock to hers like I had always imagined a mate. I wanted it all.

"Nephesh!" Justine's voice was high, gasping, as her muscles began to go slack, and I knew this was it, where I let everything close. And so I did. My orgasm hit me with the power of a hurricane as I pulled her down against me, thrusting myself as deep as I could before letting everything go.

"Sweet mate," I gritted out, emptying myself inside her, feeling the demon's lock settle into place as my body quivered into relaxation. I stroked a hand down her back, feeling the light sweat on her skin as she fell forward, wrapping her arms around my neck as her body bowed over mine.

"Wow," she said finally, her eyes still closed against my chest. "Are you sure it's not better in dreams?"

"It might be worse, actually."

"You lie."

I grinned. "Only one way to find out."

16

Nephesh

Bliss was not something I was familiar with. Right now, in Justine's dream, with her sprawled across me, my hand tracing the lines and ridges of her spine as she told me about her first time driving a car, I knew this was as close as I might get.

"What did your parents do when they found out?"

"Oh, I was grounded for weeks. I thought my mom's head was going to explode when I came clean."

"I can't believe you told her."

Justine laughed, the movement making her body shake a little against me. "She knew every inch of that car. There was no chance she was going to miss the giant neon green paint on the side door."

"Good point. Is it better to confess or be found out?"

"With my mom or the world?"

I paused my strokes as I considered. "Both."

"Always confess, because then there's a chance you can still make things better."

"A chance?"

I felt her smile rather than saw it. "A chance is all we get in this world."

For a long moment, we lay in silence, just thinking. We'd been here for hours now, wrapped up in each other, talking, trying to find peace in the unknown of what would happen after we left here.

"What would your mother have done?"

"Probably cursed me to the ends of the Underworld. Between her and my father, she was the one with the temper."

She turned to face me, rising up on an elbow. "You're kidding. I keep picturing your father as some kind of fire-breathing monster."

I booped her nose. "I didn't say he wasn't. I just said that between the two, Mother was always the more explosive one. Father always said that it was a good thing he was nearly impossible to kill."

Justine grinned, and then her face grew solemn. "Will I ever meet them?"

Dread uncurled in my gut. The need to show her off to my family battled with the obsessive need to keep her far from danger. "I imagine you might." I didn't know if that would be in this world or the next, but maybe there would be a time it would be safe for us to be together.

Justine dropped back onto my chest, and my hand moved back to combing through those strawberry red locks. "I'm still punching the brother who locked you up. That was a dick move."

I snorted. "Arafel? Feel free, but don't forget he's the one helping us now too."

Her shoulders moved in what might be a shrug. "Still."

I chuckled, and we fell back into a comfortable silence.

After a moment, she said, "Nephesh?"

"Yes?"

"You're leaving after this, aren't you?"

Ice trickled through my veins. But I'd promised her the truth. I would give it to her, even if it nearly killed me to do so. "I am."

"And our deal is done, so you actually *can* leave, right?"

"If my theory is correct, yes. I've essentially failed to protect you from myself. So the deal will dissolve."

I could see her holding her wrist up, examining the mark there. "I'm a little sad. I've gotten attached to the tattoo."

"That's the only thing you're attached to?"

Justine giggled. "The only thing."

I rolled my eyes, settling back into the pillows. "Good to know."

"Will you come back?"

I wanted to promise her yes. I wanted to tell her that I would rather tear the boundaries between the living and the dead than be apart from her. But that didn't matter, and it *wouldn't* matter because I couldn't let that happen.

"When it's safe, I can try."

"Will you be able to find me?"

I blinked. If I had my magic back, finding her would be nothing. Let alone the pull that I knew would exist between soul mates. "I will always find you."

"What if… What if I need you before then?"

I sat up, pulling Justine around until she straddled me against the blankets tangled between us. "The bond between our souls will always allow me to find you. But if you need me…"

I carefully picked up her arm, below the tattoo that would be fading as soon as we left the dream realm. With a flicker of fire at the tips of my claws, I scrawled my name down her arm, the lettering tiny and minute under the lily.

"Oh." Justine held the scrawling text up to observe. "It's beautiful. Is it… Is it like what your brother did with his mate?"

"A little. This is a sort of calling card. You just have to press on this, call my name, and it will tell me that you need me. I will come as soon as I'm able."

Justine nodded, but her face was hidden as her fingers traced the new tattoo once again. "I'm going to miss you."

No pleading. No begging.

Just her missing me.

The place deep in my chest where my heart and soul resided nearly buckled with the need to give it all up. To stay in this perfectly imperfect world with her for as long as she allowed me.

"I could…"

But her fingers were pressing against my lips, warm and firm, locking the thought deep inside my mind. "You are a good person, Nephesh. A good demon. And you have to go back and help your family."

I remained still under her gaze.

"And if we are meant to be together, then we will be, when the time is right." She laughed after that, and the sound was a little ragged. "God, did you hear me? I sound like I know what I'm doing."

"You," I said, removing her hand from my mouth and pressing a kiss to the new tattoo on her wrist, "are more than I deserve."

Her smile wobbled but then held. "If you truly believe we are soul mates, then I'm exactly what you deserve, Nephesh."

I lunged for her, my mouth hungry and desperate for hers. We didn't talk, save the whispered pleas and soft noises that I tore from her mouth for a long time after that.

***

Justine

The world seemed decidedly less vivid today. It didn't matter that the fall sun was shining in through my crappy side window or that it was the middle of the day. After our night last night in the dream realm, where we'd spent far, far longer than the eight hours of sleep together, I wasn't sure I could adjust.

Not in time for him to go. In a matter of a week, he'd completely thrown my life into chaos. And shown me exactly what I needed in a partner.

And now he had to leave. I glanced down at the tattoo on my wrist. Nephesh's name scrawled across my wrist bones still looked up at me. But the lily was gone.

Our deal was done.

Now that I knew what it was, I could feel the bond in my chest screaming to stay close to him. But that wasn't possible. It didn't matter how many times I'd brought it up, he refused to bring me to the Underworld until he was sure it was safe.

I swallowed. Who knew how long that might be. Unable to hide it, I ducked to the ground, kneeling at Cerberus's side and pressing my face into the softness of his scruff. "I'm going to miss you too, Clark."

The dog barked at his nickname then tried to lick my face again. I laughed, pushing him away as I heard Nephesh walk up to beside us. "I'm going to send him back as soon as we figure out a gameplan. He can protect you until I'm able to get back."

I nodded, eyes on Cerberus. I couldn't look at him. If I did, I would break. I would give up and tell him I wasn't strong after all. That I needed him to stay, or to take me with him, but that I couldn't do life without him anymore.

"Justine." His voice was soft, gentle. "Come here."

He gripped my elbow, pulling me until I was standing against him. "I can't," I said, unsure of what exactly I couldn't do. Life without him—couldn't do. Say goodbye—also could not do.

"I know," he said, his hands dropping to circle my waist and pull me closer. "But you can. You stole from a police detective's girlfriend. You reclaimed your freedom back from your landlord. You tamed the Underworld's guard dog. You went toe-to-toe with the heir to Hell on a daily basis."

"I did that because of you."

"You did that in spite of everything else. We are better together, little thief."

"How am I supposed to say goodbye to you?"

"My father once told me that history is told in chapters. This, my mate, is only the beginning of ours."

I nodded, pressing my face to the side of his, my toes cramping until he took pity on me and picked me up so I could better feel him against me. Memories from last night, from the time we'd spent, were so real that I simply couldn't believe that it would be the only chance we'd have to be together.

"Only the beginning," I repeated. Then, digging my hands into his heavy silver hair, I tugged his head back. "Tell me how to do it."

His amber eyes warmed mine, and a slow smile split his mouth. "You simply have to give it to me."

With a whimper, I covered his mouth with my own, letting my mind wander to the place deep in my chest that had always fluttered and hummed in his presence. There was heat, fire-red and gold, and at the center, a flame that fluttered like a candle in the breeze.

He kept kissing me, his lips careful and loving as I carefully let that fire rise inside me, until suddenly, I was breaking away gasping as something pulled from me in a pinch of heat and pressure.

My mind whirled as I stared down at the tiny flame that burned between us, flickering and dancing in the air. It was red, and gold, white and violet, as it twisted and burned in on itself Beautiful and deadly. Fragile and dangerous all in one.

My lips quivered, even as tears lipped down my cheek. It was him.

Our eyes met through the flame of his soul, and then slowly Nephesh released me until I was back on the floor. With shaking hands, he reached out, his hands cupping around the fire and bringing it closer to his body.

In the presence of his hands, it immediately bloomed higher, making me gasp and step back as the heat in my apartment rose quickly.

"Wow," I couldn't stop myself from saying.

Nephesh immediately stepped back, his face tense. "Stay back."

I smiled at him and his fiery soul and then took a purposeful step back up to him, reaching out to cup his hands with my own. They were so warm, nearly burning, but I didn't back down. Together, we raised his soul up to his chest, where he hesitated just a moment.

"It's okay," I said, watching as Nephesh curled his hands closer, slowly clasping his fingers until his soul disappeared into his palms, my fingers still securely wrapped around his.

"It is done," Nephesh said, but there was something odd in his expression as he jerked his hands free of mine and down to his side. "I should go now. No telling what will happen."

"Nephesh…it's going to be fine."

His amber eyes snapped up. "You don't know that. And I'm putting you more at risk every moment I'm here."

"Oh, okay." I awkwardly stepped back, my bare feet curling against the worn rug. "I guess this is goodbye for now."

Nephesh's chest was rapidly rising and falling, his body so stiff that I wasn't sure he wouldn't break the moment I hugged him. But I did it anyway, looping my arms around his middle and getting one last touch in before he left.

I could feel his hands on my shoulders, but he didn't clasp me to him like I thought he might. Instead, he merely brushed his fingers over my shoulders a moment then stepped out of my arms.

"I'll be back," he said. Then he nodded jerkily and moved towards the door.

"Don't you want to take Cerberus?" I asked, gesturing to the dog who was still lying by my feet, staring at his owner.

Nephesh's mouth tightened, and a wan smile appeared on his lips. "Oh yes, of course. Come here, Cerberus."

The dog pushed up to a sitting position but didn't get off of my foot or approach his owner. Nephesh blinked, surprised.

"Cerberus, come." This time there was an echoing command in every letter.

The dog stood, walking quickly to his side, his stumpy tail wagging slightly when Nephesh placed a hand on his head.

"Bye 'Rus," I whispered.

My throat felt tight. In all the strange comments, unusual conversations that the two of us had had. This was the first time he'd lied to me. I could feel it as clearly as if he had admitted it out loud.

Nephesh turned his hand on the knob, and I couldn't stop the rest of the words from falling free.

"I'll be waiting for you. You're worth waiting for."

His sharp amber eyes dropped as I spoke, staring at the floor until he was sure there was nothing else to be said. And then he was gone. He and Cerberus disappeared out of my doorway and down the creaky hallway.

A hot tear slipped free, racing down my cheek before I could brush it away. Then another. That one I let fall, enjoying the simple reminder that although I was all alone again, at least I hadn't lost my ability to cry.

Or to truly enjoy a person for who they were.

I sniffled hard, my phone finally vibrating with a text from the diner. They needed me. Correction, they needed me to work today. Clearing my throat, I moved out the door, and after staring down the empty hallway, I locked the door.

No one else was going to need back in.

***

There was nothing like coming home to a barren, bone-cold apartment. For some reason, it hasn't felt the same as it had before Nephesh had come into my life. For all that he was the definition of prickly, he had filled this space with conversation and peace and, in many cases, laughter. Even if it was at his expense.

In the day since he'd left, I'd attempted to keep busy, but nothing could fill the hollow feelings that ached at the center of me. At first I was worried about the absence of Nephesh's soul damaging me somehow. But I knew now, it was the absence of the demon himself. Of my soul mate. I had had him, and now I didn't.

And in the quiet moments walking home from the diner, the only thing that kept me putting one foot after the other had been reliving those quiet, beautiful moments in my dreams. When we had just been us.

I shut the door, bolting it behind me, and then stared around the space. A sudden compulsion to go running back out of the room hit me, and I braced my feet, swearing loudly. "There's nowhere else to go."

But deep in my chest, something hummed, a desperate compulsion to open the door, to bolt out of this building. Because something was wrong. It wasn't just Nephesh leaving.

I hadn't felt this in years. It reminded me just like that day… A sharp chill swept down my spine, fear filling my heart.

Oh God, what had I done? I'd been distracted, too distracted. I must've missed something. Hurrying, I zipped up my jacket, the straps on my bag suddenly slick with my sweat.

I needed to go. I turned, unbolting the door I'd just come through and swinging it wide. My mind was already racing with backup plans when I realized that there was someone in front of me. Multiple someones.

There, standing on my doorway, stood Rocky, his white hair tousled and wild. But I wasn't worried about his hair or the way that his clothes were knocked askew and looked as if they'd be just thrown on. I was distracted by the man in a dark suit, standing beside him, looming over him, and as soon as my door was open, the stranger leaned in, palm flattening on my door. Another man, depressed identically, moved to stand behind them.

My eyes took them in, heart rate climbing as I read the warning, the plea in Rocky's eyes. Fury, fear, frustration all boomed in my belly.

"They know you took the meds, Justine."

I blinked, adrenaline coursing through my veins. "Wait, what?"

Rocky cleared his throat. "The medicine you stole for the kids. They know it was you."

I stared at him, incredulous. "Rocky, you think these people are with the police? Look at them! Do you think they send them out here for petty crimes like that?"

Rocky quivered, his eyes anxiously jumping from me to the palm on my door and back again. "I'm sorry, Justine. I have to protect the kids."

"And you've done a wonderful job, Mr. Rockford. You can go now."

Rocky hesitated. "Justine, I—"

"Go Rocky," I snarled. He had to go. He had to go now, to protect the kids, to protect himself. Even if he was too stupid to realize he must've gotten involved in something bigger than himself. Bigger than me.

In my chest, that warning blazed, hotter and heavier than before. Run, it begged. Run far. I braced my legs for what would come the moment we were alone.

I listened to Rocky's hurried footsteps, to the slam of his door. I heard the chain of his extra lock slide across the fixture. I frowned up into the face of the suited man. "What happens now?"

"You have to come with us, down to the station, ma'am."

"Drop the act. I know we aren't going anywhere like a police station. Might as well tell me the truth." I grunted a little as the handcuffs pinched my skin, flinching as I remembered the scars on Nephesh's wrists. He'd endured enough. I could manage this.

Besides, it allowed me to press my thumb against the name tattooed in dark ink across my wrist. Hunching forward, I whispered, "Nephesh, please, they're here."

Nervous about what they might've heard, I chattered on. "Do I have time to get my bag? You really don't want to have to deal with me without my skincare routine, I will be looking rough in like two days. So if I could just have a moment to grab that."

"Shut up. For God's sake."

I didn't stop, letting my words fall fast and furious, half of it nonsense. But it was better than letting them see the way my body trembled in fear. The men ignored my chattering as they shoved me down the hallway, my shoelaces causing me to stumble as we passed Rocky's closed door.

When I recovered, I hissed at them, surprising the one on my right enough that he stepped back from me. I saw it then, the hesitation, the fear that flashed across his face.

"You're not after me, are you?"

"Move," the other one barked.

I grunted in my most Nephesh-ish way, letting them shuffle me forward once more, my mind whirling with the possibilities. What were they doing here? That feeling that I'd had, the one that had followed me the way I'd always believed I was cursed. It had been a warning. One I hadn't taken enough into account this time.

And now they had me. But something told me there was more to this. If Nephesh had been there, this wouldn't be happening. Was it possible they knew about him? They had to have. Something in the timing was too coincidental.

He would come for me. And until then, I had to do what I had always done.

Survive by any means possible.

Taking a deep breath, I reached the stairs that zigzagged down my building all the way to the street. Closing my eyes, I let my body go limp. If they were going to take me, fine. But I was going to make it hard as hell to do so.

Life has always been chaotic. Why should my death be any different?

Justine

I'd pissed them off well and completely now. After my trick on the stairs, I'd been hurled into a dark sedan with tinted windows. I only remembered a moment though, since something wet and thick had been pressed against my nose as soon as I slipped onto the seat.

I'd inhaled, unable to control my impulse, and moments later the car moved forward. I'd fallen into a deep, anxious sleep, only to wake up here in what I could only assume was their version of a jail cell.

It was only a fraction smaller than my apartment, honestly, and had a cement ceiling and base, which had thick iron bars lining the front side of it. The other three sides were dark cement as well. When I leaned against the bars, I could see a sliver of another cell next to mine. But it appeared empty.

I was alone, unless you counted the two rotating guards who appeared directly across the warehouse-styled room that my cell had been dropped into. Beyond them, a single door led out of here, and they'd done a great job concealing any bits of the hallway beyond when they rotated.

Which left me with absolutely no idea who these people were or why they wanted me. Inside my cell, I had a little camping-style bed with crisscross legs that held a mattress and a sleeping bag. I wasn't stupid and could see that there were two there.

They had meant to catch someone else. Not sure if it meant Nephesh or if I was still expecting another guest, but either way, I would almost welcome the company now. Anything was better than the swollen silence that seemed to echo back at me from every side.

It didn't help that I was still struggling with motor functions after our little ride. I had no idea if it was a reaction to whatever they'd given me or something else, but I was still struggling to stand or to get my body to do what I liked. As long as I sat here, propped up against the wall, my legs out flat, it seemed to be fine.

But when I moved, it felt like the whole world was in motion. So here I sat, trying to plan out my next move, one that didn't require the use of my legs. As of yet, nothing had come to mind.

Some hours later, food was pressed into my hand by one of the men who had been at my apartment. Unlike my two companions guarding the door, he looked like a businessman in his tailored suit. Maybe he was more important. Or maybe he was just a crap shot and didn't make the cut.

I hid my smile as I wobbled over to the bars to take the food.

"How are you? Haven't seen you in a while."

He glared down at me. "You disgust me, demon fucker."

My eyebrows rose, taking my temper with them, "Oh my. Can you think of a nicer nickname? I called you Righty instead of stuck-up asshole."

He grabbed me through the bars, one meaty fist yanking me forward, my face slamming against the iron. A moment later, I heard the jingle of keys, and then he was inside. My fear made me wild, and my hands searched across the cold floor to find something, anything to defend myself.

But there was nothing. The first kick silenced my words. The second drove me to curl in on myself as the pain filtered in. I bit back the cry that threatened and instead covered my face with my arm. "Fine," I whispered. "Stuck-up asshole it is."

I wished Nephesh was here. He would've shredded this guy and then laughed at my joke. And then we could've left together and never come back to this stupid building ever again.

He reared back, prepared to kick me again, when a very soft voice spoke up. "Gregory, your brother called. He needs your help."

One of my eyes, the one that hadn't taken the worst of the smash to the bars, peeked open.

Gregory, if that really was his name, was staring down at me. Slowly, every inch making my adrenaline race faster, he leaned over me. "Careful, demon whore. I know what you really are." Then he spat on me, the action cutting through my already fragile confidence.

I huffed, a single tear slipping free from my eye and running down my cheek. I heard Righty, or rather Gregory, speaking to the newcomer for a short moment before the cell door slammed. Assuming I was alone again, I slowly shifted back into my sitting position, moaning a little when my head spun for a whole new reason.

When my eyes could focus, I stared down at the thermos in front of me. The one Gregory had brought. My stomach growled when I smelled the strawberries, and I could almost feel the coolness against my parched throat.

"I don't like that flavor much."

I flinched, my head hitting the wall a little as I stared across the cell at the door. There was a girl there—no, actually, she was a woman, just tiny with delicate features. Against the grays and blacks of the surrounding room, she was in a bright teal dress, her olive skin vibrant and healthy.

In short, she looked like she didn't belong here at all. But based on the fact that I was on this side of the bars and she wasn't, that fit. I picked up the thermos, shaking the contents a little.

"Okay, well…" I gestured around the room. "I'm a little desperate here." I opened the thermos, my stomach growling.

"You won't like it."

I turned my head back to her. "Excuse me? What the hell are you talking about?"

She shifted, her high heels scraping against the floor. A section of her dark hair slipped forward over her eyes as she did, and instantly I scanned the walls on that side of her. There were cameras everywhere, but that one, it had a large device hanging just below it, the tiny green light glowing at me from the shadows. "You won't like what is in the recipe." Her words were measured, careful.

Fear, something dark and slithering, moved in my chest. I carefully put the smoothie down. The motion made the girl's shoulders slump in what appeared to be relief. I struggled to sit up again, suddenly far more interested in my guest.

"Who are you?"

She shook her head. "No one. Just a member of the Great Cause. I came to get Gregory."

I nodded slowly, my balance still off, but I swore she sounded almost sarcastic. Had I found an unexpected ally? "Got it."

She turned and began to walk away, and just before she got to the door, I called, "Wait!" I swallowed to wet my too-dry throat. "When he gets here, something tells me you should stay out of the way. We can save you, you can be free."

The only clue that she might've listened, or even heard me, was the tiniest misstep in her heels as she reached for the locked doorknob. Then loudly, her voice echoed out into the room.

"I belong to the Drude, and I always will."

I wasn't sure what she meant by that, but I did recognize his name. The Drude, the creature that was wreaking havoc on Nephesh's family and his world. I had been right, and she had just given me an enormous clue about what I was facing.

Crawling across the cell, I tipped the strawberry-scented drink into the drain there. I wouldn't be tempted now. Stomach growling in protest, I knew the best way to get rid of an empty belly was to sleep. After running some cold water over the egg-shaped lump I had across my temple, I crawled back over into my bed and curled up. The blankets were stiff, scratchy, but when I covered my head, the darkness eased some of the ache in my head. I swallowed hard, and a few tears slipped free.

"I hope you're safe, Nephesh. Far, far from here."

When I woke up again, the space was still empty but the thundering of footsteps echoed off the thick metal walls. I shifted, sitting up on my stiff backside as I stared at the door. A moment later, figures began to filter in, dressed in all black, heavy utility boots on each of their feets as they filled the barren room where my cell resided.

My brows rose. "All this for me?" Clearly they hadn't seen me fall on my way out of my apartment earlier. Physically I was more of a liability to myself than them.

They didn't respond. Most of their faces remained covered in ski masks, but for the two suited from earlier. Their faces were bare. I forced a smile to my lips, folding my legs under myself as I attempted to pretend that I wasn't moments from either bursting into tears or hysterical laughter.

Gregory. That was what she'd called him. He was back and standing to the front of the group. "That smart mouth will get you in a lot of trouble someday."

"It already has, clearly," I responded, following the two now familiar faces as they began to pace in front of their legion of soldiers.

"We have come to discuss your options with you." That was Lefty, Gregory's brother, who spoke now.

I bit my lip, the hysterical laughter from earlier bubbling up and burning my throat for a moment. "I wasn't aware I had any."

"You do," he said, his hands gesturing wide in a flash of comedic relief. "Surprise."

My laughter died in my throat. I remained silent, watching their faces for any hint of what they were about to say. Finally, Gregory, who appeared to be the chattier brother, continued on. "You have been chosen for the most dangerous role in this world. You are the keeper of a demon's soul. And if he were to come into possession of his soul, then you may put the entire living world in jeopardy."

Lefty paused his brother with a slap on the shoulder. "That's where we come in. We are here to protect you, to keep you as far from the demon as possible."

Maybe I could play dumb. Maybe they didn't know everything yet. They obviously didn't know that I had already given Nephesh the other half of his soul. Maybe I had a way to work that angle. My mind, thankfully clearer than earlier, raced.

"A demon? You're kidding."

"I believe you know him as Nephesh, or perhaps the Judge. He's had many titles in the centuries since his unholy birth, and while his monster is so dangerous even Lucifer fears his own son, he is quite capable of appearing human. When he wants, that is." They paused, looking at me pointedly, "He might have even acted human, shared human emotions. Human acts."

I could feel the soft burn of heat across my cheeks. But still, I remained still and silent.

"But as you can imagine, he is nothing but a demon, the Judge of every soul that enters the Underworld. Our spies tell us that his power has been growing again. Probably the result of him interacting with you."

My heartbeat slowly picked up speed, desperate to hear what they knew.

"You seem to know an awful lot about someone you're claiming to be a supernatural overlord who wants my soul."

I prayed to anyone listening that this man, or whatever he was, couldn't tell I had already given Nephesh his soul back. The way he continued on told me I was safe. For now at least.

"We are the demon hunters who have been entrusted by our master in the Great Cause to make sure that the sons of Hell are never able to regain their souls."

"And if they do?"

"They will bring Hell to Earth, combining the living world and the afterlife in one catalytic disaster that will undo all the good humans have ever done."

I sagged my shoulders dramatically. "I had no idea." Perhaps I had missed my calling in theater.

Gregory moved forward, and again I heard the jingle of keys, but when I looked up, I took note that it wasn't just a key keeping me in here. It was a key and some kind of glowing identification pad that he pressed his palm to.

With a pop, the door unlocked, and Lefty gripped my shoulder, pulling me out into the room. The armed guards and the newcomers all stared at me from the eyeholes of their masks. The front row was heavily armed, each with their trigger fingers at the ready. Dread filled my belly, and I was worried I was going to be sick.

"It's going to be alright, Justine. You are safe now. He'll never be able to get through our defense. And in a few hours, we will have you in front of our master, where we can safely dispatch your souls."

"Dispatch?"

The hand stroked my shoulder as ice grew in my belly. "We can't let you die. Your soul would be lost again. But our master is very gifted. He can take the demon's soul from you. We can use it to grow more powerful, to spread our cause to even more of the living world."

I was briefly surprised and confused that so many of the words that Nephesh used were the same that these two used.

Living world. How many times did someone refer to this world like that?

I turned slowly, staring up at him. "You're insane. All of you. You don't know anything about this world or his. And you definitely don't have any rights to destroying his family or their way of life. They didn't want this war. Your so-called master did. He's the one who started it. When he gets here…" My voice cut off, and my breathing was sharp and painful.

He cocked his head. "Do you believe he'd come for you? Little girl, these demons do not understand relationships as humans do or even love as we understand it. They understand only power and bloodshed. They are monsters and must be destroyed."

"The only monsters I've seen are the ones in front of me. Who do you think you are, to determine a whole world's fate?"

Lefty shook his head. "You poor thing. I knew he had gotten to you. The master will be able to make you understand. It's the least we can do before you give your soul to the Great Cause."

"The Great Cause?" I laughed, but the sound was too high and thin. "Don't you know, there is no good or bad. There are only those who continue to fight and those, like you and your little posse, who roll over when things get difficult."

Gregory's hand slammed into my face with a ringing slap.

I moved slowly, eyes watering as I turned to face him again. "Guess which one I am?"

"Gag her. I'm tired of hearing her love for the Fallen. It's making me sick."

My heartrate spiked again as I leaned back, away from the individuals who split away from the group to raise a gag to my lips. "Nephesh is not evil. He and his family are merely keepers of the souls. They are guardians and teachers, and I—"

The gag slipped into place between my teeth, and the rough fabric bit into my lips as they lashed it tighter and tighter. I grunted a little as I was heaved off my feet and carried back towards the cell.

"If you think a gag will stop me from calling for him, you're so far from reality that nothing I do will change your mind." The words game out garbled and strange on my lips as two more gripped my arms, lifting me and pulling on my shoulders as they hauled me up and dragged me back behind bars.

A moment later, the door was shut, and one by one the soldiers disappeared back out of the space, leaving just me and the brothers, who looked between themselves then to me.

"What if he comes for her?"

Lefty nearly squirmed in delight. "Master will be so pleased. Can you imagine what he would say if we deliver the Judge of Hell to him as well as his soul?"

I stared, my breathing labored as panic rose in my belly.

"You see, Justine, if your demon shows up, then we win. And if he doesn't not, we will still win. It is fruitless to fight us. You're entering a battle that was lost hundreds of years ago."

And then he smiled, stepping away as a small remote appeared in his hand. A moment later, the bars hummed softly, a sign that they were electrified. A new layer of horror and disappointment nearly choked me.

I whimpered a little when they closed the door after them, the lights slowly fading to a dim gray. Between the darkness and the claustrophobia of the gag in my mouth, fear warred common sense in my mind.

As I lay there, staring up, I let my mind wander. U realized for the first time that the hum in my chest, the thing that always connected Judge and me, was still there. He'd taken his soul, yes, but something remained. I closed my eyes, feeling that soft hum, the rustle of power that reminded me of the way his wings had felt against my palms when we flew together that night. It was so real. It was so tangible, I could almost pretend that he was right here.

Here, I could admit it, even if it was just to myself. I wished he was here, grumpy face, beautiful. I would give nearly anything to see him for more time. Especially knowing what I knew now. That when they found out what I'd already done, then I was as good as dead. For the second time in my life, my soul was suddenly the biggest bargaining chip I had. Too bad I'd already given it away.

18

Nephesh

I stared at my missing soul.

"Do you know what you are risking?" Atlas's voice rose in pitch as he leaned over in the chair he'd taken upon entering the courthouse apartment. I'd not bothered to even snarl at him when he barged in just a few moments before. I was transfixed. And now, it seemed so was he.

"You are carrying your soul around? Why don't you put us all out of our misery and absorb it?"

"You know why I must be careful."

Atlas raised a hand as if to stroke the flame that danced at the center of my palm but then thought better of it. Maybe it was the fact that every one of my teeth was showing as he flopped back in his seat once more. "You were a very bad guy, once upon a time. I know. We all know. We are trained on that, just as we are trained to avoid you in that state."

"Your point? It seems you are only proving mine."

"The demon who acted that way was different, untethered and wild. You are…" Atlas paused, his hands circling midair as he searched for the word. "Different now."

"How so?"

"You want me to spell it out?'

I snarled.

"Fine, okay, so you have spent your entire existence judging others, a task that eventually left you acting as a weapon against those who were bad enough to warrant it. You didn't have a path of your own. When you took on the Courthouse, when you built the dam, you started to change. Everyone noticed. The magic changed too, brought more jurors, brought more peace."

"And then Anna died."

"She did, and you got off the rail a little. But now, Nephesh, I barely recognize you. You are grounded." He nodded to the soul I held. "You are complete, and I'm not just talking about the soul."

I glared at him. "Careful, soldier, or I will smite you where you stand."

"Go ahead and try," Atlas growled, leveling me with a harsh look. "You know that I'm right. All you have to do now is let it happen. Trust in the good."

I snarled in response, surprised once again that my teeth remained human, flat and useless in my threat. "I know what I'm doing."

"Do you?" Atlas leaned back once more, eyeing my clothing for the day. "We know what happens when a demon stays in the living world too long. And now you return, holding a soul and pretending that it is completely ordinary."

Her gifted soul, the half of mine I'd been searching so long to find, leaped in my hand, the soft red flame dancing on my palm. It wasn't often that souls appeared like this. When a living being passed, their soul, mimicking their early forms, was carried here looking nearly alive in the Underworld.

But not mine. It was pure fire, wild and unbothered as I held it. But at the same time, I knew there were differences. Because Atlas was correct. In only a few years within her, my soul was forever changed. She hadn't just carried my soul but improved upon it. And improved upon me.

Yet, I still knew what it meant. What I could do once my soul was complete once more. To put this soul back inside of me, it would mean that I would be restored. My future as the heir of Hell settled as surely as if I had built the world myself.

I stilled. "I am afraid."

"You're afraid? Of your own soul?"

"You were not here when I was at full power. Before Anna, before Kadmiel was even born."

"I don't understand."

I cocked my head, moving my fingers around the soul. "The firstborn son of Hell, bred and raised to do my father's bidding."

Atlas leaned forward, elbows to knees. "I don't see the problem."

"You wouldn't, would you? Not until you have seen what I can become once I am whole. What I will become again."

"We need every bit of power now, my lord. To fight the Drude and drive the Corrupted back into the river. If you can't handle that, what happens at the courthouse? What happens to all those souls at the bridge waiting on judgment? I know the risk is high, but so is the reward."

I knew this, she had said as much, daring me to love her. Knowing that I may never be able to return.

"Not yet. My brothers will make do." I glanced out the window, the sunlight flickering through the trees. "My father is more than capable of assisting as soon as he chooses to get off his throne." My fist closed on the flickering soul, and it vanished, waiting under my skin, not a part of me in the way it craved to be. Simply stored there held far from my heart, which ached more than I'd been prepared for.

"I'll miss you," she had said. The memory was burned across my mind like an arrow. Just as sharp, there was tightening on my wrist, and I turned it over, staring down at my skin as a dark tattoo began to appear, as if an invisible hand was writing.

Justine, in looping, feminine handwriting appeared on my wrist. Before the line on the final letter was even complete, I was racing to the door. Blinking, I tested my magic, knowing the full moon was soon, when it would be easier to get into the living world. I could count on that to help me. I refused to arrive where she needed me and not be ready to do whatever it was necessary.

Atlas stumbled down the stairs after me. "My lord, where are you going?"

"Justine needs me."

"You are needed here, Nephesh. No one can do what you can. Besides, you are not bound to her any longer. How will you find her?"

I decided not to mention the tattoo, instead focusing on tugging my boots on as I throw open the front door of the courthouse. "I'm the Prince of Hell. I can manage."

"And if you can't?"

I snarled, fangs flashing. "Then I do it the hard way."

Atlas's brows rose. "And that is…?"

I glared at him. "Unless you are my father, I don't owe you any kind of explanation. Now, get the fuck out of my way. My mate needs me."

Atlas's wide eyes were the last thing I saw as I let my magic bloom up around me. Flames of gold and red consumed me whole, taking me to the place I was needed most in any world.

I kept my fist pressed to my chest, over the aching place where my own fear pierced my heart. Monsters did not deserve soul mates, but I would protect her to my last breath. No matter what the consequences were.

My magic rippled, the soul I had tucked away growing ever more hot under my flesh.

But then, there it was.

A call. Not unlike the one I had once felt while making deals for my father. I studied it, straightening as I did.

It was her.

Something was wrong. My fangs filled with deadly venom and it took only a minute to send a message to my brothers through the mental connection we always shared. I didn't owe them an explanation, but I offered them my forgiveness, and I wanted to grant it before we braved whatever evil had come for my mate.

Justine had once said all we needed was a chance. I hoped to Hades that we got two.

***

Nephesh

Something was very wrong. I stood outside of the apartment building that had somehow become home with Justine.

Something felt tainted. Like metal on my tongue, I tasted it everywhere I looked. Fear. *Her* fear. It invaded every one of my cells, driving my heart rate up and my power to my skin. Ignoring the burn as the flames of my power leaped about under my skin, I moved around to the side of the building, where the fire exit was. Where our window was. I cast a shielding spell, strong enough to keep whatever had scared Justine from seeing me, and then released my wings from their place.

Snapping them to wakefulness, I shoved air down, sending myself skyrocketing into the air. I landed on the ledge of the window a moment later, and the lock opened with a wave of my hand. I knew it was empty the moment I slipped inside, the metallic traces of her fear less here than outside. I moved around, noting the discarded bag on the floor and the unlocked front door.

Something slithered through my veins, beneath my power, making it throb and pulse ever higher. Fury, it called to me, to the monster deep inside that lurked and thrashed in the cage I barely managed to withhold. The desire to unleash him, the me deep inside, nearly undid me. I reared back, my head falling back as I sucked in not just Justine's scent, but the fear that coated it too.

I wanted it all. I needed it all to do what I needed to do. For the first time in over fifty years, I let down the walls of my cage ever so slightly. My eyes burned then sharpened into the nearly telescopic vision that my innermost form carried. The monster there snarled as I held the chain that still restrained the secret part of myself.

There was more of me showing now though, and with it something I could've only ever dreamed of seeing. The softest glow, the glowing power and gift of a soul mate. My connection to her, it threaded into my system, wrapping around my monster, my soul, and even my heart. Not as a leash but as an anchor.

My head snapped forward. My eyes glowed with my magic, casting a dim red glow across the room as I stalked to the window. My glamor covered me without a second thought, and I stepped out onto the ledge. My wings opened, the white

feathers twitching and spreading as the breeze moved around
me.

"I'm coming, little thief," I whispered into the darkness, and
then I sprang forwards, my wings catching me and thrusting me
towards the nearly whole moon. My power throbbed through
me, the monster inside screaming for vengeance upon anyone
who had touched our mate.

For the first time in my existence, I agreed with it
wholeheartedly. And as I turned my face to the wind once more,
I let the tether she would forever hold on my soul pull me
towards her.

19

Justine

"I want to know everything that you know."

My brows rose, and I shifted in the chair.

He quickly amended his statement. "About the Fallen."

The ties that kept me bound to the uncomfortable wooden seating bit into my skin with every breath. I flinched before I could stop myself then leveled another glare in his direction. Gregory was back, dressed in a posh tailored black suit, his tablet on his lap as he stared at me. He looked more like he was sitting in some corporate office then in this dingy, dark warehouse, talking to a prisoner.

"You know more than I do," I answered simply, bracing myself for this reaction.

Lefty smiled, which immediately made me nervous, "Oh, come now. I'm sure that's not true. We might know more about the Fallen and the Morningstar, but you know about the man behind the demon. Or at least the human portion that is left of him. Let's start there."

I remained silent, and he made a big show of sitting back in his chair, crossing one leg over the other. He was wearing chili pepper socks. What an odd choice.

I yanked myself back into the present. He was talking again.

"You must've had some kind of shock when he told you who he was."

"What? No, it wasn't a huge shock. He saved me, and we struck a deal."

"You just accepted that he was a demon, and…what, went back to life?"

"Yeah, I guess we did."

Gregory tapped something into his tablet, the glowing light illuminating more of his features as he did.

My tongue burned as I tried pulling my hands in closer once again. The ropes bit into my skin, and I muffled the noise by ducking my chin. "He's a good person, you know. Just leave him alone."

"Well, to start, he's not a person. And I don't think you really know that much about what he can do. Who he really is."

Gregory shifted, leaning forward, his words coming out in an excited rush. "Did you fuck him? I know they are capable of reproduction, so there must be some kind of male aspect to him."

Instant nausea. I recoiled, ducking my chin to my chest so that I didn't have to look at him and reveal my truths. My heart ached as I did, images of our time together hurtling through my mind as I fought to keep my breathing even. "That's none of your business."

Gregory snorted. "He is a monster, a prince of Hell. The child of a witch and the Fallen. He's not a morally gray villain in some love story, Justine. He is the bad guy, nothing outside of that."

"If he's the bad guy and you're the good, why am I tied to a chair? Doesn't that kind of mess up the storyline?"

"You are here for your own protection. And ours."

I looked away, my chin jutting out.

"I'm sure he's told you what happens if he retains his entire soul once more?"

I focused on the memories, those stolen moments. At my apartment, cooking scrambled eggs, holding hands on the street, his protecting me at the diner. I filled my mind with Nephesh, my chest aching more and more as I fought the urge to shout at Gregory. But then, he wanted that. He wanted me frazzled and upset.

"I'm going to assume that's a no." He sighed. "We have reason to believe that Lucifer's firstborn is the most dangerous of all of them, not on purpose of course, but once they had him, well, he was the perfect weapon, wasn't he? Together they tore the whole living world apart."

"Nephesh isn't like that."

"Maybe not now, but as soon as he has his soul back, he could be. Would you really trust a demon with that kind of choice? Imagine the opportunities he would have to wreak destruction on all of this world."

"He wouldn't do that," I hissed again, my frustration making my eyes water.

Gregory focused on the screen again, his fingers rapidly tapping. "We aren't leaving the fate of the human race in one moody demon's hands."

"And what do you get out of all of this? Do you sleep better at night?"

The man smiled. "I sleep like a baby at night, demon whore. And I do this because the Fallen have ruled the Underworld for too long. We will claim it for ourselves, return the balance to the side for good. You can see it every day. I know you did." Gregory shook the tablet in my direction, "After all, you're not exactly a shining example of a good citizen either. But that's not all your fault. Darkness from their world is seeping into ours. We have a plan to change all of that. But until then, we need to disarm their greatest weapon. And that, my dear, is the soul you are carrying around with you."

"So you're all insane. Got it."

"Say what you will. I can see it even now. You believe your monster will come save you. But I have to tell you, he will only come for your soul. He doesn't care about anything else. They never do."

"Sounds personal there, Gregory."

He stood, moving over to stand above me, and his thumb pressed against my lips and dragged them across in a painful pull. I jerked back, my body recoiling at the way his black pupils seemed to bleed into the colorful irises.

"What are you?" My voice shook with surprise. He had looked so human, acted so human. He'd been a dick, but now, knowing he was something other, it made my blood run cold.

"We are the trusted soldiers of the real master." His hand moved down, cupping the nape of my neck. "And after we free your soul, giving it to my master will be simple. And then you will join us."

"You can't just take someone's soul."

"We can if we have the witch who originally cast the spell."

I blinked rapidly, confused by his words. As if disappointed in what he'd told me, Gregory paused. His hand moved around to the front of my neck, and my breath wheezed out of my throat as his fingers continued to hold there, pressing and holding in a slow threat of what he was capable of doing. After a moment, his head tilted back, his top lip lifting in a mark of disgust.

"I cannot kill you yet, monster fucker, but when I can, I will take great relish in it."

He pressed harder, and a dark spots appeared in my vision as I fought to keep my mind clear, to focus on slowing my panicked breaths.

He thought I still had my soul.

But I didn't.

I could only buy more time. Maybe I would be able to escape. Maybe I would be able to…

Gregory's body was suddenly snatched away from me. My breath rushed back, making my still-bound limbs tingle as oxygen swept into my blood once again. In the shadows, there was movement, horrible sounds, the crunching of what could only be Gregory as soft cries suddenly stopped. Slowly the shadows slipped, gathered it seemed as a pair of massive white wings spread. The feathers quivered as I stared, awestruck at the deadly efficiency of Nephesh's movements.

I followed the crest of the wings to the straightening body; Nephesh looked back at me through a pair of glowing ruby red eyes. Below those eyes, an inhuman set of fangs dripped with red, blood staining his neck and now bare chest. The jeans were cut off at the ankle, his feet turned to claws that curled against the cement as he lowered himself into the shadows ever so slightly more. My eyes snapped up, lighting up on the pair of sharp black horns that slipped through the silken white strands that I'd buried my fingers in.

"Nephesh," I said, knowing him in an instant. It could only be right, as this was his true form. Or at least his truer form. Nephesh lifted his head again, and I could hear the thick inhale.

"Did you kill him?"

His rattling growl echoed around the room. "He touched you."

"I'll take that as a yes," I croaked, a strange emotion filling my throat at his words. "I'm glad."

The horns cocked sideways.

I struggled against my ties. "Are you alright?"

His laughter was the same, deep and rumbling as the dove white wings shifted. "You are asking me if I am alright? When you are the one who has been held captive?"

Nephesh stepped towards me. The fluorescent lights above cast a shadow over him, illuminating more of his skin, the scars that littered his flesh. The ones I had pressed my hands to, my lips to. My belly squeezed as he moved around me, and then I felt the ropes around me go slack.

"How did you get here?"

I didn't need him to answer me as he moved back around, his hands on my shoulders as the long, black claws began to rub small circles in the muscle that'd been held in that unnatural pose.

His voice was more human when he spoke again. "Can you stand? We have to keep moving."

"Where are we going?"

"Somewhere you will be safe," he answered simply, pulling on my arms and assisting me to my feet.

I weaved a little, my heart rushing with weakness as my muscles shook in resistance to my request to hurry.

"I'm sorry," I whispered as my face pressed against this bare chest. His hands smoothed over my back, both holding me up and holding me against him as I tried to regain my footing. "I'm so weak."

"You, little thief," Nephesh said, "are never weak. Only those who saw it necessary to bind you in such a way are to blame for this moment."

I glanced up into his face, seeing the man there, even with the fangs, the dark swirl of his horns.

"And I will make them pay."

I didn't say anything. I just pressed myself against him, my body seeming to grow stronger by the moment, as every stroke of his hands on my back made my mind clearer, my muscles stronger. He was doing something to me, the familiar feel of his magic seeping into my skin as we stood together.

I jutted my chin as I stepped back enough I could look him in the face once again. "What did you do?"

"A small healing, just enough to keep you on your feet."

"You didn't ask this time."

"I'm sorry. Would you like me to take it back?" His brows rose, and again I was stuck by the simple beauty of him in all forms.

"No," I said coolly. "I just want to get out of here."

"My pleasure." Nephesh held out his arm.

I blinked at him. "What are you doing?"

"We are not walking out of here. We will be flying."

"How did you get in here?"

Nephesh slowly pointed one black claw, and I stared up. The ceiling, which was already shrouded in darkness beyond the dangling fluorescent lights, seemed to shift and move, shadows moving to the side and revealing a very large, very demon-shaped hole right there in the top.

"Oh."

"Oh, is right." Nephesh moved closer then held out his arm again. I cleared my throat, trying to appear unconcerned as I moved towards him, letting him sweep his arm around my hips as he picked me up. "Are you ready?"

I attempted to look at ease, even as my stomach twisted with nerves. "As I'll ever be."

Nephesh grinned, showing of a mouthful of sharp teeth. "Such a disbeliever you are, little thief."

He bent his knees, spreading his snowy white wings wide as the tension in the room racketed up. I could feel something deep in my chest swirl to life, and I moved my hands to press against the place I always felt him.

Trust. Belief. Understanding. Something deep inside glowed with pleasure.

"I believe you," I whispered just before his wings flexed, driving the air around us down as his legs unfurled, those claws spreading wide against the cement as we were thrust into the air. One breath, two, and then we passed the lights, the shadows slipping over us as I tilted back my head and stared up at the sweet sky and clouds that awaited us. Nephesh's hands shifted, lifting me higher, and I moved with him, a smile creeping across my face as we reached the hole in the ceiling,

But then there was a shriek, something darker and more terrifying than any other sound I'd heard in my life. For a moment, I looked down at the people who had filtered into my little jail below us.

Then back up at Nephesh as I tried to locate the sound of that cry.

Only to feel my entire being shudder with horror. We were falling.

It was Nephesh who was making that sound, the wounded cry trailing off as we began to plummet back into the building. I didn't have time to do anything. Nephesh's arms banded tighter around me as we fell, and I realized now that he was falling with purpose, guiding me until I was at his front.

I didn't understand why until his body slammed into the cement floor. And my body, cushioned from the damage by his own, landed squarely on top of him.

Nephesh moved under me, his groans making my heart ache, but at least I knew he was alive. I pushed up, trying to decide how I could protect us from what was coming next as I staggered to my feet.

There were more of them than before now, lines of them surrounding us, all dressed in black. But now, they parted as one moved through, an olive-skinned male who smiled at me in welcome.

Dread curled in my gut. I knew that look. It was one of victory.

"What did you do to him?"

"I did nothing," he said quietly.

"Let us go. Please. We didn't do anything wrong."

The man was shaking his head. "You know I cannot, sweet girl. Unlike my friends here…" He gestured to the blood that had seeped across the floor. The remnants of Gregory, around which several other soldiers were poised to strike. "I can see that you've already given Lucifer's son your soul. You are no longer the innocent party here, Justine."

My breathing accelerated.

"But now we know something new." The man's head cocked, and his entire eye went black. "The Fallen can love, and isn't it a beautiful thing." He gestured at Nephesh's broken form at my feet. A flicker of laughter filled the room.

"How interesting, though, that he has not accepted the missing half though. He could just as easily have absorbed that soul and gone back to rule his part of the Underworld. But hey…" He moved his head, his dark eyes staring over at me. "Isn't love grand? Perhaps his soul was damaged? Not that it's your fault. Born to be the carrier of a demon's soul? That's a lot of darkness to carry around." He tutted. "More likely is that you had a positive effect on his soul. No wonder he cannot accept it."

Nephesh hadn't accepted my soul. Rejection threatened to flood me, but I pushed back, grasping for the reality of this thing in front of me. He was trying to hurt me, and he'd do it any way possible.

Nephesh moved, struggling to sit up, and I moved to him, careful to not step on his beautiful, bloodied wings.

"Justine," he grunted, propping himself up as best he could. "I can explain."

I shushed him, pressing my hand over his mouth as the man encroached ever farther on his. "It doesn't matter. Survive, and then we can talk."

"So many ideas and options. That's why we need you both here. The information you will give us can completely change the tide of this war." His eyes gleamed. "Master will be so thrilled."

Nephesh's eyes met mine again, and I saw the sorrow there. I wished so badly I could kiss him, I wished I could tell him that we were going to be fine. Because we had to be. Because he came back for me.

But not now. The lump in my throat grew.

Survive first.

I twisted, standing to face down the man in front of me. "You seem to know an awful lot about us. Are you the Drude, then?"

He chuckled. "Sweet girl, I am but one of his many devoted servants."

I blinked. "And your name is?"

"You can call me Niko."

"Great, nice to meet you. Now let us go."

Niko ignored me, craning around dramatically to stare at Nephesh on the floor. "Such a mighty prince to let a little human speak for him."

I stepped in front of Nephesh once more. "I speak for both of us. And if you were a real man, you wouldn't be so scared to talk to a woman."

"A real man?"

Recognition flickered in those pitch-black eyes. "You're his mate, aren't you?"

I froze, blood running cold at the joy in his words.

Niko moved away, a hand at his jaw. "Yes, it makes so much sense. You were useless to him, yet he came back for you. We weren't sure she was telling us the truth, but now it's so clear."

He turned, pacing the floor. "I need to speak with her."

Her?

"You." He gestured at two guards. "Put them back inside the cell. The master will be here soon, and he will want to see Lucifer's heir and his little mate for himself."

The guards hesitated, and I could tell why. Nephesh was on his knees now, his eyes a soft red glow.

But Niko swatted the air again. "She's spelled this entire place. He can't take another hit like that."

The guards marched forward now, and I didn't stop myself from leaning over Nephesh and putting my hands through his arm and hauling his immense weight off the floor. Holding my head high, I walked us back into my cell.

When the doors slammed shut, it was all I could to not sink to my knees. Imprisoned again. Nephesh reached for me, his claws skating across my skin.

"I need you to tell me everything."

"I know."

"Let's start with the most basic one."

Nephesh's breath caught. He knew what I would ask.

"Am I your soul mate?"

20

Nephesh

For a moment, the pain that radiated through my system went quiet, and my gaze found hers in the dark cell.

"I had not expected you to find out this way."

Her delicate voice whispered, "So I am? Your soul mate?"

"Yes, I believe so." I couldn't hide the bitterness from my voice.

"And you didn't tell me…why?"

"What life could I offer you?" I snarled back, my wings lifting weakly as my temper rose. "What life would you have with a creature like me? This…" I gestured down at myself. "This is merely a glimpse of what I can do, who I am."

That silenced her, but only for a moment. "Why wouldn't you give me the opportunity to decide for myself?"

"You are telling me that you would be okay, being with something like me? Forever. Tied to a dying land and the devil himself."

"You didn't let me decide for myself. I tried to tell you when you left that I…"

Her little fists balled up on my chest, as if she wanted to hit me but had lost direction.

My heart thundered. "That you what?"

"That I didn't want you to go."

"I had to."

"I know. That's why I let you go, you idiot. I just don't know… I just wish."

"I should've told you everything. I know that now." I trailed my fingers up her neck, making her tilt her head back up to me, where I could stare down into her eyes. They were glassy, filled with unshed tears. "I'm sorry, Justine. I was afraid. I wanted to experience you on my terms, and that was wrong. But I know I couldn't damn you to my life. Look at what's happened to you, even now."

Justine's eyes overfilled now, the tears slipping down her cheeks as her soft pink lips quivered. "I wasn't done with you though."

"And now?"

Her laugh was watery, but she didn't move away as I caressed her throat once again. "Looks like we're stuck together for a little longer."

I wanted to kiss her, but I didn't dare. Not with the heady, coppery taste of that insolent human guard still trapped in my mouth. So instead I pressed my forehead to hers. "I won't make this mistake again."

"Which one?" she responded with more than a little bite.

It made me smile, and I tucked her in closer.

"All of them. But mostly underestimating your strength," I responded finally.

"Good," Justine said, sniffing a little, "Now, I want to hear the rest. Moving down the list to what happened to us. We were almost out."

I pulled back, staring over my shoulder at the guards who were still posted up across the room. Without their master there, I could smell their fear even now. Good, I thought. That would keep them farther away while I talked to Justine.

No doubt we were being recorded and watched, but it didn't matter now. Still I hesitated. Justine had already been exposed to so much in such a short amount of time. But I had to believe that when she said she was ready to know, she knew herself.

"I believe that it was witchcraft."

"Uh, what did you say?"

"My mother was a witch, and before her kind was nearly wiped out, they were a powerful force in the world."

"She was good, then? Or bad?"

My lips quivered. "She was a good witch, her magic taken from the environment and her own genetically passed abilities. But it wasn't long until the kings of man thought that they should be able to do the same magic and miracles. She was imprisoned, taken hostage after her family was murdered. Under his control, she did horrible things. Until my father found her, and together they escaped that life. They set up the Underworld and began to rule it together."

"So they have a witch here, doing spells on you?"

"Witches are one of few who can truly injure us. Otherwise we are quite resilient. Having a spell here means that they must've found a living witch to work for them."

"Can you stop them? Or will your family come?"

"My mother is gone, taken again hundreds of years ago. While my brother claims that she visits him though the dream realm, I have no such evidence that she knows anything about what's going on. She would have no reason to save us."

"Harsh."

"She was Lucifer's bride. Compassion was limited."

"Good point." Justine suddenly plastered a hand against her chest. "Oh my God, is your father going to show up?"

I snorted. "No. If he sends anything, it will be one of his cronies." I walked to the bars, craning my head up and looking up at the sky once again. "But I'm assuming if they thought ahead enough to have a witch here, then they knew enough to hide us from my father's influence or my brother's eyes."

"Just fucking great," Justine said, flopping down on the bed.

"We will find a way," I told her, scrambling to think about what we could do to continue to make our way to freedom. But at the moment, I didn't know enough to push the edges. I needed to know more about what was going to happen to us if I were to make a bid for freedom. Justine was my priority, no matter what happened between us. Since the witchcraft in this space affected only me, I would focus on getting her to safety first. Then I could do what needed to be done.

We will worry about the whole mate bond thing after I got her out of this hole. And after I destroyed these pests who thought they could hurt what was mine.

Well, fuck. What I wanted to be mine, anyway.

My father needed to know what was happening here. We knew that the corrupted souls had made it to the living world. We had known that the Drude was gaining power, but I secretly believed that we had all hoped that with Arafel's victory at his post and the unification of his soul, we might have made a step forward.

Apparently we were misled.

This group, however strange it was, was too organized and too calm. They did not fear us as we needed them to. A smile slowly spread across my face.

"Guard," I shouted. "Give me a towel."

"Shut the fuck up, monster," he responded as I expected. Suppressing the desire to roll my eyes, I tried again.

"Fine. I guess I will greet your boss with bits of your friend in my teeth, then."

He flinched, and I knew I'd won. Smiling smugly, I waited against the bars until he stepped back in, holding two towels. I took them, the bars pressing against my chest as my claws closed over them. One was damp, the other soft and dry. I curled my arm, bringing them inside with me.

"Do you need to wash up?" I asked Justine as she crawled up on the bed.

She eyed me warily. "Not as much as you do." She paused for a moment. "Do you really have Gregor in your teeth?"

"No, I don't eat garbage."

"Cute," she said, nose wrinkled.

I began to wash my skin, getting as much of the blood off my chin and chest as I did. She watched me, her breathing slowly picking up speed. My wings ruffled and my cock twitched.

"Do you like me like this?"

"I—uh—don't dislike it. You still look like Nephesh to me, just a bit more…"

"Monstrous."

"Maybe, but not in a bad way. In a badass, powerful way."

I sprawled across the cell, turning my back to the guards. Justien's eyes widened, and she leaned back a little when my palms pressed into the thin mattress, caging her in place. "You don't know much about demons and their mates, little thief, but know that the imminent threat on your life is the only thing keeping me from claiming you again." I ran my nose up the side of her face. "And again." My lips brushed her ear. "And again."

Her breath shuddered out between us. "Nephesh…"

I smiled there, at the perfect smell of her and the pulsing warmth that pounded in my chest. We were so close to our mate. My monster crowed with pleasure as I took the moment to breathe her in, soak her into my flesh.

"You don't know yet."

"But I will?" she answered, her heart rate a scattered mess.

I pulled back, meeting her gaze head on. "First survive. Then I will show you everything there is to know about being a mate to the Prince of Hell."

"I'm holding you to it."

***

That night we feasted on what could only be known as slop, and while I could go many weeks without consuming sustenance, I ate it anyway. I wanted to share even this with her. The lack of her rejection of my revelation was a constant in my mind, the reality that I might not have to live without her pressure in my chest.

I needed to get us out of here. But this time, I wouldn't run. And as we sat on the floor, the strange globby pasta between us, sharing a fork, I told her about my brothers.

"So the River Styx is a real river, with water and rocks and fish."

"Kharon would not appreciate his magical river road being dumbed down to that extent…" I considered it then grinned at her. "But yes, unless you count its inhabitants, then it's quite ordinary."

"I cannot believe that. So much that people got wrong."

"Stories are always evolving. It is the reason we are able to exist as we can. The only souls who truly know us are the ones who have already passed."

"And you judge them?"

"I do."

"Isn't that horrible?"

I shifted a little. "Among other abilities, my magic is uniquely designed for it. I can see a soul's measure, the scales of good or evil that every person is made up of."

"Wow."

"Wow is right. Most of the souls can be sorted by the river itself, where I have fixated my magic into a dam. The good and righteous move to Elysium. The evil are moved to Tartarus."

"They don't have a chance to plead their case?"

"They do, but only those who are very close to equal. I see that more and more lately. I cannot tell whether humans are becoming less concerned about the darkness of their souls or whether my magic had faded so much that I was not able to sort them in the traditional way. The process is taking too long, the souls held up and bottlenecked, unable to continue to the power that keeps the Underworld strong and secure. Perhaps once I..." I trailed off, realizing where I'd led the conversation to.

Justine lowered her head, her eyes focused on the food. "But you don't want my soul—or your soul that I carried..."

"Justine, look at me." I waited for a long breath until her gaze rose to me. "Taking your soul, feeling it in my hand, was one of the most beautiful moments of my entire life. But to take it back, to let myself have all of that power..." My body grew tense. "I was something else before I was the Judge. Something that was taken from the history books."

"Why?"

"Because no one survived long enough to record it."

Her sharp intake only cemented the awareness that I could never show this monster to her. But as usual, my soul mate surprised me. "Show me."

"I cannot."

"Because you haven't taken the soul into you." She reached across and brushed my forearm. "Nothing you show me will scare me away, Nephesh. You promised you would not underestimate me again."

"I'm not underestimating you. I'm acknowledging the fact that to show you my true, basest form, it will forever change how you look at me." I brushed my claws over her head, the strawberry-toned strands tangling there. "And I don't think I can do that. So you see, it is I who is afraid."

I released her head, letting my fingers trail down the side of her face until I cupped her cheek. "Do you understand?"

"No, but I'll keep trying." She smiled at me. "Tell me more."

I rocked forward. "I will. I always will. But first…" I leaned in, pressing my lips against hers. The soft heat of her mouth ushered a shudder of pure need through my body. I had been kissing her for only a few moments when one of the guards began shouting. We ignored them, long enough for one of them to hurl one of their own empty food trays at the bars. It clanked loudly, and I pulled away, snarling at them as Justine let out a soft, breathy laugh against my neck before pressing her face there.

"Now, do you want to know about the smug bastard who runs the Underworld guards or the angsty one who guards the real evil of this world?"

Justine snorted. "The angsty one. Duh."

I rolled my eyes and dived into the tale of Elon and all the chaos and destruction he had raised as a young demon, far before the war with the Drude began. Justine laughed when she should've, nodded solemnly when I got to the part about the Drude's first attack on the Underworld, and when I talked about my brother withdrawing to Tartarus to heal, she slapped her hands against the floor.

"And you just let him? Obviously he needed help."

I shrugged. "I was locked up at that point.'

Her hands trailed down my forearms, to my wrists where she delicately traces the scars there. "And you got these? I just don't understand. Why would they do that to you?"

"That is too long of a story for tonight, little thief."

"You can't just dangle that little tidbit out there and then not respond!"

"I can and I will. It is late, and you're tired."

"I am not."

"You are, and I cannot count on your help to fight your way out of here unless you are rested. I gestured at the half wall behind which I knew was a toilet and rudimentary shower. "Do whatever you need to do. I'll watch them."

Justine looked at me for a long time and then stood. But before she moved past me, she trailed her fingers across my shoulders. "I don't know what happened to you yet, but when I do, I'll hunt down every single person who hurt you."

"I know you will." *That is why I know you were meant to be mine.*

But even as I stared at the guards, daring them to look at my mate as she tried to get cleaned up for rest, I wondered just how any of this could move forward.

I could have forever with her.

But she would be trapped with me.

One of us was getting the better end of the deal. The guilt nearly suffocated me, and I dwelled in that place, the depression welling up inside of me, until I felt Justine's fingers on my neck once more.

I moved habitually, rinsing my mouth and taking care of my meager bodily needs before crawling into the thin and narrow bed beside her. Tall as she might be for a human woman, I dwarfed her. Finally she rolled over, showing me her back as I curled closer.

"Always the big spoon," she murmured, her hips moving against my palms as I pressed her closer.

"I don't know what that means, but I do not take it as a compliment."

She snorted but did not press back. I smiled into the dark. Behind me, across the room, I could hear the soldiers speaking. It was a change of shift, and they were supposed to check in with their master first.

I growled slightly. I didn't like the idea of seeing "Corrupted" again. His name—I had forgotten his name. But I knew enough. Those dark eyes… He was a corrupted soul, one the Drude's forces had freed from the Underworld and implanted into a human form here. He would be hard to kill, impossible maybe, as long as the Drude's power fed him. And if I were to kill the human he was using as a prop, there was no guarantee that the soul inside would indeed die and pass back to the River.

I could hear their footsteps as they passed through the doors. They were bold now, made bolder by the witch's power that surrounded this place. Even now, it pressed against me, smothering the power that bubbled ever higher in Justine's presence.

"Are they gone?"

"Only for a short time, but yes."

Justine's voice hitched. "Nephesh?"

"Yes?"

"Show me."

"Show you…?" I didn't understand. I pushed up on an elbow so I could stare down into her eyes. My shoulder blades ached where my wings were glamoured away, but I ignored it.

"What would it be like…to be a demon's mate?"

I dropped my head, forehead pressing against her shoulder. "Justine… Not here."

"Then when? You are so fixated on the perfect moment, the perfect situation, the perfect conversation. There is no perfect here. Not in my world. And I won't keep waiting for it to not enjoy the life we are gifted now."

I stared at her. She had wanted me once, before she knew what being with me might mean. And now, she was staring back at me, truth shining in her eyes as pressed her hips back against me once again.

"Nephesh," she said, her body flush to mine.

I groaned, my hand on her hip tightening hard enough that she squirmed. I released her, trying to put more distance between us on this narrow bed. But in my head, I knew that I only moved a little bit. Inside, I was desperate to know. To know her more, to feel her against me, under me once again.

I leaned over her, pressing my forehead to the side of her head as she settled against the mattress. "You cannot understand what you would be doing."

"We were already together, Nephesh. I don't understand…"

"Because as I am now, my demon self grows ever stronger. And demons don't share."

"I don't want to be shared."

I shook my head ever so slightly, my white hair mixing with her bright-red locks. "I mean that it would be forever."

"And you don't want that…" Her voice was oddly detached.

I growled. "I'm more than ready to give up anyone else, everyone else, but I don't think you understand what it would mean to bind yourself to me."

She sat up now, twisting to glare down at me. "You keep saying I don't understand, but have you ever thought that maybe I do know exactly what I'm doing? That it's you who is scared? You are the one who backs away. You are the one who hesitates. I have been here, Nephesh, the whole time. From the deal to this moment, to the way he questioned me. I have been all in."

She plopped down again, delicate shoulder blades jolting out of her back as she curled in on herself, body far from mine now.

I considered her.

I tried to shield her from the truth, that much was true. But did I inadvertently insult her by not giving her credit where credit was due? After all, she was correct. I feared not having a mate like Arafel. If I were honest with myself for more than a second, then I would be the first to say how badly I wanted what he and Lucia had.

An understanding.

A partner.

A mate.

A chance at a real life, even as my world fought in its final battle.

But again, it didn't matter, if I let her get hurt, like I had failed Anna. My throat worked, and I leaned over her. "You're right."

That worked. She opened her eyes, rolling them to stare at me as she remained still on the bed.

"I am scared. I have failed someone important before, and my entire world suffered for it. But losing you, I wouldn't care about the world anymore. I wouldn't care about anything."

She nodded once but didn't speak.

"You understand, then, all these mistakes I'm making, they are because I know I will not survive this, knowing I let you, my mate, give up her life for the one I can offer you."

"And what life is that?"

I swallowed. "A life of war. A life of chaos. A life of damaged souls and corrupted villains."

Silence fell around us, and for a moment I thought she would back down. Then she was moving against the bedding so that she faced me. In the dark, I could see her features perfectly, but I wasn't sure if she could see any of mine. Then she reached out, careful fingers slipping up my cheekbones then down again, stroking along my jaw and tracing the lines of my frown. Her fingers paused over my lips, and I felt her press harder there.

"You listen to me, Judge. I've spent my entire life fighting. Fighting to survive. Fighting to simply get by in the world. If you say that we will be fighting, then it would be the first time in my life that I would get to fight for someone…" Her voice cut out for a moment. "Someone I love."

My heart raced. "That is the bond speaking…"

"You already hold my soul, you idiot. What I feel now is all me. Is it a little crazy? Yes. Maybe. But I have never played by life's rules."

"Justine."

"So instead of keeping me away, pushing me back… Let me in." Her fingers trailed down my throat to my collarbone, where she pushed at me lightly. "Let me love you."

The protests I'd kept. The ones I'd built up at night while I worried over her. While I punished that man in the diner who thought he could touch what was mine.

Because she was mine. Every stubborn, strong, powerful inch of her was made for me. The fates had designed her, and now, danger be damned, I was unwilling to keep pushing her away. I was a weak soul.

I let my shoulders go pliant under her hand, rolling onto my back as she raised a slender leg and shifted so that she sat over me. Her weight settled over my lower belly, and my hands rose to cup her hips as she got comfortable over me. Fuck, she felt good.

"Little thief," I warned as she wiggled around on me. Her eyes crinkled down at me, and then she looked pointedly over at the guards.

"You said you couldn't do any magic, but could you…"

My lips curled and my wings slipped free of my glamor. Healed and brilliant white against the doom of the cell, I curled them up and around us, creating a perfect illusion of privacy from those outside of the feathers.

21

Justine

I couldn't stop myself. I reached out, running a finger across one of the delicate white feathers, the silken vanes tickling my skin.

I looked down at the man, no - the male - under me. I could never mistake him for a human man. Not with those eyes. Not with that all-consuming pull that I felt every time we were close together. "You are beautiful, you know."

He snorted, but I could see by the way his eyes flickered red that there was some part of him that liked my compliment. My pulse fluttered as he moved his hands up under my shirt so that they were splayed against my belly.

"More," he said softly.

Eager, I moved my hands to the hemline of the shirt they'd given me after my first night there. It was a plain black thing, thick cotton. I began to pull it up then hesitated, waiting.

"More," I echoed, hoping I wasn't pushing him past his rather precarious boundaries. But even now, I knew that both of us needed to see everything. To lay everything bare.

Nephesh breathed out, a soft growl in the sound as he rolled his head slightly against the flattened pillow. Black, nearly iridescent black horns curled up from his temples, parting the white strands on his hair as he did. When his eyes met mine, his mouth dropped open as he dragged a dark-red tongue across a pair of fangs that had slipped free of his gums.

My breath caught.

"Now you," he said as his fingertips, which felt sharper than I remembered, skimmed over my ribs.

I smiled at him. "You know I am good for my word." Then I grasped my hemline, yanking the scratchy shirt from my body, and after a short hesitation, Nephesh lowered the feathers enough that I could throw it out of our space.

Under my body, Nephesh's hips rose, grinding against mine as his clawed hands kept me still over his belly. Against my ass, I could feel the pressure of his length growing against me.

"Nothing underneath?"

I blushed at that. "Everything was sweaty and gross. I just…" My words trailed off when Nephesh pushed up onto an elbow, his mouth pressing against my collarbone in a silky hot kiss. Heat throbbed through me, just as it did every time he was close to me, but this was more insistent, a nearly painful ache that settled somewhere at the core of me, under my ribs, where I had once unknowingly hidden away his soul.

My hands stroked into his hair, finding the long strands were tangled, but I didn't care. I wanted them more tangled. I wanted them messier. I wanted to hold him there, wrapped in him knowing that I wasn't about to leave, because we were bound together now. There was no going back.

Not for me.

Not anymore. And I knew he felt the same way. I'd heard it in the way he'd described his fear of losing me. Felt it in the way his hands had held me so desperately, even before I knew everything.

"Neph—"

His mouth settled over my breast, and I forgot what I wanted to say as his tongue, longer, so much longer than a normal man, swept out to curl around the pucker of my nipple. "Oh fuck, Nephesh."

His eyes opened, a glowing ruby red, and for a moment, I felt a sliver of fear. But instead of turning me off, it only added to the heat of the moment. He was a predator, a creature from a world I had just barely been able to understand. These people feared him, were prepared to wage war against him.

And here we were, with him worshiping me.

My head fell back and I rolled my hips forward and back, finding the thick length of him there and gasping as the head of him rubbed against me.

Nephesh's head fell back, his claws leaving tiny pinpricks of blood against my ribs as he groaned. "Little thief, you are pushing too far."

"I intend to push exactly as far as I need to to keep you for myself."

Nephesh moaned. "Such a demanding mate." The last word was soft, barely uttered in this tiny hidden space, so surrounded by our danger. But I felt it, the bond in my chest thrumming to life in my chest.

My heart lifted, nearly choking me. "Someone has to keep you on your toes."

Nephesh's red gaze met mine again, the corners softening ever so slightly. Saying what he was still too afraid to say now. But that was okay, because I could be brave enough for both of us.

Rising farther onto my knees, my hands on the center of his muscular belly, I pushed back so I could hover over the rigid length of him. Catching his eyes flashing red, I lowered myself again, letting my weight rock forward then back, slowly teasing him as I found a comfortable rhythm against him.

"Justine…" Nephesh's voice was strained as he cupped my breasts, dangerous-looking thumbs brushing over my nipples as his knees bent and he urged me into a slower rhythm. "The feeling of you… I'm afraid I will lose control."

My belly fluttered, heat tangling at the delicious pressure of his length pressing against the needy crest of my body. A moan slipped from me. I closed my mouth, wetted my lips, and tried again.

"You don't scare me."

Nephesh's smile showed off those fangs. "Maybe that's been the problem all along."

"Ha-ha," I said flatly. "Now he's funny." I pried myself free of his hands then shifted back farther. "Here, funny, let me see more of you." My fingers spread across the rippling abdominal muscles that leapt under my touch.

Blinking, I poked one. "Come to think of it, where is your shirt?"

A silvery brow rose. "I scarcely had time to procure these pants. Are you complaining?"

"Not at all. Just a casual observation, you know, because I'm still figuring out this whole *demon moving through the worlds* thing, and I—"

Nephesh cut me off by pulling me up, his mouth on mine in an instant. I smiled into the kiss, letting his thick tongue slowly into my mouth as he rolled us carefully.

I didn't want to talk anymore. I pressed close to him, not necessarily concerned about the guards seeing any of my skin in the dark cell, but more about the idea that there was anything existing outside of us. I wanted it to be only us, at least in my mind. Especially if this was all I got.

I pouted when he settled me on my back, his head immediately tucking into my neck, where he dragged in air, scenting me as his hands leisurely stroked my body.

"What are you doing?"

"You smell like…like home. It's addicting, and when I touch you like this…" His hand brushed lower, past my waistband to stroke over the top of my leggings carefully. "It is even richer."

I blushed, which was surprising at this point in my life. But I found that I liked it. "I like the way you smell too. You smell like firewood and smoke, but not in a bad way. It smells really good."

Nephesh tilted his head tilted to stare at me for a long moment, and then he was moving again, tracing his mouth down my neck, the slick slide of his tongue tasting me, teasing me with every touch and flick. When he reached my collarbone, that long tongue danced out, tracing the lines of my bone before breathing out over it, his breath sweet and hot against the freshly dampened lines.

"There are those amongst the demons who crave human flesh. It's written in our old books before my father shaped our home. But now I feel that there may have been a slight misunderstanding." His eyes were red, narrowed, as he shifted lower, his wings flickering as they moved to accommodate us once more.

"What do you mean?"

"Because I will never know another thing that I would crave more than the taste of you."

I started to giggle at his realization, but then the sound that slipped out of me was something else altogether. A plea, perhaps, as his hips rocked against me, just a teasing glance of what was to come.

"Nephesh…"

He was right, though. My craving for him ran deeper and thicker than the blood in my veins. I could feel it now, calling out to him.

I boldly drew my hands down his sides, feeling the way the muscles of his back flexed under my touch. His mouth brushed over my lips.

"I have put you in danger. I have threatened your life, simply by existing in yours. But I cannot find it in myself to regret a single second of being with you, little thief."

My heart was racing.

"And while I believe that most monsters do not deserve any kind of happiness, I find myself hoping for exactly what you always said you wanted."

"What's that?"

"A chance." He sat up, settling back on his ankles as he maneuvered me up the bed. A quick glance told me that there were shadows stretching across the bars, darkening the space all around us as if encompassed in a dark, heavy fog. "A chance to know someone completely."

"A chance to trust someone," I responded, nodding as Nephesh slipped my leggings down over my legs. My breathing panted out as my panties followed, the sharp, cool lines of Nephesh's claws trailing up my thighs.

"A chance to love someone," he said, his voice a dark rumble as the shadows billowed around us.

Sitting up, I found the line of his waistband and guided it over his hips, my mind consumed with the beautiful lines of his body, both of muscle but also the scars that he'd earned trying to do what was right.

What he had believed in.

His breathing hitched as he kneeled back on the mattress, and my fingers traced down past his belly button, lower, until the hot, hard length of him brushed my palm. I was only there a moment before he was on me again, pushing me back into the bed. Feeling the sweet weight of him over me dragged a soft moan from my lips.

Because we fit in every way.

His hard lines against my soft. My grasping fingers to his teasing touch. And when he found my lips again, I couldn't stop my hips from bucking into the long, strong fingers that teased me there. But still, he didn't give me what I wanted.

I huffed out a breath, but a smile stayed on my mouth as I responded back to him. "And be loved in return."

His massive body shuddered as I spoke, and then he was kissing me again, his tongue slick and hot against mine, teasing and playing before retreating. My fingers sank into his hair as his mouth trailed lower, across my collarbone once more, before stopping to hover over my breasts, where my nipples were peaked and begging for attention.

His hot breath warmed my flesh. I squirmed under him, hoping that he would put me out of this misery. "Nephesh."

The smug bastard smiled, and my heart fluttered. "A chance is all we need."

"And all we have."

Nephesh's eyes flashed that bright, unnatural red just before his mouth brushed over my nipple. The heat of his mouth coupled with the gentle rasp of one fang made my whole body jump. He tempered the initial attack on my senses with a slow swirl of his tongue over my sensitive skin.

"Oh God, yes, right there, Nephesh." Clasping my knees to his sides, I writhed against him. His free hand slipped up high to press against my throat.

"As much as I want to hear you call out my name, mate, you're going to bring out a side of me you aren't ready for if you keep talking like that."

I ignored the presence of his hand on my throat and moved my hand to grip his wrist. "I'm not afraid of you, Nephesh."

22

Nephesh

Fire raced down my spine, making my breath come short in my lungs as her words sank into my skin. She wasn't afraid of me, and I could feel the truth of her words as she spoke them. The bond in my chest pulsed wildly with every breath she took.

I knew then that I loved her. More than the simplicity of the words. I loved her, and I was loved in return. She didn't fear the dark parts of me like I thought she might. Instead she embraced me, even called for me as I finally allowed myself to recognize what had been staring at me this entire time.

She was mine, and I was hers. I let the tension in my magic free, allowing more of my glamor to fall. I had control over the most monstrous of my forms, but for once, he seemed content to sit back and enjoy. And so my silver hair grew longer, swirling across my shoulders, parted by the reappearance of swirling horns, which had disappeared once I'd been struck down during our escape.

And I knew when I looked at her next, sparks of fire raced through the shadows all around us, illuminating the way she looked up at me. Not in fear, but with a kind of desperate need that matched the one pounding in my body.

My hand was still pressing on her neck, and I released her now, loving the way she immediately followed my hand so that she could run a finger down one horn.

"You're beautiful."

I growled as her fingers made contact, the caress driving home just how badly I needed her. I ducked away, resuming my attempt to taste every part of her. After dropping a kiss on the breast I'd neglected before, I pressed my lips against her ribs then lower to the soft curve of her belly that flexed and quivered under my tongue.

I only looked at her a moment, seeing the way she nodded eagerly, before I guided her legs over my shoulders. Her skin was like satin but didn't compare at all to the slick, heat of her core. Letting my long, demonic tongue drop out, I traced the lines of her first, the taste of her making my cock ache as I ground myself against the edge of the mattress.

She was perfect, and I was instantly an addict for not only the way she tasted, but the way her body moved against my mouth. In all of my life, I'd never felt the rush of pleasure and satisfaction that this moment brought as I drove my mate into pleasure.

Pulling back, I pressed a kiss to her thigh, my fingers pressing into that heat, thrusting deep and watching the beautiful arch of her body as I slowly fucked my fingers into her. I knew I wanted to be inside her, and I would, but this time, I wanted to just watch her pleasure. I wanted to savor it, to soak up every moment without being clouded by my own needs.

With one hand on her hip, I guided her frantic movements, two fingers stretching her, feeling the flutter of her muscles as her soft cries grew louder.

"Nephesh, I'm…"

My mouth watered as I pressed another kiss to her thigh, sucking hard against the flesh there. "I've been dreaming of this moment since the first time you opened that saucy little mouth, thief. Been dreaming of the sounds you would make. The way you would call my name. So don't be shy, mate. Let me hear you."

"It feels so good, Nephesh. Please don't stop."

A smile curled my lips. "I am at your command. Tell me everything."

She tossed her head against the pillows.

Fed by her proximity and our connection, I could feel my power growing, circling us, protecting us from the outside. "Tell me."

Her pale cheeks were flushed in a way that I found intoxicating. It was the same pink tone that darkened her thighs where I'd kissed and licked just a moment ago. Her back was arched. My fingers were waiting, poised to bring her every pleasure when she finally spoke.

"Harder, please. I need harder."

My cock jerked, but I ignored it again, following the uttered, desperate order from my mate, thrusting my fingers into her harder, the slick sound of her wetness against my palms enough to make a sweat break out across my body.

She was perfect. And when I finally sank my cock into her, in this realm, in the living world, I knew there would be no going back.

Justine keened, her hips rolling against my hand as she drove herself higher and higher up the peak of her pleasure. I was transfixed, unable to look away, at least until her eyes met mine in a wild, uncertain moment.

I pressed my lips against the inside of her knee. "Come for me, Justine." With permission offered and then given, she collapsed back onto her back, her body shaking as her pussy clenched and spasmed around my fingers. I rode out her orgasm, dragging it out as best I could until the minute jerks of her muscles under my body were nearly indiscernible.

I withdrew my fingers, making sure she was watching when I let my tongue dart out, tasting her once again.

"Fucking delicious."

Justine let out a soft, ragged noise, somewhere between a laugh and a moan. And then she was moving again, her hands settling on my shoulders, where she pulled me up and over her. My hips slipped naturally between her thighs, the heavy length of my cock cradled against her pussy.

"Are you ready to be mine?" I asked her, one hand moving down to cup her leg and bring her flush against me once again.

One red brow rose cockily. "Are you ready to be mine?"

I growled, "I have always been yours." I arched my hips, letting the thick head of my cock slip inside her. The movement robbed me of thought for a long moment. When I regained use of my body, I withdrew then thrust forward hard, seating myself deep inside her. With a strangled cry, Justine threw her arms up and around my shoulders, wrapping her legs around me in an embrace.

"And I—" she whimpered as I withdrew again, my eyes rapt on her pleasure-filled face "—have always been yours."

I thrust hard, setting up a rhythm that left no time for talking, no time for explanation. We rode the hard line of pleasure, hands exploring, lips brushing. As our bodies fed from each other, my power swirled through my core, even as my heart nearly burst at the joy of being reunited with not just my soul, but my mate as well.

I knew she was getting close. I could feel the quiver in her limbs, hear the sweet noises she whispered into my ear. Drawing my wings closer, I enclosed us in the haze of white feathers and dark shadows.

"Others will love you. Others will want you. But only I will ever have the pleasure of hearing your pleasure, little thief. Now, let me hear you."

"I love you," she whispered. And then her nails were digging into my shoulders, her body arching and coiling against mine as she cried out in pleasure.

I couldn't hold back now, my hips dropping low and hard, seating myself as far into her slick heat as I could get. I knew my demon blood was taking over now, and while I knew that I could pull back a little, to avoid the lock that would keep us together longer, I couldn't make myself do it.

And when my orgasm overwhelmed me, nothing in Heaven, Hell, or Earth would keep me driving into her where my body released every spasm of my pleasure deep inside her. Instantly my cock locked into her, the thickening of my organ and the suction from the head meant to keep us not only locked together and increase the odds of creating another generation of demons, but to bring our mates even more pleasure.

Justine felt it, her gasp in my ear enough to send another wave of pleasure down my spine and straight to my cock.

Breathing hard, I dropped to my elbows so I could press a kiss against her relaxed, smiling lips.

"I love you too."

***

Justine

"Why did your mother split your souls?"

"She believed it was the best way to save us. We demons are generally pretty tough, but when she and my father realized they were expecting me, there was a lot of panic. A hybrid that could be easily as dangerous as either parent... They were worried. My father claims more demon blood runs in my veins than any of my brothers, but I'm not so sure anymore. When

Arafel thought we were threatening his mate, he went full demon on us."

"Arafel is the one who looks like a gargoyle, right?"

Nephesh's chest shook under me. We were curled up together, redressed after a rather long time…uh…tied together post-sex. Not that I had minded, but it had been a bit of a surprise. "He's a little gray, you're right about that. He could wear his human glamor if he chose, but since he interacts so heavily with those who are already dreaming, they are not as phased by his appearance as maybe the living might be around someone like, hmm, Elon."

"What happened to him?"

"Tartarus was the first place that was attacked by the Drude. They sought to free the most dangerous souls in the Underworld and expected my brother to be easily swayed by an offer of freedom."

"Why would he be swayed?"

"Being born to guard the worst of the worst, little thief, it changes you. But instead of joining the Drude, Elon and his warriors pushed the Drude back into Tartarus once more, where they attempted to cage him. Arafel and Khan said that he was like a possessed man. But just before victory, one of the souls that resides in Tartarus reared up, pulled Elon into the flames. The fire that burns there is unique and unusual. They resist our typical ways of healing. I haven't seen the wounds on his body, but I am sure they are a constant pain to Elon. And worst of all, the Drude was able to escape and went into hiding.

"How horrible for him," I breathed, swallowing back my emotion. "Do you think that he'll ever heal?"

Nephesh shifted uncomfortably. "My mother was a great healer. That's why the human kings loved her. They wanted to keep her as a pet, locked up in their castles, waiting to keep them alive during their bloody campaigns. It changed her, being held by them. Where once she'd been soft and giving, she became harder and more cynical. That's how she met my father. It's a long story, but he came to her with a deal. He offered freedom, a chance to expand her power. She gave him her heart. Not that it matters now. She's been gone since the Drude's first attack on the Underworld."

"I'm sorry, Nephesh. Is that when she took your soul?"

"No, that was a long time before, hundreds of years maybe. Before the slayings at Salem."

Alarm bells were ringing in my head. "The witch-hunting Salem? Is that what you mean? Why do you know about those?"

Nephesh was quiet for a moment. "My mother was the first witch."

"Okay, that makes sense, I guess, but..." I craned my head to look back at him. "Did they target your mother at Salem or something?"

"They did, or at least that's what my father believes. This was before we knew that they were a united effort. But there were humans already too interested in gaining the power of the Underworld. They spread fear and lies about the witches, driving the witch trials into action in a pitiful attempt to find the witch that Lucifer loved. They knew that Lucifer had taken a wife and he was ruling this world with her at his side. You should know, every soul that comes through feeds my father's power. They needed leverage over him since they craved his power. They knew if they could find the mate of Lucifer, his one chosen bride, then they might have a chance of defeating him and taking his throne."

"But why the soul idea?"

"Splitting them? It was a clever idea at first. By splitting our souls, it makes us even harder to kill. Of course, I believe that it might have been my father who had the idea, not that my mother would ever tell us so."

I could hear the smile in his voice.

"She was a proud one but so kind at her core. I see her in Kharon the most, that inherited kindness, even in the chaos."

Nephesh's fingers trailed up and down my spine. "Father was obsessed with her and desperate to find a way to protect her from our growing list of enemies. While being bound to him and being a full-blooded witch meant her life would be extended far past any normal woman, she was still more in danger than he was."

"You think he gave her half of his soul. To make her stronger?"

Nephew was nodding, his fingers still tracing those dizzying patterns across my lower back. "I believe so. We know it works, since Arafel's human mate continues to get more powerful. It explains Father's misery too, at least according to my brothers. I haven't been around like I should've these past few years, but I was…detained."

"Oh, a bad boy? I did not realize I was dating a felon."

Nephesh doesn't rise to my barb. In fact, he almost sank into the mattress a little more, which was shocking considering just how flat and incorporate it truly was. "Judge?"

"When my Anna was killed, I was inconsolable. Not just because of her death, but because I had failed my family too. If I had been able to do what I needed to, I could've taken the soul from her, saved the Underworld, and maybe she wouldn't have been in that place at that time."

My heart ached for him. Not only the grief of losing a dear friend, but the weight of his family as well. "Nephesh, there's no way that you could've known that."

"You're right, because I was too weak to see. I was too attached to do what I needed to in all those weeks before."

"You didn't even know how to take it from her. You can't keep blaming yourself."

"I can and I will, little thief. If not to honor her life, but also as a reminder of what can happen when I do not perform my duties."

I poked at his side. "No one says duties anymore, not without laughing."

Nephesh sighed, head falling dramatically back against the pillows. "This world is a mess."

I couldn't stop the smile that pulled at my lips. "Will you take me to see yours?"

"That's not really an option right now, darling, as we are currently jailed."

"Thank you, Nephesh," I said sarcastically. "Like I couldn't tell."

"Just making sure. As soon as we find our way out of here, I'll take you. I don't believe I'll have a choice not to. I can't possibly trust you to stay in the living world and not get into trouble. Especially now that you know nearly all of it."

"As much as you know, at least."

Nephesh's clawed fingers slipped into my hair, smoothing it away from my face. "I will not leave you in the dark any longer."

"Good," I responded, my hand going to press over his heart.

"So you must understand that whatever happens today, whoever comes walking through those doors, they are not here to help us. They want to overturn my family, to run the Underworld as they see fit. The souls there are merely a bargaining chip to gaining power. They will not protect them. They will not offer them the afterlife they are owed." His eyes flashed past me. "Isn't that right, Drude?"

23

Justine

I scrambled to roll over so quickly that I nearly toppled off onto the ground. But nothing could have prepared me for what waited for me in the middle of the room. Smoky gray shadows were cast off a tall, robed figure. They curled and moved, making my stomach riot as a strange kind of motion sickness swept over me. It was as if the elements themselves were rejecting the creature that stood in their midst. The foreboding sense of unnatural power filled the air, and I could feel Nephesh's heat and strength behind me as the bond in my chest brightened and tugged harder.

I blinked slowly, trying to re-center myself. Nephesh's hand slipped around, holding my hip as together we stared at the creature who was single-handedly trying to destroy Nephesh's world. And now my own.

"Enjoying pleasures of the flesh, demon?" asked the Drude, its voice an unnatural whisper that echoed across the chamber like the crack of a whip. I flinched as my heart burned, as if rejecting the words themselves. "Who could blame you?

Humanity can be so" —he stepped towards our cell—
"distracting, can't they?"

"Release us, Drude, and then we can discuss whatever you'd like."

"You know I cannot do that. The heir to Hell, in my very own midst." The Drude tutted, but the sound was odd and clattering, and I wondered briefly if he even had a tongue amidst the blackness of his hooded face. "Too good of an opportunity to discuss the new rules for the new world."

"And what world is that?" I asked before I could stop myself and instantly regretted it when the Drude's hooded face tilted down. I could feel that he was tilting his head, watching me closely as he took a single, awkward step forward.

My stomach curled at the strangeness of his movements. Or was the Drude even a he? Not that it mattered. I was terrified.

"My world, witchling."

Nephesh snarled, and I tensed as the Drude stepped forward. "Just like your mate here, I can see what all these humans cannot." The hood tilted a little bit, revealing gray, pale flesh. "And besides, I can smell your witch blood from here."

Witch? I was a witch? What did that even mean?

Nephesh's voice broke through my harried thoughts. "Leave her out of this."

"You know I cannot." The Drude's shadows leaped about him, tangling and touching the darkness of the room's corners. The black-dressed tactical soldiers behind them quivered as his shadows moved around them. "How poetic. Your mother will be thrilled when I tell her. Her first son, destined to love a foul-tempered witch for the rest of his days."

"I'm not...foul tempered," I finished lamely.

The Drude observed us in silence for a long moment, and I could feel Nephesh's growing tension and power. And while I knew he was strong, something inside me wanted to scream for him to stand down, to wait, because there was something bigger at play here. I could feel it. Showing his power, even without the soul he still kept separate, was showing the Drude what Nephesh's capabilities were.

I didn't think we were ready for that. Not when we were already trapped here, our backs to the wall. I reached a hand back, finding his fists clenched. "You kidnapped me for a reason. You brought us both here for a reason. If it was just to lure Nephesh in, then you would've been more prepared."

The Drude moved across the floor silently, his shadows leaping and jumping against the gray cement floor. "This one is quite bright, don't you think?"

The crew of people behind him remained silent, watching.

Nephesh moved to stand at my side then, his hand uncurling only long enough to intertwine our fingers before curling up again. "If you have a problem with my family, then you can address me. The girl is no asset to you. Let her go."

I jerked my head up. He couldn't mean that. We were in this together.

"Oh, but she is of great importance to me, my lord."

I could almost sense the smile in Drude's words, even though I couldn't see them.

"We could do great things together, Justine."

Fear clogged my throat as his attention turned back to me. I couldn't see his face or any of his features, but I knew he was looking at me. I knew he was observing me as if I were a lowly bug on the ground before him. I hated it. My legs shook as I spoke back. "I don't want to do anything for you."

"You say that now, but no matter what this one has told you, my offerings are quite sweet. And other than that sad business with your brother's pretty face—" he tilted his hooded face to address Nephesh for a moment before looking back to me "— I've always held up my end of the bargain."

Nephesh smiled, all fang, no emotion, and I wobbled in place. Here it came. The offer he must've been considering the whole time I was here. Because he was looking for an in. And I was as good as worthless with Nephesh holding my soul. Yet here they waited. They still needed something from me. I tightened my hold on Nephesh's hand, just for a moment.

"What if I told you that the reason you always felt like you were in chaos is because chaos runs in your veins? An usually large amount, especially for the time and space. Perhaps that is why you were this one's mate. I imagine it takes one hell of a person to hold the Prince of Hell's soul for as long as you did."

I kept my face carefully blank, hoping he couldn't see the rest of me as I shook. "Maybe I'm just stubborn."

"For that I have no doubt. But I'm telling you that you have the capacity to work your own magic, not just his." The Drude paced for a moment. One hand, strangely white with heavy blue veins racing through it swirled through the air. "It's true. If you let him mark you, claim you, mate you in more than the physical sense, then you share some of his abilities."

Nephesh's fingers twitched, but he didn't release me. He had told me this. None of it was a surprise. "I know that."

"Bear with me. Because I believe that you are a unique case. Out of all the other soul bounds we have located, I believe you carry your own magic. It's what made you so difficult to locate. It's why you managed to evade us all those years. Even after we took your parents."

My heart nearly stopped. "My parents?"

That sickly colored hand disappeared back under the huge, domed sleeves once again. I took a step toward him, even as I heard Nephesh's sharp intake of breath. "You took my parents?"

"We had to get to them before the demons did. To try to find a way to convince you not to join their side."

I lunged forward, screaming as my body nearly slammed into the bars. "You're a monster! I would never join you! You ruined my life." My words faded as my throat closed and tears choked me. Nephesh's hands were on my upper arms, holding me on my feet as I stared at the Drude through blurred eyes.

"How could you kill them? They were good people."

Silence fell, and somehow deep in my chest, our bond sharpened to a nearly painful point. I looked back at Nephesh, his features still blurred by my tears, but I was surprised as he slowly began to shake his head.

I slowly turned back to the Drude. The entire room seemed to be waiting on his orders. The tension only ratcheted up until finally he held out his hand, a bloom of fire inside it.

"Bring them in."

Nephesh's grip on my upper arms tightened even further, and I stared in shock as two people were marched into the room. Like the others, they wore simple, dark cotton shirts, but without the utility belts and weaponry that so many of the others did.

Something thick and hard settled in my throat as they stumbled forward. The female figure was petite, slender arms pulled back at an odd angle as they attempted to catch themselves from face-planting at the foot of Drude's swirling robes. One of the soldiers yanked back on her arms, drawing a soft cry from her lips even as the male's head swiveled around, obviously distraught at the sound of the woman.

"No," I whispered, but I knew only Nephesh felt it. Fear vibrated through my heart, straight through my veins and into our bond. It was met only with a quiet solidarity. I looked back, wondering why the bond was suddenly so quiet. Especially when a few minutes ago, I thought maybe we'd made a real point. But Nephesh's face was as blank and emotionless as the other end of the bond strung tight beaten us.

I swallowed, letting my desperate eyes turn back. The Drude was talking again, that eerie voice filling the entire space.

"Your parents didn't realize that when they met, married, and conceived you, they were merging two of the most significant and ancient witch bloodlines. The talent had been lost for generations, but the blood remains. And with that the chance of something else."

I waited, horror making me still. The Drude glanced back, and with a jerk of one wrist, the soldiers gripping the new hostages reached up and ripped the hoods off their faces.

My knees nearly buckled as I saw two of the faces that I had once loved more than anything else. The ones that I had missed every part of each day since the day they'd thrown me into a back closet of our house. I'd heard the struggle. I'd known what those sounds meant, the muffled cries, and then finally the drag marks as they were hauled out of the house.

I had waited two weeks for them to come home, going to school like I thought I was supposed to be, hoping that if I was good enough, then one day they might come back. After two weeks, I attempted to report them to the police as missing. But they'd ignored me.

That was when I realized that I was alone in this life and I could count on no one else. But now, they were there, standing in front of me. They had aged in the ten years since I'd seen them, but I imagine I wasn't exactly the awkward, gangly fifteen-year-old I had been either.

"How is this possible?"

The two figures were looking at me, then the Drude, then me again. My father's soft brown eyes were filled with tears, his mouth opening repeatedly as if he couldn't decide if he was allowed to call out for me or not. My mother, with her brilliant red hair so close in color to mine that I was startled at first. Mom's eyebrows were lowered, suspicious as she glanced around all of us then settled back on me.

She had always been the realist in my family. My father and I had been the dreamers. And I could almost see her, even now, analyzing the entire situation.

My lips felt frozen. "They've been with you this whole time?"

"With me? No. But yes, we knew that there would come a time that we would be able to find you and then they would come in handy."

I swallowed. All this time.

"You will find, witchling, that I am most adept at playing the long game."

"I hate you."

"Most do."

"Let them go," Nephesh's voice boomed behind me, making me jump as I realized that I was pressed up against the bars again. But even as the iron pressed against my face, I was unable to look away. If I did, they might disappear. Or I might wake up. Ten years. I'd been waiting for this moment for ten years.

"Momma…" I couldn't stop the soft word that slipped free from my mouth as I stared at her, wishing desperately for her eyes to come back to me. She was staring at the Drude though, her expression unreadable. But my father stepped forward at the sound of my voice.

"Are you really here? Justine?"

"I'm here," I said, my heart lurching in my chest at the familiar voice. "I'm right here."

Dad took another huge step forward, and the Drude's hand snapped out, something cracked in the air, and suddenly my father was quite still. Only his eyes moved as he stared at me. I couldn't even see his rapidly rising chest anymore. He was utterly still.

My already ragged temper was blistering. "What did you do to him?"

"Just holding him, Justine, while we talk about the terms of their release."

I opened my mouth, shock rippling through me once again. This level of cruelty was so much. Nephesh was suddenly there, his hand low on my back.

"You've made your point, Drude. Let these people go. You have me."

The Drude was silent. "Maybe that was one of the ideas, but now I want you all. It isn't common anymore to have not just one witch, but two in your council. Aren't I the lucky one?"

Two? Whatever. I didn't care anymore. I wanted to know how to get them free. My entire focus was consumed with the idea that my parents were alive. They were alive and here. Right in front of me.

"What do you want?"

Nephesh's hand stilled on my back, and suddenly the bond between us was glowing bright as he attempted to talk to me.

But I didn't want to hear it. It had been too long, and this had been too much. Everything I ever wanted, a second chance at a family… My family was staring right at me. I could almost feel the grip of my mother's hug. Or the sweetness of my father's contagious laugh.

"Join me."

Panic raced down my spine, but I was talking before I could stop. "Join you? What does that mean?"

"Join us, to fight against the tyranny of the Underworld. I have someone here who can teach you. The things we can do together… Justine, they outnumber the stars."

"And my parents, they will…" My gaze kept darting over to my parents, half-convinced that they couldn't be real.

"They will be free to do whatever they want to do."

"You promise. They can do whatever they want and no harm will come to them?"

"Justine, don't." Nephesh's voice was a desperate whisper at my back.

The Drude's voice was low, reassuring almost. "I promise."

I closed my eyes, shutting down the bond in my chest after sending one last final, desperate plea to the demon behind me.

"I'm sorry…" It felt like the entire room held its breath for a half second, and then the final word in my statement left my lips. "Nephesh."

The Drude's hand rose, snapping lightly, and before I knew it, I was on the other side of the bars, falling into my father's arms as they closed around me. A second later, another impact at my back. My mother. We were together. Tears were streaming down my face, and while joy filled my chest as I let them run hands over my hair and face, maybe, just maybe, those tears were not only for what I had just gained.

But also for what I had just lost.

24

My mate was now completely enveloped in the arms of others. First of the human who appeared to be her father, then the second one, a human woman. Her mother. That distinctive strawberry-blonde hair was a giveaway of their shared genetics.

As for the rest of them, the soldiers remained still, their weapons still at the ready. They were waiting for me to react. I didn't, of course. But then, I wasn't sure what to react to.

She was gone. She had joined him, my family's mortal enemy. And I couldn't blame her. She was experiencing exactly the same situation I was. She was trading her soul to save her family. I was searching for mine to save my own.

The fates were an evil, manipulative bunch. If I was a betting male, I would put money on them cackling to themselves at this turn of events. In the week that I had known Justine, she made one thing abundantly clear: She had always been searching for her family. For her home.

He had taken them from her. And now he had given them back.

I narrowed my eyes, my magic a living thing in my body, curling and thrashing against my hold on it. The monster in the cage, begging me to set it free. To absorb her soul, to let my true self out so that I could destroy them all.

They had played the one card that I couldn't compete with. I nearly smiled. I should've known better. I should've known the Drude would have another plan. Because as much as those souls may have been her mother and father, there was something wrong here. Maybe Justine didn't see it. But she would.

The Drude was too comfortable in my world to not at least be part demon. Which meant that promise they'd just shared was far more dangerous than it first appeared. Whether Justine knew that or not was a different question altogether.

But that wasn't what was important now. I needed to get out of this cage, to warn my father that the Drude was recruiting witches. That he had my mate—not just physically, but access to her soul as well.

My magic coiled in my chest, desperate to be let out. But that would do no one any good if I exploded here, only to have a shield or another more powerful magic wielder come out to smite me while I was weak. There was so much more happening in the living world than we had anticipated. Even Arafel's dream spies couldn't get the intel that I had just stumbled upon. If I manage to get out of here.

They were moving now, a sea of black gear and hushed voices as Justine and her family were ushered from the room back through the door. I forced my eyes back to the Drude. The air between us cracked with his power, the suffocating feel of it making my monster all the more frustrated.

"What have you done?" I snarled at him.

There was something smug about the way he stood there, watching me, waiting.

"Reunited a lost girl and her family?"

Alarm bells were tolling in my mind. Everything in my body was suddenly focused on reaching out to Justine through our bond, to beg for her to come back. Because whatever was waiting for her out there, it was so much worse than our shared cage. At least I could protect her if she was here. But now she was gone, in the hands of someone else altogether.

"And now you're wondering what will become of you?" The Drude paced a small bit, pausing and turning his hood in my direction. "I suppose you're already guessed that your parents aren't waiting on the other side of that wall."

I growled, unwilling to let him hear a single bit more from me.

"What I really need from you is some information, Your Highness. I think we might even have a few things in common. I might even be able to help you with your little 'destroys everything in your path' problem."

I simply glared at him in anger.

"Come on, Nephesh. Is this about your younger brother? The problem in the fires? I didn't intend for any of that to happen. You have to know that."

The bars were sharp against my face as I pressed my body against the barrier. "Fuck you."

"Hmm, I had expected finer diction from the Prince of Hell."

"You expected wrong."

"How about this? If you give me information, I will free your little mate from our new agreement."

Ah, so that's what he wanted. Disgusting creature.

I spat on the ground, noting one of the soldiers on the edge flinched. "I refuse to make deals with the likes of you."

"Suit yourself. There are other ways to get what we need from you."

I growled again, stepping into the darkness of my cell, hoping the Drude might get the point. I would not be giving him anything else, either on purpose or accident.

"We will talk again soon, Nephesh."

I flinched at the sound of my name on his lips, that shuddering, eerie sound of his voice. Instead of answering, I chose to stay tall and still, my eyes fast on him until he slowly moved away. His soldiers broke away to follow him, leaving only two figures in the room. One was huge, nearly the size of my human form, muscles bulging beneath his shirts.

The other was a girl, delicate and tiny. She wore no weapons, carried no additional tools. But when she offered me a tremulous smile, I knew with absolute assurance that other than me and maybe the Drude, she was the most dangerous thing here.

She stepped forward, that smile slipping just a little when I spread my wings wide. Her eyes followed them, her mouth turning into a tiny "O" as she moved ever closer.

Her shoulders rose and fell as she took a deep breath in. "Demon."

"Hello, witch…" I gambled on my next question. "Which of my brothers do you belong to, then?"

***

Justine

We were in an office. It was so different from the cold metal and cement room that I'd been in since I arrived that I would've never believed it had been only a short walk across the warehouse. But now that I was here, the guards had left, leaving me sitting on a stiff but elegantly shaped sofa, my parents on the other. Staring straight at one another.

My throat convulsed each time I opened my mouth, as if the words I was searching for were rejecting even the thought of saying them out loud. Finally, my father, who had been staring at me wide-eyed, seemed to jump then glanced anxiously at my mother before offering me a small smile.

"Justine, it's so good to see you. You've grown up so much."

Small talk. That was what this was. It felt horrible, my entire body vibrating now as a variety of dread and unease filled me.

I'd acted impulsively. For these two people. And I didn't even know them anymore.

"I thought you were dead."

"I know, honey. We just…"

My mother reached over, patting my father's knee as he began to speak over her. He hushed immediately, looking at me, his face pale as he did so. My mother, Elaine, turned back to me, fixing those familiar eyes on me. "We are so sorry, baby. We wanted to be there so badly. But the Drude insisted. He told us everything, about how our bloodline was known to create powerful witches. That you could be one of the souls bound to the Fallen."

It was eerie hearing her use these words that only two weeks ago would've confused me completely. Yet they seemed like completely natural terminology to her. "So it was those people who took you from the house."

"It was Niko. The Drude was not in our area at the time."

I mentally filed that information away, nodding absently as I let my fingers trace the seam of the couches. They were expensive, I could tell. Strange as it was, the Drude was oddly well financed. His connections must be rather secure in order to pull all of this off.

"Justine?"

My mother was looking at me curiously, and I realized I had spaced out while she was talking. "I'm sorry." I made a show of wiping my eyes. "I'm just so confused."

Dad spoke up now. "We know, Justine, but it's going to be okay now."

"Now? What happens now?"

They looked at each then, her hand moved again, resting on his knee. For some reason, it drew my attention. I loved my mom, but she had never been one for affection. Quality time, or even little notes left around the house, yes, but there were no extra cuddles at bedtime. I had not minded. I had Dad for that.

But this was what she might even consider PDA. I guessed being stuck as a master villain's hostage for ten years could change you.

"Now we will figure out next steps together."

"Together? I'm so sorry. They took the house, and I'm not sure where we would even go back to at this point," I stuttered out, suddenly feeling my cheeks heat.

My dad's jaw ticked. "It's okay. Don't worry about that. We aren't leaving, Justine."'

"Wait…what?"

"You pledged yourself to the Drude, Justine. We have to stay here."

"But I did it to free you…"

"But not yourself… You will have to stay here. I think the master means to have you train with the witch he has raised here."

Horror crept into my veins, turning them to ice. "What are you talking about?"

Again, they shared that knowing soft look between them. "There's a young witch here, another cross of the old families. She's been trained by the Drude herself. She's quite powerful. They think that she can help you."

"Help me do what?"

"Build your powers, of course. What did you think he would want you for? He already has your prince," Mom responded coolly.

"Mom, why do you sound like that?"

"Like what?"

I tried to swallow down the rising lump in my throat, but it wouldn't budge. "Like you're on his side."

She sighed. "Justine, please, you can't label things like this. The Drude has been very good to us. He has unified our family. And at great loss to himself."

"He is the one who took you originally!" I slapped my palms against my legs, my temper rising.

But my mom shook her head. "He believed there was no other way to stop the Fallen from taking more and more of this world from the living."

She sounded like she was on his side because she *was* on his side. Suddenly I was horrified because I realized what I might have done. "Is that what you think? Or did he just tell you that?"

"Honey, we have been with the Drude and his Corrupted for many years now. How long have you known your Nephesh?"

"Long enough."

"He told you he was you mate, didn't he? They are obsessed with that in the Underworld apparently. His first one died, slaughtered right in front of him. No wonder he was so invested in making sure you would give him his soul back."

I huffed, fear clouding my eyes as I looked down at that couch again. Criss, cross, criss, cross, following the seams as they crawled along the base. "I can feel it, though." I hated how I looked at them, hoping they would understand. Hoping they would agree. Anything.

But instead, they smiled softly at me. Mockingly.

I stood, pushing from that stiff, strange sofa as I did. There was nowhere to go then, nowhere to walk.

"So am I still a prisoner?"

"No, you are a student. As we once were." She reached for me, patting my hand.

Slowly, I pulled my hand out of her reach, watching the way she barely reacted, her hand still hovering there midair. The wrongness of the reaction only added to the rapidly growing panic in my mind. "He's completely brainwashed you."

"Oh Justine, let's not talk about this anymore today. I'm sure you must be exhausted. Let's get you into a new room. Somewhere you can be really comfortable."

Was he nuts? I stared at my father until he broke my stare and pushed to a standing position as well.

"This is your room." He pointed at a door off to the side, a single wooden door with panels. From this side, there were no locks, no bolts, not even a guard. Suspiciously, I moved over to it and swung the door open. Inside looked a bit like a dorm room, with two twin beds, two dressers, and even a large mirror propped up against the wall. At the back of the space, there was another slender door, and with the light on there, I could see the sliver of a shower waiting there.

"Looks nice, huh?"

"Compared to a cell." I stepped into the room because there suddenly it was quite clear there was no other option. It may not look like a jail cell, but it was. My parents both stood there, looking at me stoically, not a trace of emotion on either face. I realized in an instant that our reunion was over. I raised my chin, determined to get answers. "I thought…"

Mom's voice cuts me off in an instant and it hurts even worse than I could've imagined. "We'll have plenty of time to catch up soon. But we have jobs to take care of too."

As if my heart could break any further. "You have jobs…" Realization dawned. I had been played. "You work for him."

My dad nodded, while Mom was already craning her head around to look at the door to the office space. "We won't be far. There's no lock here, but when I tell you that you can't go outside of these rooms, I mean it."

The witch. The spells. Nausea stirred in my gut. I was going to be sick, I'd been so wrong. So very wrong.

"What's going to happen to Nephesh?"

"He'll be set free as soon as the Drude gets the information he needs."

I gagged, my hand flying to brace myself against a doorjamb as I swallowed back the bile. "What are you going to do to him?"

"Me?" Dad blinked at me. "Nothing, baby." He reached out, taking the doorknob in his hand and beginning to pull it closed. "That's not my department. Now, watch your fingers."

Then the door was closed and I was running, racing to the bathroom, where my knees slammed into the tile as I hurled up the pitiful amount of food that had been deemed edible and free of the sleeping medicine by Nephesh. Oh God, just the thought of him made me strain more, my back aching as my stomach convulsed over and over again.

By the time I sat back, letting the floor catch me with an audible thump, he was all I could see. I kept my eyes closed, suddenly so afraid of what I'd done that I was hoping this was really a huge mistake. A nightmare I would wake up from any minute then stare up into those amber eyes and kiss the grumpy, smirking line of his lips.

Focusing as hard as I could, I searched for the bond in my chest, for the connection to him that I'd severed so severely when I wanted to save my parents. It had to be there, but even now, as I sat on this cold, hard floor with nothing but silence around me, I felt nothing. Not a sliver of emotion. Not a hint of his raw devotion.

I had shattered him.

I had shattered *us*.

Fuck.

Tears ran down my face, collecting under my cheek against the tile floor. I didn't bother to wipe them away. Instead I just lay there, letting my misery drive me deeper into the dark until I could no longer tell if I was awake or asleep, alive or dead.

Nephesh was right. There was more to fate's worth than death.

And I'd just surrendered to him to endure them all.

***

Nephesh

"You told your little bedmate that the flames that burned your brother were unique and damaging."

My head lolled back, and I stared at the newest in a line of human questioners. This one appeared more scared of me than the last. I smiled. "So I did."

"What does the fire have to do with his damage? Is it deadly for all demons or just you hybrids?"

I remained silent, watching, my mind so detached at this point that I didn't even acknowledge the dramatic number of injuries that I'd procured in the however many days I'd been here since Justine left.

I had endured far worse injuries in my life and never uttered a word. Everything they might have heard between Justine and me in this cell was common enough knowledge if you knew where to look. Even this question, about the fucking hellfire that bloomed at Tartarus, was noted in a variety of texts. But no, it only burned the damned. Typically we could walk through hellfire without any issues. The day that my brother was burned was a unique occasion, or so I'd been told. I'd been locked away in a cave after Anna died and had missed the battle itself.

But one of the darkest creatures there had tried to escape. The hellfire had done its job and claimed the soul. But as my father drove him back into his jail, Elon's face was not saved.

And our magic, its continued decline, meant that he was left with a body full of scars and a habit of covering himself with a variety of wraps. He looked, as Arafel's human mate had said, like some type of mummy.

We never discussed it, Elon and me. Since fire was a source of power for me, if I had been at my strongest, I may have been able to heal him.

But now, we did not have the power to waste. It took each of us every day to keep the Underworld functioning as it was. Briefly I wondered if our time together here had fostered any more magical impulses in my realm.

I hoped so, since Justine had made the choice to join the Drude. I was royally fucked. I flinched then, looking down and noticing that my jailer, or in this case, my torture expert, was digging a long blade down my forearm.

I watched, interested as my dark-red, nearly black blood seeped out, and then I looked back up at him. He was grinning maniacally, and I knew then and there that when this soul made it to the Underworld, I was going to take him to Elon myself. We would enjoy returning the favor he performed on me now. But in his case, he would feel that pain for a decade or two.

"Monster," he breathed, "I will break you."

You won't, I thought a bit sarcastically. Because there was no way he could do enough to me without the Drude or his tiny witch to do any real damage. They needed me alive, at least for now.

Besides, what did I care? I had lost my soul. Lost a friend. Gained a soul, and yet the betrayal of Justine's pledge to serve the Drude was more devastating than any blow these pitiful humans may deliver in their questioning. I would remain quiet and alive for my family's sake.

That was it.

My hopes, the sliver of a dream I might have let take root during those days with Justine, were gone. Hidden away deep inside and replaced with my usual disinterest in generally anything.

If I could only convince them to let me sleep, I could talk to Arafel and set things into motion. But the bastard, while not good at finding the painful points in my system, was surprisingly good at keeping me just enough awake that I could not talk to my dream-wielding brother yet.

Not that he could do much physically. Maybe he could send some of the Brotherhood up to save me. But even then, that was a risk that we often didn't take.

I closed my eyes even now, letting my mind wander back to my home, setting myself at the edge of the dam and letting the sounds of the river fill my mind and take me far away from here.

Maybe, if I tried hard enough, I could doze.

Just as soon as the thought crossed my mind, the male found a new weapon and proceeded to drive it deep in my thigh. I grimaced, more irritated than in pain.

They had already found the source of my real pain, and Justine stepping away from me had been the most painful thing that I'd had to experience as of yet. They couldn't do anything else to me at this point.

I was a shell of myself, and deep inside, my monster lurked, ready to be let out.

Soon, I whispered to him. *Soon.*

25

Justine

Someone was stroking my hair. Or maybe I was still out of it. I cracked my eyes open, my eyelashes painfully glued together from the nearly constant stream of tears that had been slipping out as I laid here.

I swatted at the hand. I was sure it was my mom, or whatever strange person she had become. But the hand immediately returned, nonplussed by my attempts to make them leave.

"Shh, it's okay," the voice said. It was soft, soothing, and definitely not my mother.

I jerked away, curling in on myself as I nearly rammed my head into the base of the sink in my attempt to see who was there.

"You," I said, and I knew my voice was accusatory. But I didn't care anymore. The only person in the building I could trust now was the one I had hurt the worst. My chest ached as I stared at the girl kneeling on the floor beside me.

She looked different.. Maybe it was this light. But I could see her now. She was around my age, maybe a year or two younger.

Her skin was flawless, a lovely olive tone, with straight, serious dark brows and curling dark hair that brushed her shoulders. Eyes that were so dark they were nearly black eyed me warily.

She was in another dress, this one green with soft blue patterns woven into it. Against my stiff tee and unflattering leggings, she looked like she'd just walked out of a fancy dinner somewhere. Glancing to the side, I saw a pair of pointed black heels at the edge of the door. Had she really been wearing those? I shook my head.

"I'm sorry," she said softly. "Did I scare you?"

I ignored her question, serving her one of my own instead. "What are you doing here?"

"I live here," she said easily, laying her hands across her lap and continuing to watch me with those huge, doe-like eyes.

I held up my hand, gesturing to the room just outside of the bathroom. "You live here, here?"

She nodded.

Fuck, I had a roommate.

"You've got to be kidding me," I grunted, pushing myself to my feet, ignoring the stiff way that my body reacted from lying on the floor. "There's no way."

"You took to the ideas of demons and monsters quite easily," she answered, watching me fumble my way out of the bathroom and into the bedroom once more. "I'm surprised finding you have a roommate is so unbelievable."

I stared at her, my jaw hanging. "It's been a long freaking day. Week. Whatever."

She nodded. "I get that. I'm Faye. Faye Morelli."

"I don't give a damn about your"

"And you're Justine."

I glared at her, crossing my arms across my chest. "Now you want to chat? You didn't do much when I was locked up in that cell."

"I know. I'm sorry about that. I did warn you about the smoothies though."

"You want to argue about smoothies right now, when they are torturing my…Nephesh." I began to place the room, my anxiety making my skin crawl as I turned every few feet. This room, this strange girl with her curious eyes… It was all making me so nervous I could barely handle it. If I didn't get out of here soon, I was going to explode.

"You love him very much, don't you?"

I froze, my bare feet cold against the flat gray carpet under them. A hand pressed against my shoulders, just the barest touch, but my head spun with it, just for a second. Then there it was. Completely stillness.

I turned to her, the noise in my head far more manageable.

Faye stepped back, her hands dropping to her side as she suddenly looked sheepish. "Just a calming spell. It's one of the first things I learned."

I licked my lips, feeling the rough texture of them. "You're the witch, then. The one he talked about."

"I am."

"Which means you're the one who stopped us from leaving? Pick a side, bitch. You can't say you tried to save me then ruin my chances to escape."

Her curls shook as she made her way into the room, moving to lean against the bed. "I know you don't get it yet, but I don't have that choice, and neither do you."

"Fuck you."

Faye shrugged, unphased by my rapidly returning anxiety. "All I'm saying is that we are stuck here together. The very least we can do is help each other out a little."

"Are you going to help me get Nephesh out of here?"

Faye sighed. "I can't do that."

"Then we are not going to be friends, or whatever you think this is."

"Pity. We are two of the only witch genetics strong enough to actually manifest our own magic. We could work together. We could learn together."

"To work for the bad guy? No thanks. I'll keep my shoddy low-paying job way before I'd ever work for someone like the Drude."

Faye scooted back onto her bed, crossing her legs at the ankles and picking up a book that had been at her bedside. "Your choice, Justine."

I stared at her, suddenly wishing she'd try harder to convert me or even talk to me. Because I needed to fight with someone more than I needed my next breath. Turning to the door, I leaned my forehead against the cool wood grain and focused deep inside. Where the bond with Nephesh usually hummed with a soft, low note of awareness, there was nothing but a cool brush, like a cloud covering the sun in the heat of summer.

More tears bloomed.

He was still here. But our bond was sealed off. And I knew that could mean only two things. Either I had severed our bond for real, or he had sealed it off from me on his end.

My mind could only imagine what might be happening to him. All because I'd wanted to save two people who didn't want to be saved.

I had doomed us all.

I shifted, letting my shoulder hit the door as I slowly sank to the floor. "When do they come in to feed you?"

"Feed me? I walk down to dinner like everyone else."

I swallowed, my throat thick. "Good. I'll come with you."

Faye nodded, her eyes not even leaving her book as I settled in against the wall and tried to think of any way possible that I could get us out of the mess that I made.

***

Later, when I was sitting in a small cafeteria staring around the room, it was the most surreal thing I'd ever been in. The soldiers from earlier were sprinkled around. Some were eating and obviously off shift, based on the loosened collars and relaxed posture, while others were still stationed about the room, looking war ready.

"This is really weird."

"It's not so bad. Just pick off the green bits. I never figured out what they were."

I groaned, turning to face my roommate. "It feels like the first day of school or something and no one likes me."

Faye shrugged. "I grew up here. It feels exactly as it has my entire life."

That quieted me down. I looked down at the pasta on my plate, poking at it with a fork as I considered the young woman sitting next to me. "You've really never known anything else?"

"Nope. My first teacher…. They thought that I was around four when I came here. But I was already in the foster care system when they found me. It was too easy for them to set up some memory blockers and move me into their group."

"Nephesh calls them the Corrupted. But you're not…"

"A borrowed body?" Faye said, her expression still bright and unbothered. My stomach roiled, and I put the pasta down. "Nope."

"How many here are like you? Or like…them?"

"They don't really distinguish it. It's hard for most to see." Faye shrugged, taking another bite. "I can see before I help move the souls sometimes," Her eyes were sharp on mine. "I could show you how to look at them, you know, and see which was which."

I put my fork down, knowing full well that whatever she taught me would be immediately weaponized for the Drude.

"No thanks, I'm good. I'll just consider all of you crazy and know that I'm covered."

Faye's lips tipped up in the smallest smile, and she shrugged once more, turning back to her meal. Unsure of what my time here might mean, I tucked back into my food, trying to stomach the grainy texture of the red sauce and the less-than-flavorful vegetable medley, which was really just too much cauliflower and not enough of anything else.

When Faye handed me her roll, watching me holding mine close to my chest as I looked around, she said, "They won't take it from you, you know."

"Sorry to be a little untrusting. They were guarding my jail cell just a few hours ago."

"That was before you were one of us," Faye said simply, rising and moving to dump the remnants of her food into a bin by the door.

I followed suit, feeling every pair of eyes on me as we passed through the small room. But miraculously, no one said anything to either of us.

"What happens now?" I asked as we began the short walk back to our room. "Do we just sit around?"

"We are supposed to be learning, training, which is what I'll be doing. But if you choose not to, then I suppose you'll just be stuck watching."

I grumbled, looking down at my feet as we moved. I'd borrowed some of Faye's shoes, and they felt awkward, as everything felt too small, too tight, even the rough fabric of my clothes. Especially walking beside Faye, who floated along, her curls bouncing slightly as we moved down the narrow passageway.

When we stopped by a door, Faye swung it open to reveal the same office as before. I hated this room. With various Corrupted people walking through on their way to do whatever it was their were doing for the Drude, it felt cramped and uncomfortable. My parents weren't here today and I was surprised by the wave of relief that washed over me.

It was stupid, they were my family. I should be thrilled that I'd found them. But I just felt…nothing. I didn't know what they did for the Drude, but something told me I wouldn't want to know. Dad had been a high school teacher who coached soccer. My mom had worked as a Realtor. Not exactly nefarious. What possible use, other than their connection to me, could they be to a force of destruction like the Drude?

Once the door to our room swung closed, I found myself asking before I could stop myself, "What do all these people do, anyway?"

Faye looked at me, surprised, "We operate a bit like a business to be honest, with Master at the helm. It's important that we continue to function here, safely under the guise that we are a strange church that the government has no interest in."

I stared. "So they are just milling around, waiting to go…what, find more bodies?"

Faye frowned at me. "It's not like that, Justine."

"It is, *Faye*," I said sarcastically, emphasizing her name. "He's building an army of the undead with souls he's stolen, and you are helping him."

To my surprise, suddenly I was lifted off my feet, shoved backwards until my back was against the bedroom wall, and then slowly I was picked up until I was dangling there midair. Faye stood her ground, her dark curls blowing lightly in a breeze that originated from her steepled fingers, which glowed a soft bluish-green in front of her chest.

"Do not talk about things you don't understand, sister. You have been here a minute. You know nothing about me, nothing about why I do anything I'm doing."

My chest ached with the pressure that continued to buffet across my body. "Faye..."

"Do you understand? There is more at play here than you can imagine."

"Yes, yes, I understand," I finally gritted out, the words barely a whisper.

Faye's face relaxed, her fingers slowly going slack as the air that whirled between us softened, now barely a breeze across my panicked face as her power lowered me gently back to the ground.

I half expected her to apologize when I stumbled forward, but instead, her face went serious and she swept her gaze over me. I patted my chest for a second, wondering what she was looking at, and then took a slow step back.

"I'm sorry," I got out slowly. I observed her closely, for the first time seeing the woman beneath the sunshine exterior and knowing instantly that there was more to her and her story than what first met the eye.

Interesting, I thought as she suddenly brightened and turned to move to the small desk in the corner. My jaw loosened. The fucking girl was humming.

Was I losing my mind? Or had she? Shrugging off the realization that she had obviously decided not to kill me, I moved to sit on my bed, backing up until my spine was flush to the wall and I could watch her. She was carefully reading page by page, and then every once in a while would pull away to mutter something to herself.

"What are you reading about?"

"Do you really want to know, or are you just really bored?"

"Can it be both?"

Elbow over the back of the stiff-backed chair, she rested her chocolate eyes on me. "I'm learning more about silencing spells."

I almost guffawed at the sarcastic lilt in her voice but ignored her obvious implication by asking more. "What are you best at?"

Her shoulders dropped. "Tracking spells."

"For other people like us?"

My guess must've hit its mark because her lips quivered in a small smile before lifting. "How long did it take you to figure that out?"

"You're not doing a very good job of hiding that you're the odd one out here. You dress differently, you act differently, and you said that the Drude took you from the system when you were a child. Nephesh told me they believe he's hunting down the humans bound to his brothers. It all just kind of makes sense."

Faye lifted her hands, as if to clap, but I held up a finger, halting her. "Except one thing."

She waited expectantly. "And that is?"

"You would give up the chance to have a soul mate in order to work for someone like the Drude. You don't seem like a bad person, yet you are serving a man who means to use people's souls for ammo against a race of nearly immortal warriors." I leaned close to her. "He's going to lose, Faye, you know that, right?"

"We don't know that. And we also don't know if I'm anyone's soul mate. The fact that you are Nephesh's match is a rare oversight. Probably based on the pressure the original spell is enduring to make the soul remain split."

Why did that make something in my chest ache. "His mother's spell, you mean. And you think it's changing…"

She shrugged. "I think it's evolving to survive, just like we have."

"Why though?"

"Because demons will spend their entire lives seeking out their mates. It is a drive one thousand times stronger than that of family or fortune. Without their mates will live half a life, and not just because of their souls being severed." There was something else in Faye's voice now. Sadness, maybe.

"But if we carry both their missing soul and are fated to be with them…"

"Then there's no way they could resist the call," Faye finished with an annoying little flip of her head. "Which is why even though Nephesh already has your soul, he will always come for you."

"Because we are fated to be together." I already knew this, but there was something different talking about it in such a casual way. It was almost clinical.

"Yes, I think so. But it's more than that, isn't it? You loved him before."

I huffed, my cheeks feeling hot and tingly. "You don't fall in love with someone over the course of a few days."

Faye rolled her eyes and turned around. "We both know you're lying, so just keep telling yourself that if you need to."

Silence fell as I considered her words. "What would happen if I rejected the bond?"

"I'm not sure, to be honest. I guess that they'd continue on. Master says that plenty of demons and other Hell creatures find matches among their own kind. The fated mates thing is a bit overdramatized. It typically only happens in powerful types, like your Nephesh or my…"

"Your who…"

Faye turned her back on me. "I don't know yet."

"Hence the tracking spell, eh?"

"Leave it alone, Justine."

I chomped down on my lip, a new plan already coming into light. But first I had to keep the conversation going. I needed to know more. Knowledge was power. "What is the least helpful thing that you know how to do with magic?"

Faye's head swiveled back, looking confused. "Why?"

"Come on, just tell me. What is it?"

Forehead wrinkled in thought, Faye appeared deep in thought, her pencil tapping every few seconds against the desk. "Can I show you how to change the color of ink?"

I snorted, shoving myself off the edge of my bed. "That sounds safe."

Faye sighed but held up a pen for me to take. "I almost regret telling Master I could teach you."

"But you did, and now you're stuck with me."

Faye's mouth opened then snapped closed. "Fine. Place your pen on the desk like mine."

Grinning, I did as she asked.

26

"Your mother was quite clever, you know, splitting your souls. It does indeed make you quite hard to kill. I'm guessing that you are a little upset right now."

I turned my head, spitting blood from my mouth as I grinned at my captor. "I thought we were just getting to know each other."

This one, I think his name was Shane, wrinkled his nose at me. "You disgust me."

"You're the one who keeps insisting we spend so much time together. If you let Justine and me go, you wouldn't have to see me ever again." Or anything else, I said silently, because there was no way that this one would be allowed to live after this. He threatened my mate. I would relish every second of his death.

"Shut your mouth, demon."

"You keep asking me questions."

I didn't have time to flinch as he whirled back, slamming a steel pipe against my temple. The next breath, I was standing in the courthouse, looking down at the row of my jurors, Peter at the helm as if they were all waiting for me.

Wait. Not me.

Her.

"Mother?"

"Nephesh." Her hands were ice cold against my cheek as she pulled my head down to press her forehead against it. Our bright-white hair blended together as she sighed against me. "We only have a moment."

"Arafel said you came to him, but I didn't believe it. I wasn't sure…"

"You have to get out of there, Nephesh. Not just you, but Justine and the other witch. They need to be freed. The souls there are corrupted beyond all reason. They must be dealt with."

"I'm trying, but they seem to know too much about us. More than they should. It doesn't make any sense. They know what spell works, too, Mother."

Then I see it, the pain and regret in her face. "Oh Nephesh."

Realization dawned, and I wished more than anything else that my body would wake up. I couldn't face this reality. Not when it would decimate my reality. Let alone the way it would destroy my father. "You were with him, weren't you? That's why they know so much, isn't it? It's because of you."

She shook her head, moving away from me. "I did what I had to."

I laughed, the sound mirthless and painful to my damaged rib cage. "Of course you did. Does he still have you? Are you his captive?"

She shook her head again, moving farther away now. Peter and the others were stock still, watching us both. "Mother! Fuck, don't go. I need to know!"

"You are the lifeblood of the Underworld. It is your souls, your system, that powers us all. Without you, and without her, there will be no chance to push them back."

"Justine? But she said…"

"She said that as long as her parents were safe, then she would serve him."

I scrubbed at my face, my eyes burning as I stared at her soft glow, her form becoming less and less distinct as she stepped away. "You don't know what you're asking."

"I know exactly what I'm asking. Love is sacrifice. Her parents sacrificed themselves to keep her safe once… They would never want to live like this again."

"I understand."

Her form halted. "I'm quite proud of you, Nephesh. I always knew that you would love harder than all of them."

"What? Why?"

"Because unlike the others, you understand what it can mean to lose that love."

"Mother…please."

But then she was gone and the pounding in my head was coming back again, pulling me from my sleep and back into the world of the living. This time when Shane started in on me with more questions about entry into the Underworld, I kept my eyes on the door, waiting, knowing that however it had happened, my mother had already been here.

She might still be here.

And I needed to warn my father.

Soon. The livelihood of the Underworld depended on it. Because not only was she our queen, but she was maker and ruler of the land too. And the one person who would know exactly how to bring my father and my brothers to heel.

I could only hope she hadn't told them yet.

***

Justine

"I think we've deduced that your magic is quite a bit different than mine."

"That's putting it lightly," I said, patting the tiny flame that had ignited along the edge of my bedspread. "Yours does what you want it to, and mine does not."

Faye was eyeing my movements suspiciously, avoiding the sparks that continued to issue off of the flame. "I was trained for years and was taught control first and foremost. Your magic is a bit like your mate, I think, fiery and foul-tempered."

"He's not like that all the time." I glanced sideways at her. "Are you going to tell me whose soul you carry?"

"Frankly, I'm not completely sure. The Drude is aware that the Dream Realm's Lord has found his mate and she is his soul bound. You are with Nephesh. That leaves only a few others."

The flame was out now, and I quickly rotated my bedcovers so that the charred edge was hidden in the bottom corner of my mattress. At least if someone came in, they wouldn't immediately see the burned edge. "And you don't want to know?"

Faye was looking at her nails as if they genuinely interested her. But I knew it was a front. In the past few days living with this girl twenty-four-seven, the one thing I could say for certain was that she was always watching. "From what we can tell, carrying their souls makes us uniquely interested in them. That they are our perfect match."

"Okay…so what's the problem?" I flopped across the floor, picking at a loose thread on my shirt.

"That can never happen for me."

"Why not?"

"Because the Drude would use it against him."

"You're sure?"

She nodded, looking away. "He wants you too. He thinks he can convince you to find my soul bound and then somehow act as bait. To pull them in so he can take them."

I shivered as I thought of the plan. Nephesh had said his family had welcomed Arafel's mate into their fold with no doubts. Would they do the same with me, only for me to turn around and destroy everything?

Faye continued, "Which is why it's safer for me to remain cut off from the bond and why I have to work harder at my magic. Yours is like wildfire. You can redirect it, but it has a life of its own. I imagine there's this kind of element that would make the power bigger and more dramatic if you and Nephesh were reunited."

"We enable each other."

Faye's forehead wrinkled. "If he ever takes the rest of his soul into himself, then he will be virtually unstoppable. He was Lucifer's first weapon, a beast unlike anything the world had seen before. At least according to my teacher."

I thought back to Nephesh's face when I called the soul forward. The fear that had shown there. "I don't think he's meant to be that beast, all the time at least. He's more than some weapon. He's a person."

"I get that completely." Faye shuffled across the room, collecting her shower things as she did. "The Drude kept me only because of the potential I might have someday. I serve no other purpose."

"But you have someone wishing for you."

"Wishing for my soul."

"Wishing for you," I echoed again, raising my brows for emphasis.

"Whatever. I'm going to go shower." She pointed at the match on my desk. "For God's sake, work on your focus."

"Faye?"

"Yeah?"

I kept playing with that string, channeling all my worries, all my anxiety, into the fabric. Grounding myself, shutting off all my doubts. "How long would you be in the shower?"

She stared at me long and hard. "I imagine twenty minutes. I always hurry because the guards are so sweet at the end of shift, and I want to steal an extra dessert."

I glanced at the blinking digital clock against one corner. "Six o'clock, right?"

"Yeah, I think so."

"Cool." I pushed back against the bed, feigning that I might lie down. Not that she would buy anything I said at this point.

Faye's voice was soft, gentle, when she spoke again from the door. "See you when I get out."

"Uh-huh. See you then," I said noncommittally, waiting until the second the door closed before slipping out the other door. There was no one else in the small common room office space, and I was instantly relieved as I stepped out into the hallway. The guards glanced at me, but they seem to be somewhat used to me at this point. And since I stupidly pledged myself to the Drude, they obviously thought I was either on their side or close enough to it.

"I'm going to grab some food," I tell them when the one on the left looked at me funny."

After that, he shifted his eyes back to the hallway, adopting his earlier pose as I headed down the labyrinth of plain white walls that tunneled around this immense building.

When I reached the hallway leading directly to where they had been keeping Nephesh and me, I paused, waiting. Their shift would change, they had to report back, and then two new guards would be taking up residence there. I would have only a minute or two inside. And that was if anyone wasn't already in there with him.

God, I hoped I'd gotten the timing right. I'd been asking Faye questions constantly and had put together something of a plan to see Nephesh. Not to break out, there was no way I could od that on my own. But I needed to see him. This may be my only shot. I ducked into a small utility closet, leaving the door open only the tiniest amount as I stared out at the pair of guards who stood on my side of Nephesh's door.

I was glad they were on this side, so I could see when they left to shift posts. But it did mean they would have to walk right past me. Clamping my eyes shut, I hoped to God that luck would be on my side this time.

My heart leaped in my stomach as the two guards glanced at their watches, an alarm clearly going off as they nodded to each other. As one, they stepped off, walking down the hallway. I actually held my breath as they passed, my heart hammering in my ears as they marched past my hiding spot, then turned left, towards where I imagined the armory and guard quarters were. Faye said they kept the Corrupted away from the humans. I wasn't sure why, and I didn't ask.

The doorway was empty now, and I knew it had to be now or never since the other guards would be here any moment to replace those two.

Walking to the door, I felt a cool brush of air over my skin. I'd had that magic against me over and over the past few days, and I knew in a moment it was Faye's. Holding my breath, I kept walking, pushing the door open and feeling her spell sweep over me, harmless as I entered the darkened room.

Nephesh was back in our cell. Tears leapt to my eyes as I stared at the prone figure on the ground, his white hair standing out so dramatically against the cement floor.

"Nephesh?"

His elbow rose, and in a moment, he was pushing to his feet, hsi body plastered against the cell walls. "Justine, you can't be here."

I rushed to the cell, my arms slipping through to run my fingers over the cuts on his face, the dark stain of his blood that seemed to cover the entire top half of his bared body. I tried to be gentle, but even then I could see where his stomach jumped and flinched from my touch.

"Oh my God, are you okay?" I whimpered, "Sorry, I know that's a dumb question. Of course you're not okay."

'I'll be fine as long as you are." He pressed his forehead against the bars, and I climbed up to the first rung of the cell, pressing my forehead against his, the slick cool touch of his sweat telling me just how bad it really was.

"You have to take the soul," I whispered, my words fast and frantic. "You have to."

"Justine, you don't know what you're asking."

"I do, and I'm so sorry to put this onto you, but Faye, she thinks there's a connection there. A reason that I was chosen to carry your soul."

Nephesh brushed his thumb over my lips. "Because you're the only one tough enough."

I captured his hand. "Well, yes, but she thinks, and the Drude too probably, that there's meaning behind it. Maybe I can help. Maybe I'm supposed to."

"The only thing you're supposed to do is be safe. I'm begging you."

"But I screwed up. I pledged myself to him."

"Shh. We will find a way." Nephesh's voice was rough as he tried to soothe me.

I ran my fingers into his hair, my entire body aching as I pressed against the bars separating us.

"They're hurting you."

"I can take it."

"This is all my fault. If I'd never called for you…"

"Then *I* would've never found you." Nephesh leaned in, his nose brushing my temple. "Cerberus might have though."

I let out a wet laugh, one hand mopping at my face. "What are we going to do?"

"You are going to listen to me, little thief."

I swallowed hard, my hand still clutching his.

"You, my beautiful, kind, wild mate, you would've always been worth it. I'd happily endure all the pain in the world is worth it to spend that time with you. Even if it's all we get in this lifetime."

"Shh, Nephesh, please. Don't talk like that." I pressed my body against the bars, needing that reassurance that he was still here. Because I couldn't imagine a world without him in it. I needed him to know that. "Nephesh, I-."

"Go, Justine." His voice was as ragged as my heart felt.

"No, I can't."

"Now, before they catch you."

With a cry, I turned, stumbling off to the rung I'd been standing on and taking three jogging steps towards the center of the room before I rushed back to him. Reaching in, I felt the heat of his skin under my palms as he pressed close once more.

"You listen to me. I love you, and I'm going to find a way out of this, and then I'm going to spend the rest of your life showing you that I'm not only capable of loving you at your best, but loving you at your worst too."

Nephesh's exhale shook his whole body. "I can't wait to see it."

With a sob, I pushed away from him, rushing back across the room, out the door, and down the hallways. I didn't stop until I was back in my room, and when Faye came out of her shower, I knew she was pretending that she didn't hear my sobs.

27

Nephesh

Justine should not have come here. She should've stayed away. While the idea of her being here at all still gave me a wealth of anger issues, I knew that for the moment, she was safe. They wanted to keep her. The Drude believed that in his quest for power, the witches would be an asset to him.

And honestly, he wasn't wrong. While most bloodlines were washed out, the ones that remained should be even more powerful than before. If Justine was trained properly, by someone like Mother, she would be a force to be reckoned with.

Arafel needed to know to keep his mate close by as well. While his soul bound had only a small fraction of witch blood remaining in her, there was a chance the Drude would still be interested in her. As soon as I got us out of here, I would warn him.

I sagged against the cell wall, still unwilling to leave this space since Justine went sprinting back out of the room. It was the corner closest to her, and the ache in my chest was far less pronounced when I was actively attempting to get closer to her

327

again. Even when I needed her to stay away from me, I wanted her closer.

What a fucking paradox. This was why I hadn't wanted a mate for so long. I was so sure that I was okay alone.

Now, I would be lost without her. And this ache, this worry, it only reassured me that the bond in my chest was true. That she was meant to be mine. And there was no way the fates were cruel enough to use this soul bound to introduce me to my best friend and my mate in the same breath that it also took them away.

It couldn't be.

The monster in my core growled to life, checking my control and then curling back to wait. I was going to have to release him soon—something I'd never wanted to do again. Being harnessed to the monster, with no control, with no say in his reactions, was one of the most terrifying feelings I'd experienced. He was a bloodthirsty creature, made of fury and hatred. And that was how I treated him even now, laying my power between the regained half-soul that Justine had had and my own.

I wasn't ready to accept it.

When I did, everything would change. I could get out of here on my own. I didn't need to become that monster to save us. At least, that was what I believed. And I hoped to Hades that I was correct.

"Hello there, Fallen," a deep voice said. Niko again. The well-dressed man kept the door open for a moment, ushering the other witch in behind him. She was pale-faced and grim, her lips a flat line as she followed Niko into the middle of the room.

He gestured with his hands to the ground then at me. "You know what to do."

She began to draw against the concrete, her fingers leaving a charred line, slowly arching around until it was a complete circle on the ground.

I knew what it was in an instant. After all, how many times had I seen my mother draw one for an errant soul or for a demon who had lost control. Only, I had never been the one standing in the middle. I shifted, my lips parting so he could see every inch of the fangs I let slip free from my gums.

"Can I help you with something?" I kept my voice light, even as my wings fluttered in agitation behind me.

"You and I are going to have a chat, Fallen." Niko approached the cell, hands behind his back. He rocked back on his heels as he stared into the darkened cell.

"My name is Nephesh, but then, you know that."

The witch approached Niko again, but he didn't look at her. "I do, and now that we are on a first-name basis, I really want to ask you a few questions. How do you feel about that?"

"I feel like I want to rip your heart from your chest and feed it to my dog, but that doesn't seem like a good idea just yet."

Niko blinked, his self-satisfied smile only wavering an instant. "Lucky me."

I grunted. "What do you really want?"

"I just wanted to ask you a few questions." Niko pressed a button on a brightly lit cell phone and then looked back to me. "But we need to rearrange you a little to get the correct response."

Pain didn't scare me. But the fact that these people had Justine did. I could only hope they would continue to focus on me. Niko moved to the cell door, his hand pressing against it in a series of soft beeping noises.

"I'm going to let you out, but if you can't play nice, I'll have Faye here put a stop to that cursed heart in your chest."

I blinked at him as the door swung open.

"And yes, she can do that. Don't try me."

I moved out the door and over to the circle that she'd drawn, pausing at the edge.

"You can step over it right now," her soft, barely audible voice sounded in my ears.

I nodded, looking into her wide eyes, surprised to find her boldly looking back at me. She might look and sound meek, but I could feel the burn of her power under that stare. He wasn't bluffing. That much was sure.

I stepped over the line, turning to face Niko once again. Slowly crossing my arms, I waited for him to speak.

"We have some questions for you."

I remained silent for a moment. I was already tired of this conversation. Finally I said, "I'm sure you do."

"Tell me, Prince of Hell, what does your father know about my Master?"

My brows furrowed. That was not the question I was prepared for, and it was simple to answer. "Not as much as he'd like."

Niko chuckled as if I'd pleased him. I blew air through my nose, watching as the man stopped by Faye and leaned in. "Do it."

The air around me suddenly crackled with energy, spiking down my skin with a burn. I grunted in surprise, pain pulsing in my mind.

"Don't be cute, Fallen. We don't have time for that."

I shook my arms out, glaring first at him and then at the slender witch at his side. "That hurt." I grunted at her pointedly.

To my surprise, she blushed and then stepped farther behind Niko.

He rolled his eyes. "Witches, I swear. Such emotional creatures. But then, you know that since your mate is one as well."

Alarm bells were ringing in my mind, and I kept my face carefully calm. When I didn't react, I could see the visible disappointment in his gaze. He tried again.

"You should hear what it took to break this one into her powers, even with a teacher as powerful as…" He trailed off, grinning at me wolfishly. "Well, anyway. We always find a way to get what we need."

He circled me. "Those who do not bend at the knee, often break, Fallen. Why don't we work together to make sure that doesn't happen for your spicy little redhead."

I grunted, steeling myself for the next wave. This time I could see the way the witch shifted, her gaze flickering ever so slightly to the man standing beside her. And then, a caress against my mind. Not a knock. Not an invasion like my family's communication. Something else.

I focused on it for only a breath before it broke in.

Faye's voice was soft and hushed inside my mind. "Close the bond to her."

"Why?" I met her eyes, seeing the fear invade them now as Niko looked at me with such hatred.

"Because what he will have me do to you…" Faye's eyes met mine, even as her lips remained unmoving, her voice speaking directly into my mind. "It will hurt her too."

Horror filled every part of me. "What?"

"I'm sorry" was all she said, and then she was gone from my head.

Panicked, I threw my magic against the bond in my chest, closing it down, keeping it far away, putting pressure on it until it was nothing but a tiny speck against the very core of my soul.

Only then could I hope that she would be safe from their hands. Meeting the witch's eyes, I nodded. Fangs dropping, I snarled at Niko. "I am a prince of Hell, the heir to my father's kingdom. I won't tell you anything."

Niko's handsome face turned dark in an instant. "We will see about that."

***

28

Justine

I ran through the halls, my feet slapping against the cold floor as Faye shouted my name. I could hear the loading of weapons as the soldiers for the Master—fuck, I meant the Drude, trailed after me. They only jogged, which made sense because they knew that I couldn't actually escape.

I ran anyway. Deep in my chest, I let my bond rip open, flooding desperate love and need down the tremulous bond between Nephesh and myself. There had to be a way. There had to be a connection still. If Faye could still feel hers, even after shoving it down and hiding it for most of her life, then Nephesh's attempt couldn't be the end of us.

It could be a beginning.

But I had to get to him first. I charged down past the furnished part of the warehouse and into the cold, dimly lit space that had been home for those first few days. It had been only last week, but it felt like forever, especially knowing what might have happened to Nephesh while I was there, unable to reach him.

Too fucking afraid to reach him.

But I was done waiting. I was going to save him, and we were getting out of here. The door in front of me looked unapologetically solid, and as I raced towards it, I raised a shoulder and prayed to God and even Nephesh's dear old dad that I might make it through. Surprise spiraled through me when I arrived at the door, and instead of slamming into it, I seemed to slip right through, my flesh chilling to ice then heating to three hundred degrees all at the same time. As I dragged air back into my lungs, I slowed my feet and realized that I was standing in the middle of the jail area once again…but with one large difference.

Nephesh was dangled from above, his limbs strung wide as he hung unmoving in the thick metal chains. A cry was torn from my lips as I realized he was limp, asleep or passed out or… I swallowed. He couldn't be dead. I would know if he were, right?

I lurched towards him. "Nephesh! Nephesh, please. I'm here." I rushed to where he was suspended in the middle of the room. Panic gripped me as I wrapped my arms around his middle and tried to get a grip on the floor enough that I could prop him up. I couldn't let him hang there a moment longer. Anything so that he wasn't hanging like that, like a puppet with no matter, an eagle trapped in lines.

Nephesh groaned in my ear, his face shifting as he ran his nose into my hair. My muscles shook under the weight of his body as I attempted to lever him up.

"You came back."

My heart felt like it was being shredded. "Yes, yes, I'm here. I'm so sorry."

Nephesh's beautiful smile surprised me. "You saved your family. I'm proud of you."

I sobbed, his weight heavy in my arms as my feet continued to slip against the cement floor. Frustrated, I looked down then wished with every bit of my heart that I hadn't. I was standing in a thick puddle of blood. His blood.

"Monsters," I whispered, my words slurred by the onslaught of tears that continued to race down my face. "We will make them pay."

"Hmmm," Nephesh groaned, trying to pull away. "You are supposed to be somewhere safe."

"*We* are supposed to be somewhere safe. And this is my fault. I'm getting you out of here."

That statement caught his attention, and his eyes focused on me. "Justine, what are you talking about?" Then, as if in slow motion, he rolled his head back over his shoulder to look at the sliver of bright light spilling into the room.

I whimpered, realizing I hadn't heard the door open, but sure enough, it was wide open, and at the front of the squad that filled the hallway were my parents.

"They are not your parents," Nephesh said behind me, his voice soft and gentle. "They may look like your parents, they may even act like your parents, but they are Corrupted. Souls that were taken from the Underworld and placed in those bodies for one purpose and one only."

My mom moved into the room, a club in one hand, a cell phone in the other. Dad was following behind, weaponless, save his height and bulk, which I imagine would be quite formidable.

"Wh-What do you mean?"

"Look at them," Nephesh said. "Really look at them. They may be the bodies of your family, Justine, but their souls are not here any longer."

"No…" I shook my head. It was too much, too far. No one could possibly be that evil. Could they?

"Yes," Nephesh said. "Close your eyes, little thief. Let me show you."

I backed into him, my back to his front as a sudden burst of warmth was lit between us. His soul—the dark, devious part of himself that he feared so much—flared between us. "Nephesh…what is this?"

"Let me show you." I could feel the fear in his words, the ominous warning in his voice.

I blinked down at the dancing flame between us, at the soul longing to be reunited with the half that burned at his center.

Nephesh breathed in, a small bit of that flame rising and flicking across the lower part of his face before lowering again. But I didn't watch what he did next, because as soon as he breathed in that bit of his missing soul, Nephesh leaned in and pressed his forehead flush to mine.

"Look at them," he said again, but this time his voice echoed in my mind. Slowly I turned, my feet careful on the slick floor. When I spotted my mother, I leaped back, impacting Nephesh as I took in the creature that had once been my mother. When I looked hard, I could see the smooth outline of her form, the familiar one that I had protected. But at her center, it was an ugly writhing mess of black tendrils, curling over and over at the core of that form, as if unhappy to be confined in such a small place.

My stomach rose in my throat, and I almost threw up. But as soon as I blinked again, my vision was normal. My family had never come back. They were safe in the Underworld, where they belonged. These were Corrupted souls, using my parents bodies for their own benefit. Rage lit up my powers like gasoline.

I didn't owe the Drude anything. He had made me swear allegiance to save people that didn't exist anymore. Relief tempered the rage I still felt as I stared at the soul who had pretended to be someone I had loved so dearly.

I was free. And I was going to make it worth it.

"Justine, honey, don't listen to him. You know what he is now. Come back."

"You are not my mother."

Tension filled the air, broken only by Nephesh's rasping breath at my back.

Finally, the thing that was not my mother rolled its eyes wide then popped a hip out. "Took you long enough. But no one

cares, Justine. Just get over here so we can dispose of this thing."
She was pointing at Nephesh.

I reached back, my hand settling over Nephesh's wrist as I
recognized what we had to do. "Can you always share those bits
of power with me?"

"I can. But—"

Opening my hands wide, I let every tiny bit of magic that I'd
felt building in my system loose. I didn't know what it would do,
but I knew that for this group of people, a supernatural
distraction would be necessary.

Fire—ruby-red, shocking orange, and vibrant sunshine
yellow—flickered free from my hands, falling to the floor and
sweeping around Nephesh and me before streaming towards the
rapidly approaching soldiers.

"Impressive," Nephesh said, his voice tired as he sagged
against me.

I didn't bother telling him it was the extent of my abilities as
of now and it may only last a few moments. "We only have one
chance of getting out of here, and it has to happen now."

One of Nephesh's amber eyes flicked closed.

"And how precisely is that going to happen?" he asked. There
are more people coming now, filtering into the room.

I pressed my hands against his chest. "Let me see your soul."

"What?"

"Just do it!"

Nephesh breathed out slowly, his body curling forward until my forehead was leaning against his chest, my breathing ragged, lungs aching.

His head dropped until it was pressing against me once again, where he inhaled me over and over again. "Justine…"

"I'm here, and I know you're hurting, but you have to show me your soul."

Nephesh's entire body shuddered, as if he knew what I was about to do. I could feel him drag in one more breath of my hair before he exhaled out, and as he did, something appeared against his flesh, the scarred flesh seeming to spark as a flicker of fire appeared, first as only a tendril, then growing until a small flame hovered in the air, protected from their eyes by our bodies.

"You have to take it," I said, licking my overly dry lips. "You have to return it to its half."

"I cannot do that. You know that."

"You don't have a choice. They've been training, they have weapons, and they know how to hurt you. They know how to…" *Kill you.* I couldn't get that last part out.

"I will be a monster," he whispered.

"You will be mine, just as you are now. I have loved you as a human. I have loved you as a demon. I will love you in this form too," I hissed, swiping at angry tears as the flame danced. The air shifted. They were coming, maybe with Faye this time.

We were out of time. I raised my hand, the flames harmless as I dragged a finger through the flames of his soul. My other hand snaked up to tangle in his white locks, holding tight as I leaned in. Braced for what I had to do.

And who I was about to meet.

"I love you," I whispered, and then before I could regret my choices and right as the door behind me burst open, I rolled a palm over the flicker of his soul and shoved it into Nephesh's chest, right below his heart, right where our bond glowed brighter than ever.

It didn't melt into him as it had come out. This time it was a visceral, nearly violent reaction as Nephesh's entire body whipped back, the chains going taut as he first flinched away from me and then writhed at the ends of the cursed chains.

I stepped back, covering my mouth with my hands as I watched his pain and suffering. Had I thought wrong? What had I done?

I didn't bother to turn around, but I could sense the squad of soldiers who now stood between me and what had been my temporary freedom. Something inside told me that Faye wasn't here yet. I hoped she wasn't.

I hoped she would understand. Someday.

Smoke bloomed from the chains as they struggled to contain him, and I backed away, coughing a little as the smoke invaded my lungs. Nephesh was invisible in the cloud of shadows and billowing darkness in front of us.

A sob freed itself before I could stop it, the sound strange and sharp in the silence of the room. "Nephesh?"

"Turn around, Justine, and no one will get hurt." Not Nephesh's voice. It was another human, one of the dozens of nameless soldiers.

Tears streaming, I slowly turned, raising my hands to my shoulders as several raised their weapons. I looked down, seeing that dots were appearing across my chest and belly.

Red dots.

A calling card for the death I was about to endure. I closed my eyes. At least there was a chance that I could see Nephesh again in the Underworld. Tell him that I never meant any of this.

"Captain?" one of the men shouted, a sharp edge of hysteria clear in his voice. "Orders?"

"If she moves, she dies."

I could hear, with inhuman perfection, the sound of a finger twitching on a trigger. Adrenaline shot through my system, and I braced myself for the worst, when suddenly there was nothing. It was as if time slowed down. One minute there was a bullet coming for my body. The next there was a surge of heat and I was looking up into the chest of…of something I could've never dreamed up in a thousand lifetimes.

"Nephesh," I whispered to the creature in front of me. He faced me, hunched over, balanced on two legs as glowing red eyes swept my body. He was immense, even hunched over as he was, with a heavy silver coat that rippled over a thick, heavyset body. A snout had replaced Nephesh's features, parted to reveal a set of vicious white teeth, the fangs dripping lightly as he huffed in a short breath. In my mind, he was something between

the heavyset polar bears of the north, and the gray wolves I'd
seen on television. Yet the horns I'd been so enchanted by just
days ago still spiraled up over the doomed head, right next to
sharp-pointed white ears.

He was built for speed and destruction, four-inch-long claws
at the tip of each pawed leg. And I could see the exact moment
the rest of the group saw him for what he was. A predator, for
sure. But still mine.

Slowly, carefully, I realized, the creature lowered his head to
my level so that those red eyes were looking right into mine. I
smiled up at him. "You're still beautiful, Nephesh."

"Stand down, lieutenant!" another voice shouted, breaking
the tension in the room, as Nephesh whirled around, his heavy
front end slamming into the earth as he twisted to face our
attackers. He was the size of a horse like this, moving forward a
step as he settled on all fours. The picture of a villain from a
fairytale.

He was flesh and blood, the scent of smoke and flame still
lingering on his fur as he leaned down, taking the opportunity to
wrap his body around me.

I reached up, one hand digging into the soft, fluffy fur at the
base of his neck, and clung to him. "We're leaving," I announced
to the group.

Nephesh's rumbling growl followed my words.

"Now," I stated.

29

No one moved. The one barking orders, the one Faye had glared at the other day, shifted forward a little. "You're staying right where you are." He raised his gun. "Don't think about it, monster."

I blinked, my eyelids slow and lethargic as the bond in my chest thumped back to life with a ferocity that shocked me. When my eyes closed, the world slowed, and while I couldn't see, there was a visibility that flickered to life, as if staring into the darkness of night and seeing shadows. Only, I saw them as figures, shapeless, and at their core, a small scale, constantly shifting. But the others, they were less solid, more blurred lines, and at their center something inky and dark twisted around the soft glow of what I knew instantly had to be their soul. I was seeing the difference between the Corrupted and the human souls.

Letting my head turn to my mate, I reached a hand out. Instincts I'd never felt before rose up, overruling all else.

So many were hurt. So many souls were lost.

And I was here to fix that.

"Nephesh…"

Yes, his voice echoed in my head, low and rough.

"Can you see them?"

"Always."

For a moment, my eyes went wide open in shock, taking in the massive wolf-like creature that leaned against my side. Then back to the soldiers in front of me. They looked so ordinary with my human eyes, just frail, scared people who were staring down the personification of what they feared the most. Without their master, they were pawns left to die in the trail of destruction that the Drude was weaving.

"You should run," I told them, but my voice was different now, the power racing through Nephesh's body into mine, making it a dark rasp. Or was that my power running into him? I couldn't tell any longer.

"Stand your ground," the captain barked out when several of his soldiers attempted to flee.

My heart pounded for their loss, even as my eyes closed again.

"I don't know what I'm doing," I said in my mind, hoping Nephesh could hear.

There was a rumbling growl under my palm, and I knew that the soldiers had opted to stay. That they were still facing us with guns loaded.

"You were born for this, little thief," Nephesh answered. He stepped forward, the extension of my power sizzling down our

bond until his silvery fur nearly glowed with it. My muscles shook, and after a quick look back at me, Nephesh's inhuman arm reached out and picked me up, swinging me over his shoulder, where I could rest against his back.

I dug in, my legs in front of the powerful joint of his shoulders, my hands deep in his scruff as he squared off against these men.

"Are we going to die?" I couldn't stop myself from asking very, very quietly. So quiet I knew only Nephesh could hear me.

The beast under me shuddered, and then that rasping deep voice spoke in my mind once again. *"Close your eyes, little thief."*

I obeyed, my chest heaving with anxiety.

"Look at them. Tell me which are the Corrupted and which are living souls."

I nodded, my eyes still clamped shut as hard as possible. The pounding of blood in my ears made it nearly impossible to think of anything else. But fraction by fraction, I raised my chin to look out through the magicked film that I felt wrap around my body. I stared at those faded lines of people.

No, not people.

Souls.

And just like Faye had said, just like Nephesh had known, I could see more clearly now which were the living souls and which were more faded, their inner glow tangled in more of that black inked vise.

I must've been translating some of that to Nephesh, because then his front legs were bending. I could feel his breath catch just before he launched forward.

"That one," I said, jabbing a finger at the one on the left with the mustache that slipped from the ski mask. *"He's corrupted."*

One swipe of Nephesh's paw, and I saw the inky tendrils disappearing, retreating into the edges of the soul. And without that tie, the human form collapsed straight to the floor. A moment later, a soft glow ignited from there, burning hot and bright before vanishing in a spark of light.

"Oh!"

Nephesh growled. "Focus, Justine. Which one is next?"

I tore my eyes from the rapidly darkening form and stared at the next. Without hesitation, I pointed at another corrupted soul, their forms becoming easier and easier to discern from the living souls that were sprinkled through the room.

One by one, I pointed them out in my mind, Nephesh bringing them down with a combination of teeth and claws and a burning-hot magic that appeared even in my hazed vision.

At some point, the living souls must've started to leave, and when my eyes opened into the bloodshed and destruction that we'd brought into this chamber, I could see easily that Gregor wasn't there.

My stomach lurched, a combination of the blood that dotted my skin, Nephesh's silvery hair, and the idea that the arm of the Drude escaped. My mind wandered as I wondered how many of those people were left. Not just here, but everywhere. Slowly, I slid to the ground, and after a deep rattling sigh, Nephesh's body curled into smoke, his flesh shifting in a transfixing snap as suddenly the Nephesh I had met all those nights ago in Omaha stood before me. He was dirty now, his skin bruised in several places, although I wasn't sure if that was from the Drude's soldier or the fact that he'd been tortured before.

I reached out for him. "Are we okay?" I swallowed. "I mean, are you okay?"

Nephesh reached out, one rough thumb tracing the lines of my jaw. "You came for me."

I choked out a short laugh. "Of course I did." My voice caught at the look in his amber eyes. "Can we get out of here now? I don't think I'm ready to fight any more battles today."

Nephesh nodded, suddenly stiffening and glancing over my shoulder. A growl ripped through his chest, and I turned in time to see Faye standing in the doorway. One look, and I knew something was wrong.

"Faye?"

Her eyes found mine, and for a moment, there was the softest brush against my mind.

"Run."

"Faye?"

Nephesh's arms snapped forward and whipped me around as Faye's hands suddenly surged upwards and out, her magic crackling through the air as she hurled something at us, crystal and shining. It wasn't until it broke against Nephesh's back and fell around us in a cluster did I recognize she was shooting ice at us, as sharp and deadly as she could make them.

Nephesh released me, turning to block me from her attacks as he spread his arms wide. I knew that pose in a second. I looked from him to her and back again, suddenly so sure of what I was seeing.

"No, Nephesh, don't! She can't help herself."

I looked around Nephesh's arms at Faye, who, while her arms moved in a sort of starlike motion at the whirling blue air in front of her, her face was lifted, staring right at us.

"Faye…" I whispered. I could see the tears slipping down her face from here.

Her lips moved, her entire body quivering as the magic in front of her continued to build. Bits of ice broke away, flinging themselves at Nephesh as he shoved me back behind him, before dropping with an eerie ease into this creature form, one immense leg pushing me back as yet more ice flew our way.

"Nephesh," I screamed, begging. He was going to kill her. She may be my friend, or maybe just an ally, but I understood her the same way I understood him. I knew her. I would've been her if my parents hadn't given me that extra time.

Nephesh couldn't hear me, and one by one his massive feet carried him towards Faye. I could see her face fall, her magic falter for a moment, before the whirling wind grew ever larger in front of her.

"Nephesh," I screamed. Desperately I clamped my eyes shut. For whatever reason, maybe the connection to my magic, but I could connect better with the creature who ruled Nephesh right now while I was using my magic. I held my hands wide, my eyes shut fast as I focused on the bond in my chest, at the soft flicker of red that bloomed there whenever we were close.

"Nephesh, please," I whispered aloud and into that bond. "Don't make me. Please. I don't want to hurt you." Knowing what this might mean and asking him to do it anyway. I could only pray we were strong enough to weather it.

The creature's gait broke, and Nephesh slowed to a halt as he cast one glowing eye in my direction before swinging around to stare at Faye once again. I could see the shudder that ran over his body as he leaned forward, bracing himself against the onslaught of power that suddenly snapped free from Faye's hands and covered the demon in front of her.

I felt each stab and slide of the icy daggers that flew into his pelt. Screaming, I fell to my knees as Nephesh's great form let out a scream, rearing up and then falling to the side as the daggers continued to fall. Just as suddenly, Nephesh shoved me away from our bond, the magic of our connection tight, as I could no longer feel his pain.

Rolling to my feet, I took off running, making it to Nephesh as Faye stumbled back, her face bright white and her mouth open in shock and despair. Behind her, Niko moved forward, his handsome face twisted in fury as he leveled his weapon at us.

"Good job, Faye," he said, his voice smug as two of the uniformed souls that were left appeared from behind him, wrapping their arms around the other witch's slender body and dragging her back into the hallway behind them. Faye was slumped over, more tears running down her face as she was dragged out, her stare on me for as long as she could see me.

"As you can see, witchling, the Drude truly does know each of your weaknesses."

I couldn't answer. My hands shook as I stroked Nephesh's form, at the soft muzzle, the eyes that were no longer glowing red, but rather wide and black and more afraid than I'd ever seen before. His chest rose and fell, but only barely. And I knew then that his limited magic was gone. Even with his soul reunited, he needed time to regain that power. And I'd ruined it by interfering. I'd ruined everything .

The only thing he could do was to remain in this form and try to protect us that way. But nothing could protect us from the array of bullets that were coming for us. Niko nodded at his group, and three more soldiers stepped into the room.

"Ready."

"Aim."

"No!" Something deep inside of me shattered, and the men in front of me roared, two dropping their weapons as they clamped their hands over their ears. And the sound kept coming, splitting me wide as my magic was released from the years and years of withholding, of holding back. It was now free. It manifested in the form of fire, the flickering flames crawling down my arm and igniting the ground around us. It needed no fuel because it was as much a part of me as my own arms. I could feel it thrumming around my body, reigniting the bond in my chest, and even curling over Nephesh's body as I took a breath then screamed once more. This time an order. Not a plea.

An order.

"Save us."

And the world around us shattered. I threw myself around Nephesh's body, covering as much of him as I could. My flames did the rest, blanketing us as we fell straight out of the living world…and into somewhere that I could've never imagined.

30

"She's waking up!"

"You're hovering, Kadmiel."

Feet shifted, boots scraping against something as I pushed a hand out, feeling for something. Anything. All I felt was something soft, a blanket maybe, as I slowly pushed my eyes open.

I was staring right into a pair of curious blue eyes, one dark brunette braid slipping over a shoulder as she leaned over me. I blinked then started again.

"Hi," she said. Her voice was soft, almost a whisper, but it rang through my mind like a gong. I cringed, sitting up slowly as she retreated. First to an elbow, then all the way as I cradled my head in my hands. "Move slow."

"Ugh. I don't have much of a choice," I mumbled into my hands. "My head is killing me. "

"We'll get you something for that in a minute," the girl spoke again, her tone still soft.

"Why do I feel like I just spent the night drinking cheap tequila?"

There was a snort from elsewhere in the room, and I parted my fingers enough that I could look through them. The girl was still there, a hesitant smile on her lips. But she was flanked by two others I had never seen. The one on her right looked like he just walked off the stage at a runway show. He was so beautiful it nearly hurt to look at him, his golden hair swept back off his forehead, bright-green eyes sharp on my face.

The other had a strange quality to him. He was slender, shorter than the other man, with fingers that twitched towards the blades hanging at his waist.

The girl followed my gaze, her chin ducking for a minute. "These two are totally harmless," she said, elbowing the one who continued to narrow his eyes my way.

"Paran is my mate's trusted soldier. And Kadmiel here—"

I cut her off, my eyes wide as I stared at the beautiful one.

"You're Nephesh's brother."

Kadmiel looked between the girl and me and back again, nodding.

"Which makes you Lucia."

The girl in question grinned. "He's told you about us. I'm flattered."

I shrugged as much as I dared with my head throbbing like this.

"Oh good." Lucia let out a long sigh, her shoulders dropping with relief as she turned to Paran. "If he trusts her enough to tell her about us, then there's no way she's going to spring from this bed and do any of us harm." Her emphasis was clearly on him relaxing, but he didn't budge.

"I promised, my lord, I would remain by your side. Besides, from what I've learned, it's not weapons that make her dangerous."

Lucia rolled her eyes with a soft groan. "I don't think she's going to be attacking, are you?"

"Not yet," I said sarcastically, but this seemed to thrill her, and she immediately grinned once again.

"Perfect."

Panic slammed into me. "Oh my God, where's Nephesh?"

Lucia's smile was gone in a moment, her body language changing in an instant. "Arafel is with him, as well as their father."

I stared. "Here? He's okay?"

"He made it back home. You dragged both of you through the boundary and landed in a heap near the Pier of Kalos. Atlas, that's Nephesh's guard, brought you here though."

"Where is *here*?"

Lucia cringed. "You're in the Court of Hell right now. That's where Lucifer lives."

I stared. "You have to be kidding."

"Bear with me. It's more of a government center than fire and brimstone."

My breathing slowed but only slightly. "Is Nephesh okay? He was—" I remembered the blood, the way I'd held him back when he tried to protect us. A lump rose in my throat. "He was hurt…"

"His father is there, treating him," Lucia sighed. "He wasn't in good shape at first."

"There? As in, not here."

Lucia nodded slowly, and Paran twitched a little.

"I need to see him. Now."

Kadmiel moved closer. "He's dangerous right now. It's not a good idea."

I stared up at him, my jaw slack. "I know you think you're making sense, but I don't know you." I pointed at each of them. "I don't know you. Or even you. So forgive me when I say that I want to see him. Now."

No one moved.

"My mate. Now," I snarled, ignoring the pounding in my head as I shoved my legs over the edge of the bed and stood. Pain rose through my body, but I gripped the edge of the bed and leveled my best glare at the group.

Lucia sighed. "We will take you to him. But you need to brace yourself. It's not what you think."

I didn't know what she was talking about, nor did I care right now. I needed to see Nephesh. I needed to tell him how sorry I was. How much I loved him. "Now."

Kadmiel nodded, stepping forward. "There's a portal in the great hall."

I stepped forward, wobbling a little as all the muscles in my legs seemed to give out on me all at once.

Lucia reached for me, her expression kind. "Can I help?"

Tears threatened at the back of my eyes. All that power, all that force that I'd been so strong with just a little while ago. But now I was a weakling, begging people to take me to my…my Nephesh.

I nodded jerkily, suddenly unable to speak. Lucia looped her arm through mine and then towed me out of the immense bedroom. I didn't ask and she didn't offer to take the time to change from the pair of loose sleep shorts and soft shirt someone had put me in.

"Are these yours?" I asked.

Lucia moved to the door, her head held high as someone on the outside swung the doors wide. "Yeah, we're close to the same size. I thought you would be more comfortable that way."

I nodded. My cheeks felt hot as I considered who might have dressed me, but there would be time to be awkward about that later. As we walked down a wide, stone-walled hall, soldiers passed dressed completely in black with bright red threading across their throats.

It would've reminded me of Drude's soldiers maybe, if not for the variety of sized horns twisting over their heads. They eyed me with black, pupil-less gazes that made me shiver. But none of them moved our direction. I could feel Kadmiel behind us, as well as more soldiers like Paran who seemed to file in as we made our way towards Nephesh.

"Are you doing okay?"

"They are…demons?"

Lucia's grip tightened. "They are. I don't know how much you know about the Underworld, but these are among Lucifer's most loyal. You are safe here."

I nodded again, awestruck as one that was nearly as tall as the immense vaulted doors stooped down to open it for us, leathery wings snapping back as he moved to bow lightly to us.

"I can't believe…" There were so many things I couldn't believe. But the bottom line was: "I couldn't believe that we made it."

Lucia led me down a wide hallway, stopping by the arched entry. "I've heard you showed the Drude and his crew what's what."

I shook my head. "I barely did anything. Nephesh, he…he fought so hard. And I didn't let him kill her."

"The girl, the other witch there?"

"Yeah." I suddenly jerked away from her. "How do you know any of this? Did Nephesh tell you?"

"Nephesh isn't talking a lot right now, but Arafel has been able to get a few things out of him. Including how you, Justine, returned his soul to him. You made him whole. You saved him."

"I just did what we had to, to survive." I swallowed hard as we entered a vast room with stained glass windows. Lucia's grip softened as we walked through the room. It was empty now, chairs lining the front, all surrounding a massive centerpiece.

A throne, shining under the glow of row after row of chandeliers, all swinging from a vaulted ceiling, the candles thick, black, the dripping wax leaving lines along the iron holders. It was dark here, even with all the candles and the stained-glass windows that should be letting in a variety of light from outside.

I swallowed, another realization hitting me as our group slowed by the throne.

"How is there light here? There's no sun, is there?"

Lucia glanced at me, biting her lip. "This world is of Lucifer and the first witch's craft, but it's not really 'under' anything. This is a world within your world, so to speak. And when the first deal was struck and Lucifer was put in charge of the souls, his power began to fuel this place. In return he likes it to run similar to the living world."

"Oh."

Lucia's cheeks pinked a little. "I know this is a lot. Nephesh will be able to explain more, when he's…uh…able to."

"He's still in creature form, isn't he?"

Lucia nodded. "Arafel said that it has happened before. He lost control when his soul bound died. He tore apart his home, wrecked the pier…and then was trapped. And that was without the other part of his soul. Now that he is whole again, we aren't sure…"

"What he will do?" I stared at her then at the others. "Oh my God, is he chained up again? Did you see what his arms look like?"

Lucia looked worried, especially as my temper flared again, the bond in my chest warming my skin as I pivoted to glare at

Kadmiel. "Were you there? When they chained him up, held him down, told him he was a monster?"

Kadmiel's face was impassive for a long moment, and then the mask cracked, revealing an expression of regret. Slowly, he nodded.

"Take me to him. Right now."

Kadmiel breathed out, one of his hands rising up as he moved to one of the stained-glass windows. At first I barely looked up at them, so focused on sending every bit of my hatred and fury into Kadmiel's head. But then we stopped in front of the second one. In the middle on one side, a rushing river was full of soft blues and vibrant greens as the tiles tumbled over each other across the glass. At the top, there was a building with a tall bell tower perched at the river's edge.

Kadmiel raised a hand. Soft white plumes of smoke slipped from his palm, swirling through the air until they brushed up against the stained glass. In an instant and as I watched, the river slowly awakened, the angular lines of the tiles becoming more and more fluid until I was staring at a real river, surrounded by tumbled stones. That immense building gained details as the vision sharpened, and I was sure that I was simply looking straight out a window into that very river. I swallowed, knowing damn well there was no way that's true.

"This is a portal," Paran said from behind me, but I couldn't turn my eyes away from the view in front of me. "We're going to step through, and we will be in Nephesh's realm. Are you ready?"

Biting my lip, I nodded. "To see him? Yes." I had been hoping for some kind of vehicle that would take us there. Walking through a massive stained-glass window hadn't been first on my wish list. But I had seen so much these past weeks.

Kadmiel moved aside. "Lucia will go first," he said. "Arafel is waiting."

Lucia stepped up, gripping his hand with a delicate hold, putting one foot up on the benches that lined each of the walls, and then standing up completely on it. It made the perfect step up to the edge of the stained-glass window. With her booted foot sitting on the edge of the glass, she turned back to me.

"Just close your eyes," she said, her eyes flickering shut as she turned back, her foot to push up through the glass as if it was nothing but air. I could see her there, on either edge of the portal as she began to walk along the river, her figure a little pixelated almost but still visible. Even as I watched, I could see a dark shadow circling above her.

Arafel. I remembered him. The dark-winged brother of Nephesh. He was the one who was talking to Nephesh. Urgency filled me, and I climbed awkwardly onto the bench, the wooden base wobbling slightly as I braced myself on the frame of the stained glass before focusing my eyes on Lucia as she waited alongside that strange, vibrant blue river.

I can do this, I told myself, forcing the thought through my ice-cold veins. Then, following Lucia's example, I forced my quivering muscles to obey and stepped up onto the edge of the window. And without giving myself a moment to think twice, I stepped into the glass. Just as my knee should've broken the thin glass, I was simply tumbling, forced onto my knees, into the tall grasses that tickled and waved against my face as I kneeled there.

It had worked. I looked behind me and saw no evidence of the stone castle I'd been in a second ago.

"Easy there. I've got you," a deep, rough voice said, just before big, strong hands landed on my upper arms and easily picked me up, dropping me back on wobbly legs.

I looked up, straight into the soft gray features of…I didn't know what he was. But I knew *who* he was. This had to be Arafel. His bright-blue eyes were nearly electric colored this close, and while his features were more bold, more pronounced than his brother's, I could see some elements of Nephesh hidden there, in the shared genetics.

"You're Arafel."

"I am," he said, smiling and showing off white fangs as Lucia walked back towards us. "And you are Justine, my brother's mate."

Remembering what had happened right before I dragged us here, my throat felt tight. "If he'll have me."

Arafel tilted his head, but before he could speak again, there was a soft whoosh of hair at the nape of my neck and I knew that more were coming through. I let Arafel guide me forward, steadying me as I looked around the wide, sloping hills, my eyes catching on the vastness of the river, the soft sandy beaches that were only a few dozen feet away from us.

The water appeared like some rivers I'd seen before, but there was something odd about the color. It was so blue, so brilliantly blue, that I could barely stand to look at it for more than a few seconds. I broke away, staring at Lucia as she came to stand beside her winged mate.

"How is he?" she asked.

Arafel's eyes snapped to me and then back to his mate. "Father is with him."

She crossed her arms over her chest, chin jutting up to stare into his face. "That doesn't answer my question, Arafel."

"Healing. His wounds are nearly closed now. But as for the…situation, there's been no change."

"The situation?" I stepped up to the demon male. "What situation?"

"Come with us. You can see for yourself."

***

31

Nephesh

The pain was easing now. Whether I'd just gotten used to it or whether I was truly healing was still questionable. Groaning, I rocked back and forth, the pads on my feet sore from the odd position that I remained in while my father moved about in front of me.

"That's as good as I can do right now," Father said. "Your magic is too out of control for me to do much else."

I nodded, my beastly form still fresh in my mind. While my magic was returning, filling my chest, making my flames dance and move under my skin, it refused to give up the new hold it had in my mind. Maybe it was because I was here, in this place again. I couldn't really blame the creature for remaining nervous, at the forefront of my mind. After all, it wasn't long ago that I had been chained in here for nearly fifty years.

Maybe it was because my mate was still in danger. Father had said she was safe at the Court, but I knew no soul was safe anywhere. Not without me. The primal part of me raged to see her, to tell her everything that remained between us. Then to protect her. Always.

Far from that ice-wielding witch. Far from the Drude.

I eyed my father's cool expression as he observed me. Far from him too. There was so much that I'd learned from my time jailed with the Drude. And I couldn't believe my father hadn't known about most of it already. And yet, he'd still allowed all of it to happen.

In his eyes, we were nothing to him but ungainly children, unworthy of his knowledge.

I growled a little, remembering the bright, sharp power those ice daggers had brought with every touch. They had been too close to hurting Justine. If she had been injured, it would've been my father's final mistake.

"You can stop growling at me anytime, you know. I get it. You're pissed and don't want to talk to me."

I made a point to tug on my wrists. The chains that were so familiar to me made a soft jingling noise against the welded keeper at the ceiling of the cave. "Let me free, and we will talk."

"I wish I could."

"Liar."

Hurt flashed across my father's darkly handsome human features. "I never wanted to see you like this."

"Yet you never came by to say anything. You just sent Arafel and Kharon here when you were concerned your monster might be dead."

His chin dropped, and I could see the way the veins on his neck stood out. He was mad, irritated, or a bit of both. Good. His precious Court might not tell him the truth, but I would.

"I never thought of you like that. I was terrified of finding you because I knew that if you were dead, it was because of what your mother and I had done. Not in creating you, but in stealing from you. Something so important that I wasn't sure you would ever recover. And then you did. You showed us what it might be like if you were to find your souls again."

He turned away, his eyes on the tunnel that led to the hidden entrance to these caves. "To watch you go through that pain, without being strong enough to stop you. It was the worst thing I'd ever been through, Nephesh."

Something in his voice changed, and I couldn't stop staring at his profile. But before I could say anything or even process what he'd just confessed, Father spoke again. "She's on her way, and it sounds like she's tearing Arafel apart. But then, I'd expect nothing less of a Lady of the Underworld."

"She can't stay."

"Because you are afraid for her, or because you are afraid for yourself?"

Arafel's deep voice echoed through the tunnels, needlessly announcing himself. "Father, we're coming in."

Father stood, tugging down the cuff of one sleeve before moving to the other. The picture of elegant danger. When he caught me staring at him, a smirk appeared on his face.

"I'm meeting my new daughter-in-law, aren't I? I need to make a good impression."

But I was ignoring him now, my entire body completely focused on the footsteps I was hearing through the very real pounding of my heart as I stared at the tunnel. My pain was forgotten, my entire being so completely devoted to seeing who would be coming down that tunnel...

First there was Arafel, his opal-colored wings nearly blocking out everyone behind him as he led the way into the cavern. My magic slipped free of me, spreading across the floor in slender lines, as if attached to the wick of a long-buried explosive. They lit the path for her, keeping her safe as I heard her come closer and closer.

I couldn't stand just yet. Whether it was the healing spell that my father had performed or the fact that I was simply too weak, I lay there. Waiting.

I didn't have to wait very much longer. As if summoned by my thoughts, I heard her feet—bare, I thought—racing along the edge of my flames until they reached me. Then my eyes remained closed as she flung her arms over me, her body falling into the waist-deep water with me.

My arms and shoulders ached as I buried my face in her hair, unable to hug her back but needing her to know how badly I wanted to.

"Nephesh, Nephesh, Nephesh..." Her voice cracked as she breathed out my name over and over into my chest. "What did they do to you?" Her fingers raced up my forearms and over the heavy cuffs that kept me suspended.

"Justine, you should get out. It's quite cold…"

"I'm not going anywhere," Justine shouted, twisting to spit the words at where my family stood looking down at us. "Not until you take him down. This is inhumane, and it has to stop now!"

No one moved. I continued to breathe her in, letting the bond in my chest hum happily at the way she felt against me after our days apart. She was pissed, sure, but she was safe. And for the first time in a very long time, I had someone protecting me.

"He was injured when you two got here. We were able to convince him to release you and let us take you to Court to heal."

"And you so you brought him here?" Justine was staring around the cavern, and I could see my clever mate putting the pieces together. I almost felt bad for my family. "Oh my God, this is where you kept him all those years, isn't it? You disgust me. Family does not trap family in a fucking underground jail."

"We aren't a normal family," Arafel said after a long moment. "But you are right, Justine. We made a mistake."

"And so you did it again?"

"Justine," I whispered, "they know about my soul."

"So what?" She jabbed a finger at Arafel. "He has a complete soul, and no one is chaining him up."

"Nephesh's soul has always been more volatile than the others."

My father's cool voice drew Justine's attention back to him.

She blinked at him, her voice flat when she said, "Maybe because you have him locked in a cave? Did you think of that, genius?"

I cringed, the chains clanking slightly as I leaned forward. "Justine, meet my father, Lucifer, King of Hell."

To my utter pleasure, Justine's face didn't change for a second. If anything, her eyes narrowed farther. "My pleasure. Now let him free."

"We can't do that." My father sat down on the edge of a large stone, a sigh rattling the air after his words.

"Why not?"

"They were never locked," Father said, his eyes finding mine. "Not once."

"What the hell does that mean? Or what the— What does it mean?" Justine's frustration was palpable, and it matched mine. Based on the way Arafel and Lucia were looking at Father, they were confused as well.

"What do you mean?" I echoed, the question directed towards Father.

"These chains, it is true that they are among very few types that can hold us and the upper-level demons. But this particular set was made by your mother, specifically made to keep you here, locked and held until you believe that you are no longer a danger to anyone else. The moment you'd trusted yourself to not lose control, they would've released you."

Shocked silence filled the cavern, and then Arafel was snarling, stepping towards Father with his wings fluttering wide in agitation. Justine was repeating my father's words as if trying to puzzle them out, even as I let my mind wander back.

"Of all the dirty tricks, Father," Arafel growled.

"I still should not have put you here, knowing the guilt and worry you held over your powers. But I thought that it would help you. I thought you would realize that the only person here who is truly scared of you hurting someone is you."

Justine finally spoke, this time her voice was barely a quivering whisper. "You are punishing him because he has a conscience? You're insane." But instead of continuing to berate my father, suddenly she was back in my arms, her body pressing wetly against mine. It calmed me instantly, soothing the burn in my heart that I knew was grief and a self-awareness that I suddenly had come face-to-face with.

"Nephesh, listen to me. Listen to me."

I finally met her gaze, her hands on my face as she rose up against me, her legs tight around my waist.

"You are not dangerous. I've seen the good and I've seen the bad out there, and you are the perfect blend of them both. No one is perfect. No one is asking *you* to be perfect."

"I could never risk hurting you."

"Don't you remember? I'm stronger than I look," Justine said. "Let me prove this to you. Let me show you how life can be when you aren't afraid."

"How?"

She pressed a kiss against my jaw. "I have a new deal for you."

"What?"

"Well, more of a rendition on the last one." She held up her wrist, showing the lily that was still inked there. "You, Nephesh, heir of Hell, Judge of the Underworld, and all your other titles, will continue to protect me for the rest of our lives. And in return, I will be there, always, to make sure you remember to see the good in yourself."

My chest was heaving. "What did you say?"

"The good in yourself?"

"And what happens if we default on our deal?"

"I don't know, but whatever it is, we will face it together. Always."

I stared at her, absorbing the feel of her against me, the waves of love and affection that flowed through the bond and into my body. She didn't understand, maybe she never would, that somehow in my quest to keep her safe, I'd allowed her to protect me as well. And she'd found a way to not break down my walls around my heart, but to steal it for herself.

I could trust her. She was mine, and I was hers. A match made out of necessity but that had bloomed into so much more.

My arms suddenly flopped downwards, the chains releasing me in a splash of water. The muscles were sore, but not enough to make me stop as I lunged forward.

"Fascinating…" Arafel's voice was filled with awe.

"Your little human just trapped you in another deal," Father said calmly.

"She can't do that. She's not a demon."

"She's a witch though, isn't she? Their magic is just as binding, though it usually manifests slightly differently." His gaze fell to my wrist, and he gestured at it.

I turned it over to find a lily inked there against my pale skin. The deep-red ink looked close to the color of blood, as if my veins were just rerouted there to create the lily on my flesh.

"It's been a long time since we had a living witch in Hell," Lucifer said calmly. "I wonder what my wife was thinking when she set this one up." He stood, dusting off his pants and clearly planning on leaving.

"She was probably thinking she would need help down here, and clearly you demons can't be trusted to handle it on your own," Justine spat at him, her face an angry snarl.

Father's dark brows lifted as I bit back a laugh. "I think I see exactly why she chose you."

I looked at my mate. Anna had been soft. She'd found me when I was unwilling to let anyone in. She'd shown me love, compassion, and kindness. But Justine had shown me everything. She'd let me in, let me become a part of her from the beginning. Two souls always meant to be together, the witch with no family and the demon with no hope.

Together we'd found both, in each other.

My hand on her lower back, I guided her out of the frigid water and up onto the rocks. Arafel reached for her, his hand extended, before I growled a soft warning and helped her out myself.

"Demons," Lucia huffed quietly, but she was smiling.

Justine's lips, which had begun to turn blue around the edges, quirked in a very small smile. Once we were standing aground, I looked straight to my father.

"The Drude is going to come for us. For all of us."

The shadows in the cave shifted as he slowly smiled. "I'm looking forward to it."

"No, Father, there's more. He knows too much. He knew who Justine was. His people had been following her for years. And he's collecting powerful souls and has his own witch."

Justine shifted at my side but remained silent when I looked down at her.

Father sighed. "That's a good point, Nephesh. There seems to be an abundance of Underworld secrets making it to his group. I know that Arafel has his very best creatures attempting to find the individuals responsible for sharing our details with the Drude. But it will take time."

"We don't have time, Father. There's more you should know." I licked my lips, my arm snaking around to hold Justine closer. "I want you to know that there was nothing we could've done."

Father's head tilted, but he waited silently. Around us, water dripped from the stalactites far above.

"Tell him what you told me."

Justine fidgeted again but looked boldly across the cave to where Father stood. "There's another witch being held there. She's been there since she was a kid. She's one of your soul bonded too."

"And?"

"She said that when she first arrived, she was taught magic from another great witch."

I stared at my father, waiting to see his reaction. His eye twitched, but he remained relaxed. The picture of controlled power.

"She claimed that her teacher was the first witch."

Shadows leapt, and I pulled Justine back into my body as my father advanced on us. At my side, Arafel's wings snapped out, Lucia crowded to stand beside Justine.

He slowed, seemingly aware that he was threatening. "That's not possible, witch. She was taken from us years ago, long before the Drude. I would've known if she was still alive. I would've sensed her."

"Faye, the witch, she was sure of it. She said the witch was the keeper of the Underworld but had refused to give up her mate. The Drude had taken her somewhere else. Faye studied on her own after that."

"Where did he take her?"

"She didn't know. After that, she trained alone or with the other witches who came through to serve the Drude."

Father whirled away, his magic a dark swirl. "We need that witch."

"Father…" Arafel reached out.

"I need to find her." He snapped his fingers, and two immense red figures appeared. They wore heavy black-plated armor, their red flesh nearly covered by the material as they turned as one to bow to my father. "My wife may be alive. I want you to find her. Now."

"Yes, my lord."

"Failure will result in your destruction. Do you understand?"

"Yes, my lord."

"Then what are you waiting for?" Lucifer snarled. And then together, all three disappeared in a snap.

Justine cleared her throat. "Sorry about that. I think I might have…"

"It doesn't take much, honestly," Lucia said, stepping forward. "Does this mean you are planning on staying in the Underworld? Your deal will protect you—you know, from the elements here."

Justine's fingers interlaced with mine. "I'm staying with Nephesh. He's my family. So whatever that means."

"If you are his family, then that means you are ours too."

My mate wrinkled her nose, and Arafel let out a huff. "I understand that isn't very appealing right now. But if you ever decide to forgive us, we would welcome another human into our fold."

"What about a witch?"

God I loved her.

Arafel smiled broadly, "Absolutely."

32

Arafel was watching Nephesh, one side of his mouth curled in a very familiar smirk. "Mother would be so proud."

"That my mate is a witch?" Nephesh looked unconvinced.

"No, that you allowed yourself to find someone. That you allowed yourself some peace. That's all she ever wanted for us."

Nephesh slowly brought my hand up to his lips, where he brushed the back with a light kiss.

"She is everything. My peace. My chaos. My love. My future."

My eyes burned, and suddenly I felt like everyone was watching. With a flick of my wrists, I sent flames soaring up around us, leaving us in a flaming all of our own design. When they started to go too high, I could feel the soothing balm of Nephesh's magic wrap around mine, calming it.

"Are you embarrassed?" I whispered, even though I was sure Arafel and the others were leaving outside of the flames.

Nephesh grinned, full and beautiful and full of trust. "To be yours? Never."

I stepped into him, ignoring our wet clothes as I wrapped my arms around his shoulders. With a soft noise, Nephesh bent at the knees, scoping me up so that my legs could lock around his waist.

Holding him tight, I kissed him, pouring every bit of myself into it. Letting him feel the way I hoped for our future, the way I wanted to protect his past. His lips captured mine, teasing and pulling away again and again until I sank my hands into his hair and dragged him deeper against me.

When we finally broke away, I was shaking—and not from the cold water. Slowly, Nephesh released me, letting my feet rest against the cool cave floor.

Amber eyes sparkling, he found my hand with his own. "Do you want to see your new home?"

"I'd love that."

The flames fell and we stepped apart, my lips still tingling from his kiss. Together we walked out of the cave and into the Underworld, where above us, the clouds swirled an ominous black. Nephesh looked up at it, his face worried for a moment.

But then I pressed my hand on his chest, over the bond that burned bright. "Let's go home."

He turned me towards a large building overlooking the river Styx.

"You don't have a bunch of roommates or something, do you?"

"Oh, I do." Nephesh flashed a grin at me. "Twelve, in fact."

"Excuse me?"

He spun me around, stealing another kiss as he did. "Don't worry. You'll love them."

Epilogue

Justine

My back cracked as I slowly stood from my chair and then straightened, every muscle screaming as I did.

"I heard that. I can't believe your human bodies can be so…loud."

I glared at my mate as he leaned against the doorjamb. "Sorry that we all can't be…well, whatever the fuck you are."

He grinned, white fangs glistening. I'd been in the Underworld a few weeks now, and other than the obvious struggles, like getting used to seeing souls floating around on the daily and having to share my breakfast with a variety of strange creatures, I was happier than I had ever been.

Lucia had immediately sought me out as a friend, and I recognized that the bond that tied her to Arafel, and Arafel to Nephesh, somehow looped the two of us in as well. Nephesh said it was a tiresome old demon thing from when demons traveled in packs. But it was nice. Unlike Faye, Lucia and I had a lot in common.

And while she practiced her flying, I had taken to working on my control. My power had grown exponentially since coming here, and while it occasionally scared me, Nephesh assured me that nearly everyone here in the Underworld was at least partially fireproof. A quality I didn't appreciate until my flames exploded on me a few days ago and I nearly fried Kadmiel as he came by with news from the Court of Hell.

Nephesh's brother had merely ripped the blackened shirt off his body, given me a glare, and then carried on with his message, ignoring us. Lucia and I had rolled around the ground, laughing hysterically.

It was Lucia who had found these books for me too, old spell books and journals from Nephesh's mother. She had been far more powerful than I was, but it felt good to try. That way, if I was ever separated from Nephesh, then I would be able to stand on my own.

"Did you need something? Or did you just come to gloat about your five-hundred-year-old body's perfection?"

"I don't gloat."

My jaw dropped. "You gloat constantly. It's one of your most dominant features."

Nephesh rolled his eyes, a habit he had picked up from me, and let his wings loose from his glamor. I'd gotten used to his ever-evolving form in the past few weeks, but it didn't mean that I loved seeing it any less. Every part of my mate was stunning, but the wings were positively swoon worthy.

"Are we going somewhere?"

"There's a Corrupted by the Sleepy Mountains. I wasn't sure whether you wanted to handle or if we should send a reaper."

I frowned. "Still no Kharon?"

"No, not yet."

Nephesh's younger brother, one I still hadn't met, was missing. He'd been gone for weeks now, and I knew that the weight of the River Styx was wearing on all of Nephesh's family, myself included. Since the river was where most of the souls attempted to escape from we'd taken to patrolling it. Nephesh in his creature form, and me with him, helping to direct his magic.

It was a thrill still, to not only have something to contribute, but also to have another way to bond with Nephesh. When we were out there, it was like nothing I'd ever experienced. The two of us against the world and only for each other.

My grin was instantaneous. "Of course. Tell the reaper to stand down." I didn't like Kharon's creatures very much. The reapers, while helpful in delivering souls to the Underworld, also were the most like what horror movies had made them out to be. They were tall, with tattered, torn black robes wrapped around their thin forms. They didn't swim the river like I heard Kharon did occasionally but patrolled alongside it. Great black shadows, usually carrying a sickle or staff in their pale hands, they were known to be aggressive to anyone who got in the way of their tasks.

I much preferred to be on Nephesh's monstrous back when we got close to them. And while he never said so, I think

Nephesh also preferred it. In his monster form, they steered clear of us, and I appreciated every extra inch between us and them.

There was just something ominous in the way they glided along, herding souls back into place, driving the dead to their judgment. It always made the goosebumps rise up on my arms.

When I'd told Nephesh that, he said that the reapers were among the first things his father had built. There were seven of them, and each had once ruled a part of the Underworld with Lucifer at the helm. Something in his voice gave me the distinct impression that neither Nephesh nor Lucifer was terribly fond of them.

Today I was glad to call them off and send them back to the river where they belonged. Nephesh and I could track this soul with our eyes closed.

"Well, let's go, then!"

"Always so eager."

"Hmm." I leaned up, pressing my face against his neck then kissing a long line from his jaw to his collarbone. "Are you disappointed?"

Nephesh growled, his hands on my waist as he hitched me up higher. "Justine."

I slipped free, his claws harmless against my skin. "Shall we go?"

Nephesh growled again.

"The sooner we go, the faster we will be home," I teased.

His lips quirked in a small smile that sent my stomach tumbling. He always did that when I called the courthouse home. Or even the Underworld home. But I didn't say it for him. I said it for me.

Because for the first time in a long time, I did have a home. And a mate. And I would do everything in my power to protect both of them. Even if his dad was a dick.

A few minutes later, we were out the door, Nephesh's immense strides eating up the ground as he loped towards the Sleeping Mountains.

"Which way?" he asked me silently, mind to mind.

I brushed my hand down his thick neck, letting my eyes close for a moment, focusing on the missing soul, for what I knew they might be feelings.

"That way," I responded to him, my shuttered eyes turning towards the tree line before us. "A little bit longer, and we might lose them in the rocks."

"Then let's not lose them, shall we, mate?"

My throat clenched at the warmth, the love that radiated through his words.

"Don't worry," I whispered into the Underworld air. "I'll protect you."

Nephesh's howling laughter joined mine as we plunged deeper into the Underworld. It was time to get to work.

The End

Want a steamy bonus scene from after Nephesh and Justine find their happily ever after? You can get it from Maggie White's website: www.maggiewhitebooks.com.

The Lords of the Underworld series continues on in book which will be Kharon and Faye's story coming in 2024. Preorder River of Hope and Hatred on Maggie White's website.